ASK NICOISE

by

Dawn Durrell

To my lovely friend Diane, enjoy! love Dawn x x

1

Published in 2015

© Dawn Taylor (nee Durrell)

ISBN 978-1-849-14609-8

Printed in the UK.

DEDICATION

Karen,
Always believe and never give up.
Love,

Dawn

Chapter One

The cooler is not a pleasant place to spend your 'Fairday' (probably better known as a day off work), it's so annoying, however to be fair I guess it is my own fault, basically I'm not very good at my job ...I'm a trainee guardian angel, and even I have to admit at this rate I will remain a 'trainee' for a very a long time yet, possibly never qualifying – a very scary prospect indeed, not really a lot of work here for angels that don't make the grade as a guardian angel.

Every case is the same, I start off enthusiastic and then I get distracted, lose interest. Then I get behind with writing up the case notes, but this last time and the reason that I am now sitting feeling sorry for myself in this small, dingy and grey room is that I forgot to turn up for a crucial 'watch' on my case, not very clever as my job title suggests 'guardian' (you can't guard your cases if you don't even bother to turn up to the event!)

It's just honestly I sometimes find humans a little irritating (well that's not strictly true I should say I find very irritating) – I mean they get into allsorts of messes in their lives, and wow we really do see some cases, they then get really stressed out, worry their friends and families and then they expect someone or something else to sort the mess out! That's when we get called in and I mean they expect miracles and I just can't see sometimes why they can't sort their own mess out, breath Nicoise breath! I sound awful and I know I should be saintly, but on the other hand I have to be true to myself and my true feelings, however, these feelings could lose me my job and I guess I need my job, (humans seem to think that angels just float around the skies sending light rays to needy people and then we float around some more – wrong, we work and we have strict rules to adhere too!)

If only I could float around all day, flying high into the clouds, meeting my friends at the Sparkle Bar, yes then life indeed would be a breeze!

Reality check … I wouldn't have a purpose, I mean if humans were perfect they wouldn't need angels help, and flying around, sure that would be cool for a while but in the deep midst of a cold winter believe me it does not hold the same appeal (yes even angels feel the cold and we don't have extra layers to put on… coats yes that's the word, we don't wear coats!)

So I guess what I am saying here or trying to say is that on reflection I guess we would need something to occupy our highly developed minds (well some angels have highly developed minds, mine is say still in the process). So the point of me sitting in this awful place is too reflect on my actions and I guess I am saying that we angels and especially trainee guardians need humans, we need to feel wanted, we need humans to want us and ask us for help, that makes us special, that unleashes our powers of angelic qualities that ultimately help humans solve their own problems. In turn, humans definitely need us, some may not believe that they do, because not many believe we exist (perish the thought!) and some just don't know how to go about asking for our help.

My head is aching with too many thoughts whizzing round, being in solitude does not suit me, it gives me too much thinking time. I know that is the whole point, I know I need to grow up and embrace my guardian role bestowed upon me, which I should add is an honour, not every angel gets to be a 'guardian' and the ones that do are very special beings indeed.

"You would be well placed to remember that thought young Nicoise!" bellowed a loud thespian voice that almost made my wings fall off with the thundering vibrations of my mentor Hibissa's voice, who had as normal read my thoughts (a really annoying but cool skill).

"Hibissa Sir, you startled me" I scrambled to my feet as quick as I could to greet my mentor who was now standing directly opposite me after just appearing in only a way that a specialised qualified angel can.

Hibissa smiled, not a pleasant smile, not a welcoming smile, no his smile was mean and knowing, he was after all one of the most powerful Angels up here and boy didn't he know it! "Nicoise, pleasant few days I trust here in the cooler?"

I nodded meekly knowing there was no real point to speak as Hibissa always knew what I was thinking, I concentrated hard to keep my mind blank and calm without giving away my true thoughts.

"Here" he handed me a large dusty case folder. "Your new case, thought you could have a read through in your last few hours in here"

"Thank you Sir, very thoughtful" I replied with a heavy heart, although I was also relieved that he had given me another case, I was a little worried that he might put me on white wash duties here (everything here is white, whiter than white in fact, so when angels go off the rails one of the community projects that they may be assigned to is painting the walls of the endless white corridors).

"Can I ask you to remember your earlier thoughts and remember that you are a 'Guardian Angel,' well trying to be anyway, and that I just will not tolerate anymore of your recklessness and laziness from you! It is totally unacceptable! You have the ability in my opinion to do a good job Nicoise, you just need to keep focused on the case, in turn you will be rewarded with satisfaction of helping meeker souls, do I make myself clear?" Hibissa boomed (he had real problems speaking quietly in my opinion).

"I understand Sir" I nodded

"Well, I am not sure that you really do Nicoise, sometimes I despair of you, I feel that you have no concept of what your role really entails and how you should conduct yourself in such a prestigious role, however, being the soft angel that I am." He paused and stared directly at me to see if my thoughts had any smart comment on this last comment, I kept my mind blank and Hibissa continued "I am giving you one more chance before changing your career path. I mean lets look at the evidence, your last case, 4126000, you completely managed to ruin her chances of her staying with her true soul mate, does that not make you feel sad?"

I bowed my head to stare at the grey marble floor of the cooler, of course I felt a little sad, admittedly case 4126000 had gone a little wrong, but it was not all my fault. I mean her friend seemed to have her thoughts and was always one step ahead, which meant she eventually ended up with my case's allocated soul mate. As an angel I do not have the powers to reverse peoples thoughts, this is what I mean about humans, some are so uncaring and relentless and will stop at nothing to achieve their own goals, never minding who they step over or hurt in the process (I would never sacrifice friendship for gain, but humans do time and time again).

"Well speak out loud Nicoise, don't mumble in your thoughts, what is your answer to my question?" Hibissa grumbled impatiently.

"Yes Sir, sorry Sir, I understand that I failed and need to try harder and promise I will do better on this new case and thank you for giving me another opportunity, which I know I surely do not deserve?" I said pathetically, appalled with how cringey I must sound. I read the name on the case file that was in my hands 'Katie Johnston' I groaned inwardly hoping Hibissa would not sense my despair, not another female, they are always so more emotional, which always makes it a lot harder.

"Good, that is the correct answer, now have a good read and take care of your new case 4126999 ... and Nicoise not all females are more emotional than men counterparts, it is wrong of you to discriminate between the sexes".

"Sorry Sir" I replied almost sarcastically, I mean what does he know he hasn't met as many of the modern females as I have!

"You have two hours left in here Nicoise, put it to good use and read the file before the guard lets you out, I want you to report to me in three days" with that Hibissa was gone just leaving a cold whirling breeze of air circulating in the already cold grey box of a room.

I looked at the file and dusted off the surface layer of dust, before opening the file and sitting back down on the cold uninviting marble floor. I flicked through the pages, scan reading bits and pieces but not properly reading as Hibissa intended. Katie looked pleasant enough in the picture although she looked quite a lot younger in the picture than her 36 years, probably an out of date picture judging by the amount of dust and unturned pages. Although she was smiling, her eyes looked sad and there was a hint of loneliness and rejection (oh not this). I squinted my eyes to see if she had an aura, and yes it worked, I could see she did have an aura, she had a light green aura, so she was a 'giving' person, well that's a start I guess.

I continued flicking though the heavy pages and read only words that jumped out to me like *'chocoholic'* *'boring job'* *'broken relationship'*... whatever Hibissa may say about females he is wrong, these words indicate to me 'emotional'. But no, I need to keep focused and positive here, I have to succeed, Hibissa had said this was my last chance before he considered a career change. The very thought sent goose bumps all down my spine causing me to shudder! Just before I closed the file having seen enough the worst words jumped out at me: -

"Katie does not believe in Angels"

"Well Katie I'm afraid that you are going to have to start believing otherwise my job is going to be a lot harder. And that will not be good for either of us - you have a chance now to solve your issues here. I am not going to miss any more Fairday's basking in clouds or light sky races because of humans not helping me to help them!" I grumbled out loud. "You will need to ask me for help Katie".

Chapter 2

Katie woke up to the sound of her untuned radio hissing out a noise from various different stations. She quickly flicked the off switch groaning and making a mental note to sort the radio out later. She lay there motionless for a few moments looking up at the white cracked ceiling, and then decided to turn over and hide under the pink flowery duvet. But the radio was relentless and the alarm sounded again, happily hissing out an awful noise. The sound was just too awful so reluctantly Katie got up realising it was Monday morning! Always the hardest morning to be cheery about, knowing that a long tedious week was about to start all over again. However, that was life and at least she had a job to pay all the bills.

She slowly ambled to the bathroom, cursing as she bumped into the leg of the table at the top of the stairs. She was always stubbing her toe there, she really should move the table out of the way and she reminded herself to do this later. She limped into the bathroom feeling a little sorry for herself. She already had a feeling it was going to be one of those days. Actually, no she corrected herself; it was going to be one of those weeks!

Finally arriving at the office Katie switched on her PC and whilst it 'warmed up' which always took forever, she went and put the kettle on for that very important and necessary first cup of tea. By the time she had finished making it her computer was slowly starting to wake up. She smiled to herself, knowing the feeling.

Katie was a PA to Ms Carla Red, one of the junior partners in the Accountancy firm that she worked for. Carla was an incredibly ambitious woman, demanding and really quite rude. Not that anyone would ever say that out loud. Carla was a stickler for detail and Katie often had to recreate work which to her eye seemed more than adequate, she was sure that Carla sometimes purposely corrected her work just because she could and she seemed to get a kick out of talking to people as if they were stupid. In fact Katie often found mistakes Carla had made yet she never dare bring these up, she would just quietly amend them.

At 36, Katie was the oldest of the secretarial support staff, and the other two sure did like to remind Katie of this at pretty much any opportunity. They were both in their early 20's and life to them was just one big social event, consisting of shopping, going out, meeting men, more shopping...and so on. They never seemed to wear the same clothes twice, unlike Katie who strictly rotated her 'office' clothes; there would be no point in trying to keep up with their fickle fashion because nothing would ever be right. Katie kept herself to herself as much as she could, ignoring the younger girls giggling and whispering. She knew she was a good worker and an asset to the firm, however she felt deep down like an outsider at work, and unfortunately this did cause her to be a bit of a clock-watcher – daydreaming at any suitable point about life beyond this dull existence.

Katie checked her PC, which was still not quite up and running so she walked out to the reception area to check on the plants. They looked a little droopy, and sad after a few days of no attention, and no doubt no one had thought to water them whilst she had been off on Friday. She filled up the water bottle and gently sprinkled water over them.

"There we are, that's better," she said out loud to the plants not realising that Sara was standing behind her.

"You want to watch that talking to plants," giggled Sara

"Oh yes hi, I've heard its supposed to help them, thought I would give it a try as they look a little droopy"

"Interesting I'm sure, is the tea ready?" asked Sara.

They both went back into the office and were soon joined by Jayne the other Secretary who was wearing the loudest cerise pink jacket – it was so bright and so Jayne.

"Wow, love the coat, it's totally..."

"Pink" Katie added, both Sara and Jayne threw her a disdained look and then ignored her as they continued to talk excitedly about the pink jacket.

"I know it's so me, I saw it and I thought I have to have it," said Jayne, who really was a 'pink' kind of girl, a sickly pink girl.

"Is the kettle on, I'm parched?" Jayne asked Sara

"Katie is sorting it out" she turned to Katie "Is the tea ready, could you bring it over?'

Then whispering started. Katie never really could work out why they had to whisper. Honestly it was like being back at the school playground at break time. Katie shrugged it off - she had no desire to know what or whom they were talking about. No doubt it was about a man or men, it usually was. Jayne seemed to think that every man on the planet was attracted to her it was quite laughable really. They probably looked her way then, once they heard her speak if they had sense they would look away - she really has the most annoying high-pitched voice, although admittedly she did have a good figure!

The door suddenly crashed open and in entered the two junior partners, Carla and James (Sara was James PA –and Katie was a little jealous of this because she had a secret little crush on James and wished she worked for him and not Carla).

"Morning ladies" greeted James with a cheery smile

Carla's greeting was somewhat terser: "Katie, file on Pippa-Smiths in my office now. I have that meeting with their Director this morning".

"It is on your desk waiting Carla," replied Katie calmly

"Excellent...bring in a black coffee," she barked as usual with no please or thank you. Katie never let this worry her; it was just the way Carla was even if it was a little rude. James always said please and thank you, had manners, and he was probably one of the most laid back bosses you would be likely to come across. He was also very hands-on believing that Sara was too 'snowed under' so he often did some of her work, which suited Sara fine, as she was a very lazy girl. Sometimes James even made tea for her!

Jayne on the other hand did have to work a little harder than Sara, as she worked for Mr Kyle who was the Senior Partner. He was not in the office an awful lot, being out and about with clients, speaking at seminars, going out on 'business lunches' etc, which meant Jayne had a lot of calls to answer, lots of meetings and hotels to book. However, even though Mr Kyle was the Senior Partner, even he was not so picky about work and seemed quite a fair boss on the whole. Katie definitely had the hardest taskmaster to work for and Sara and Jayne were eternally happy that Carla was not their boss. They hated it when Katie took any leave, as they had to cover. This would really shake them up and make them appreciate their bosses. Well maybe for a day anyway, then they would revert back to their lazy ways.

The morning dragged on and Katie constantly peeped at the clock, which seemingly refused to budge. Towards lunchtime Sara strolled over to Katie's desk.

"Katie" Sara spoke sweetly, too sweetly, and Katie knew she wanted something.

"I have an appointment at the dentist at 12.30 and you know how freaked out I get about going, so I may need more time over lunch in order to get there and get over it if I go into one of my panic attacks. I promised James though that I would type up the Henson report. Do you think you could be a real sweetie and type it up for me and cover the phones, there shouldn't be many calls.... I'll cover for you in return ...soon?" she cooed flashing her recently whitened teeth.

Katie knew only too well it was a story, undoubtedly to cover one of Sara's frequent 'extended lunch breaks'. Suddenly Jayne joined in the conversation.

"Hey you two, remember I am at lunch at 12.30 today"

Now Katie knew for sure the two of them were scheming to go out together leaving her to do all the work and cover all the phones. She bit her lip wanting to reply with something along the lines of 'No. Unable to help today' but instead she heard herself kindly replying "of course, not a problem". How she wished she could say 'No'. Surely it's not that hard a word? She would have to practise saying it ...but to whom, she never said 'no' to anyone. The only consolation for Katie would be peace and quiet from the two giggling women.

"I am walking that way, why don't we walk down the High Street together?" said Jayne to Sara. Katie smirked under her breath, acutely aware of the play-acting at hand.

Katie sighed and took out her cheese and tomato sandwiches she had made earlier. They did not really look that appetising but they would do. After finishing the sandwiches Katie made a start on the report for James that Sara had delegated down for her to do whilst Sara and Jayne were out enjoying themselves. The phones had a mad half an hour, even James answered a few calls, realising that Katie was alone. Gradually the calls subsided and Katie managed to complete the draft report. She took the report in to James.

"Hello Katie, what can I do for you? Phones were a bit mental weren't they?" he laughed.

"Sara asked me to pass this too you" she said handing over the report she had just typed.

"Thank you". He flicked through it quickly "Sara really is a diamond you know, I really don't know what I would do without her. Where is she anyway?"

"Dentist ... apparently" replied Katie

James looked down at the report. He had a feeling that Katie had typed this for Sara. He knew what went on but he never said anything, he wasn't one for the managing staff side of the job, he just wanted a quiet life and everyone to get on. So he said nothing on the matter, and just smiled at Katie instead.

Katie went back to her desk and not long after the 'terrible two' returned again together like they were joined at the hip. Before having a chance to speak with them, Katie was summoned by a very loud Carla.

"Katie!" screamed Carla

"Coming" Katie, replied scurrying to Carla's office

"You have three typo's in this, and I don't like the change of font in the sub paragraphs. Change it!" Carla abruptly handed the document back to Katie.

Carla continued, "Katie, I am not sure what you have been doing today but this is really not up to standard. Did you have a late night last night or something?" Carla pretended to joke, but Katie knew it was deliberate spitefulness.

"I'm sorry, I'll do it straight away" responded Katie.

"Lovely, and Katie some coffee would be great and if you have any headache pills I would be really grateful because I have got an awful nagging headache" she moaned.

Katie walked back to the office and flicked on the kettle, overhearing Sara and Jayne who rather than working, clearly just chatting about their lunch episode.

"Did you see the way he looked at me?" Jayne giggled

"He really liked you," said Sara munching on some cheese and onion crisps – really the sort of food you would be eating after a dentist appointment. Sara looked up at Katie, but did not even say thank you for typing up James' report.

The afternoon gradually disappeared at finally it was 5pm, home time – what a lovely time of the day. Sara and Jayne were always first out of the door. Katie peered out of the window it was dark and cold. How she hated the winter evenings when it got dark so early. 'Roll on spring' she thought.

Katie felt she should make herself go to the gym or do a class, even though it was really the last thing she fancied doing. She fumbled through her oversized handbag and finally found the aerobics timetable that she had been carrying with the best intentions. She looked at the evenings classes:

- *6.00 pm Step*
- *7.00pm Body Combat*
- *8.15 Salsa Aerobics*

Katie groaned. She really had hoped it would be something gentle, not involving much moving about. Something serene like Pilates or a gentle candle light stretch to ease away the day, but no, only full on hard slog classes. The idea of exercising soon start to fade and the thought of a nice glass of wine and some chocolate in front of the TV seemed much more appealing. Katie wondered what was on TV that night, and she made a mental note to get a TV magazine when she stopped for the chocolate!

Chapter 3

I had been watching intently one of Katie's usual workdays. Nothing very exciting to report, although, she had some pretty unpleasant colleagues in my opinion. Her evening did not really get any better either; she was in her teddy-bear pj's by seven o'clock, slumped in front of her flat screen television watching a documentary on lion cubs, followed by a re-locating house programme then the news, whilst munching her way through a few bars of chocolate and a glass of wine (or two). Oh yes not to forget, she did have a phone call from her Mother, and what a Mother she has! I'll come back to that later.

I glanced around my Chamber, which I share with two other 'Trainee Guardian Angels', Pascolli and Willow, not only my room mates but my best friends, kind and funny. Well I'm not too sure if Willow would qualify as funny because he is incredibly studious and ambitious unlike Pascolli, and myself who ... well let's just say love life!

The Chamber is a total mess, with books just about everywhere, piled up in the corners, stacked on the old desk, and hidden under the beds. Like I say 'everywhere'. The serving angels never come into our room, they peep in and then beat a quick retreat. They are not allowed to tidy up if Chambers are too unruly and messy. This is supposed to teach us a lesson, and make us more disciplined, but to be honest it doesn't really bother us, (we're not awfully chamber proud like some).

Then there are the notes all over the wall to the left of the room. These are Willow's, he is note obsessed I would say, always scribbling away, and making a collage of his notes ideas and thoughts on the wall. Thinking about what I just said it occurs to me that it might be useful to have a peep at his notes, as they might inspire me for my new case, which, in all honesty seems dull. I'm sure Willow would understand, although he can be a little protective over his work on occasions.

So I started to read Willows notes, unfortunately I was unlucky here on two counts. First his writing is so tiny that my eyes can hardly read the scribble and, second, as I was concentrating on making out the tiny words I failed to hear Willow and Pascolli enter the Chamber.

"Nicoise!" exclaimed Willow sternly, causing me to jump up in fright

"What do you think you're doing reading my notes, they are confidential"?

Willow is such a good and gentle angel, no doubt just how you humans would expect angels to behave, but believe me he could occasionally have a moody moment. And right now seemed to be one of those moments!

However, some angels are actually a little cunning, even devious and maybe prone to telling small fibs to help a situation, which was exactly what I was planning to do now.

"Not very confidential if they're on the wall" laughed Pascolli, always making light of a situation.

My turn. "Willow, I was not reading your notes, how could I your writing is so small. One of the notes fell off as I closed the door. I was just popping it back up for you". I smiled my most cheesy smile.

"Oh sorry ...thank you, very kind of you. Perhaps I should consider getting a folder?" Willow replied apologetically.

"Or a less nosey room mate" added Pascolli winking at me.

"Pascolli, what do you mean I was just..."

"Having a nose, trying to get some inspiration. Come off it Nicoise you know Willow is far more qualified than you or I"

"It really doesn't really matter" Willow interjected "Like I say I should put them in a folder. It's just I find it useful to spread them over the wall like that, I just know that we'll get into trouble if we share case notes".

"Share, don't you mean copy?" Pascolli went on like a dog with a bone. He was intent in trying to wind either me or Willow up.

"Fancy getting some Twinkle rays?" I asked changing the subject and knowing Pascolli could never resist some fun.

"Excellent thinking" both Willow and Pascolli said in unison.

In case you're wondering, Twinkle rays are probably the equivalent of you humans going to your local bar, socialising with friends and having a good time over a drink. You see, just like humans we are very social and like to meet up, chat and catch up with old friends. The Twinkle rays are situated in a beautiful amazing setting, very white, very still, very calm. In long corridors of clouds small pockets exist and as you enter you get a spray of twinkles the mist of light, which, makes you feel really happy. Mind you, too much can make you a little light headed which is not allowed, as we have to fly everywhere...rules rules. However, it is just the best place.

We made a speedy exit from our chamber, and flew quickly to the fourth cloud pocket our favourite. It was less busy than some of the other pockets and the younger students seemed to prefer the later more rowdy pockets. It felt good being enveloped in mist in the pocket. If life were always full of sparkles and twinkles how great things would be.

"You would soon be bored if that was the case," Willow said randomly

"Willow, were you reading my mind?" I asked, impressed with his developing skill.

"Yes of course I was" replied Willow with a mischievous grin.

"How do you do that? I just can't seem to do that," I said with a frown.

"Practise you idiot!" added Pascolli somewhat critically.

"What I meant anyway if you're interested in letting me finish, is that life has to have its ups and downs; if life was all sparkly we would have nothing to do nothing to compare it with to appreciate" said Willow.

"Lighten up will you" Pascolli said

Reading minds and thoughts is an important training process that we as guardians have to master, and I really have not mastered this skill yet, I was a little envious of Willow sometimes, he was so good at everything, but he was also very cool, and would always help.

"What's your case load like this week?" I asked Pascolli

"A man going through a tricky divorce, wife seems a bit fearsome really taking him to the cleaners, and she is trying to distance his children from him. Yet actually it was her that originally left him to go off with some younger guy who has since left and gone with a woman his own age, I think."

"Sounds complicated, what an awful woman," I said

"There's always two sides to a story Nicoise, you should know that" Willow said knowingly.

"Erm, not too sure sometimes" I said

"I've also got this teacher bloke that is so stressed out and none of his students take him seriously and are always playing tricks on him" Pascolli continued.

"That's bad" I said "Anything else?"

"Got one lady whose daughter has gone missing, which is particularly pretty sad, oh yes some weak Accountant chap who, lets people walk all over him. Shameful really. How about you?"

"Well I have old Hibissa on my back and he has only allowed me to do one job at the moment, an important one that I have to get right or I am..."

"Finished?" interjected Pascolli

"You've got it. Finished, consigned to the life of serving ..." I shuddered. I deeply and genuinely wanted to be a Guardian Angel, but it really is hard work sometimes.

"Did you say one of your cases is an Accountant? My case works at an Accountants, and there is a chap there who does seem a bit woolly".

"Hey you two" interrupted goody two shoes Willow " You know you should not go any further with that information, you could get into case crossing and you know only too well the trouble you will get into if you go down that route!"

Pascolli and I looked at each other and nodded. Poor Willow, he really did despair of us sometimes, he played everything by the book, and to be fair always got results. I would speak to Pascolli later when Willow was out of earshot.

"I have a lovely lady who believes her son is stealing off her, but she is scared to confront him for fear of losing him" added Willow feeling he was acting a little too high and mighty, and he did not want to be totally left out of the conversation.

"That's awful, humans make me sick sometimes" I said crossly.

"Me too" added Pascolli "Shall we race?"

"Last one back cleans the Chamber!' I grinned, and with that all three of us shot up high into the blue sky, zooming as fast as our wings would carry us. Flying is just the best feeling, alas something humans will never experience. That is a shame because flying makes you feel so good, and you think of nothing but freedom whilst in the air, no worries, no Mentor on your case, no report writing ...pure unadulterated freedom.

Chapter 4

Katie woke up to the sound of someone shouting very loudly outside, and an engine running. She slowly ambled out of bed and peeped through the blinds, noticing the man across the road-getting cross with someone parked in 'his' space. She glanced at her clock and sighed as it was still quite early for a weekend, but she was up now thanks to that loud man, so she thought she might as well stay up and make the most of the weekend.

As always, Katie's first job (after cleaning her teeth) was making that all-important cup of tea. As she rummaged through her cupboard for new tea bags she came across lots of herbal teas. She knew she should opt for the herbal option, but no, only a cup of proper tea would do this morning. As she switched the radio on to listen to the news the phone rang. It was her brother, Nick.

Nick really was quite a pain to Katie he probably didn't intend to be, it was just the way he was and to a certain extent to how Katie had let him get away with treating her badly. However, Katie just couldn't bear to hurt his feelings and just couldn't say no to him. After all he was the baby of the family being nine years younger than Katie. Nick was totally self-centred, he never did anything unless it benefited him, and he was lazy and had never held down a job for more than a few months. Yet he was pretty intelligent and did really well in his exams at school, not that he ever studied. He was someone who was naturally clever and things just seemed to fall into his lap. Nick believed he was destined for greater things and felt that, in the meantime he did not need to work.

Katie had heard Nick's story millions of times about how he would be a millionaire by the time he was 35. She had to smile though because Nick had no idea of what he was going to do in order to get there. She didn't think he even did the lottery, so he didn't even have that tiny chance of securing his fortune – a chance that Katie herself clung onto each Saturday when she handed over her money for her lottery ticket.

Nick never had any money, and the only time he ever really called Katie was when he wanted something - money mainly! Katie always helped him, even though she knew she should say 'no' but that simple word was so hard to say to Nick; it just did not seem to want to come out of her lips.

"Morning Kat" Nick chirped, way too cheerily for such an early morning call.
"Hi Nick, how you doing?" Katie responded in not such a cheery tone.
"Not bad, not bad. Listen - two things. Could I give you some hand bags to sell to the girls in your office, or your friends?" Nick asked.

Katie knew this was one of Nick's dubious business enterprises and replied, "Oh I don't know, the girls at work are really fussy, I don't think..."

Nick didn't let her finish "You don't know till you try" he interjected "They are the latest fashion, have tassles and charms, they are really cool, they'll love 'em. If you could try and sell say four that would be such a help, I don't want to be left with them"

Katie gave in again "Sure no problem. Leave them at mums, I'm popping round there later, so I'll pick them up"

"Diamond sister" Nick paused and Katie knew what the next question would be. As always she was right, Nick was totally predictable.

"Any chance you could lend us a small sub? I can pay you back...once I have sold two of the bags" he said in his 'I'm such a cute brother' voice.

Katie sighed and tried to will herself to say 'No.' A voice in her head chanted "Say no! Say no! Say no! But somehow the voice stayed within and, as usual, she heard herself saying, " Yes. How much do you need?"

"Well £40. No actually Sis £50 would be better cos I'm so skint and I've got this hot date tonight with a really fit bird. You would love her"

Katie was not really listening and she laughed to herself at the thought of meeting one of his 'dates' like jobs, girls came and went very quickly with Nick.

"I'll leave the money at Mums then?" She said.

Nick said "Cheers" and with that he was gone, having got what he wanted as always.

Katie cursed herself wishing she could be more assertive. Now she would have to go into town. She took a sip of her tea, which had now gone stone cold and was pretty disgusting; another cup would have to be made.

Next on Katie's agenda was to pop round and see the lady next door. Katie had seemed to inherit the task of checking on Mrs Hogan a couple times a week, (she felt sorry for Mrs Hogan living all alone) not that she minded. Mrs Hogan was a dear old lady who had lived on the estate since it was built some 45 years ago, originally with her dear husband, Mr Hogan who had sadly died some eight years back. They had not had children and Mrs Hogan did not have a large family, her sister-in-law and nephew visited, as did a few friends from the wine tasting circle she had belonged to many years ago.

Katie knocked really loudly on the brass 'pixie' doorknocker, and then let herself in with her key; she just liked to knock to alert Mrs Hogan. The hall of the house was very cluttered, but kind of interesting too, full of Mrs Hogan's knick-knacks, all telling stories of her long life. Katie passed the lounge that was immaculate and unused apart from on Christmas Day and special occasions, and went through to the Kitchen/diner where she found Mrs Hogan.

"Morning" Katie smiled at Mrs Hogan.

"Morning dear" Mrs Hogan grinned; Katie smiled at Mrs Hogan who had not yet put in her dentures so her face looked quite funny without teeth to fill it out.

"Do you want me to get your teeth?" Katie asked.

"Beef?" Mrs Hogan asked, not hearing Katie "You have some beef?"

"Teeth" Katie pointed to her own teeth laughing.

"Oh yes, sorry I probably look a sight for sore eyes I am sure" laughed Mrs Hogan

After sorting out the teeth, Katie made them both a cuppa and made some small cheese and cucumber sandwiches with the crusts cut off for Mrs Hogan's lunch. She did have Meals on Wheels during the week, but not at the weekends.

Katie sat down with Mrs Hogan for about an hour and told her all about her week at work, Mrs Hogan loved to listen to Katie even though often she had no idea what or who Katie was talking about. Sometimes she could not even hear her, but she just nodded and enjoyed the company. Mrs Hogan was always sorry when it was time for Katie to leave, and Katie always felt a bit mean, but she could not stay there all day.

Next was the gym, Katie was not a natural gym bunny but tried to go reasonably regularly. She found it easier to go at the weekends rather than the evening after a long day at the office. On arrival at the gym

Katie was dismayed to see that it was really busy; she preferred it when it was half empty and she could get on the equipment without queuing, plus she did not like it when there were too many 'body beautifuls' strutting around making her feel inadequate. She had a quick look at the classes and noticed that a Pilate's class was just about to start so she opted for that.

Saturday afternoon was generally the time Katie popped to see her parents and today was no exception so after the very calming Pilates session, she made her way to her parent's house which was in the next town and not too far to travel. It was the same house that they had always lived in well that Katie could remember. Her bedroom was still very much the same as it was when she moved out, apart from her mum now using it as a 'store' room making it a little untidy, Katie loved that room, it was very cosy and safe.

"Can you believe the price of my special coffee? It's gone up yet again," her Mother moaned as she was putting her shopping away. "I only went out for a few bits and I spent £25. Where does the money go, everything keeps going up!" she continued.

Moaning was something Katie's Mother was very good at. She rarely had a good word to say about anything or anybody; she was always right and a little scary. Unfortunately she was one of those 'know it all' types, which used to drive Katie mad; not that she ever answered her back, she would just like for once to see her Mother happy and not moaning.

"Where's Dad?" Katie asked

"Where do you think? Out in the garden as usual" her Mother answered.

"I'll pop and see him" said Katie, making her way to the back door.

"Tell him to come in Katie, he has been out there ages, its chilly outside and he hasn't really got over his last cold. I don't want him getting another one and giving it to me...I will put the kettle on"

Katie wandered out into the spotless garden, half of which was laid to lawn (which still had her swing in it that she had enjoyed for years as a child). The other half comprised of a vegetable patch and small greenhouse and a wooden potting shed, which was big enough for a small table and chair. This is where her Dad often retreated to.

Katie's Dad loved his garden. It was his pride and joy, especially since his retirement a few years ago. He had loved his job and was pretty upset when he had to retire and be at home 24/7. The garden gave him a purpose and kept him sane.

He was busy digging some hard earth when Katie found him, but stopped when he saw her, prodding the fork into the earth and leaning one of his feet on it.

Katie thought he looked like a farmer. He really did look the part; he had a wax jacket on that was splashed with mud and because the zip was broken he had a bit of string tied round his waist to keep the coat done up and to stop Mother moaning about him getting cold.

Katie could not resist tugging the string "When are you going to treat yourself to a new coat Dad?" she asked.

"Years in this, you're as bad as your Mother keeping on at me; I like it - its comfortable" he replied indignantly.

"But it looks a mess" protested Katie, half joking half telling the truth.

"Well its ideal for the garden and I like it!" replied Dad, completely seriously.

Katie thought it was wise to change the subject "Did you go out on Thursday? I tried to call and there was no answer"

"Thursday?" he replied "Erm yes, we did go out. I took your Mother to the sea front. Had a nice walk, bit chilly though. And we had a bite to eat. Very nice, oh apart from the milk which was off apparently, in your Mothers coffee." He raised his eyebrow to Katie, who visualised her Mother nagging her Dad at the Coffee shop.

Despite her constant moaning, Katie's Dad totally adored his wife, he worshipped the ground she walked on and always had, and although her Mother rarely showed it Katie knew she also adored her Dad, it really was quite sweet.

"Mums making a brew, and she said that you are to come in now" Katie said sternly mocking her Mother. He nodded and followed Katie back down the path to the house, and into the kitchen where her Mother was busying herself with her opera music loudly playing.

"Take your boots off outside" Mother yelled, upon which Dad dutifully slipped off his wellies and replaced them with brown slippers, she then handed everyone their mug of steaming tea, and passed Katie a nice piece of fruit cake.

"No cake?" Dad asked sadly, knowing only too well what the answer was going to be.
"You know you have to lose those few pounds, you know what the doctor said"
"Yes I know, but a little?"
"No, here are your tablets" Mum handed him three coloured pills, which he dutifully but gloomily took them one by one.

After a while when Katie had really had enough of her Mum keeping on at her Dad she decided to head home - her 'visiting parents' duty fulfilled. On route she popped into the local shop and brought herself a box of chocolates and a bottle of wine ready for her evening slumped in front of the television. She felt she deserved a treat she had been to the gym after all, well Pilates anyway! She could work it off next week. As Katie put her key in the door she could hear her phone ringing. She dashed to answer it but annoyingly it rang off just as she got there. She listened to the voice-mail message that then clicked in.

"Hi Katie, Carrie here. Just wondering what you're up to tonight? Lucy and Mick are coming over and we are getting a takeaway from the new Chinese on the corner. It would be great to see you, about 8pm...call me"

Lucy and Carrie were Katie's long time friends whom she had known since primary school. Amazingly, although they were all totally different personalities, they had kept in touch over the years and were still all very close friends.

Carrie lived with her partner Tony and their two young children, two dogs, one cat and lots of goldfish! Lucy was married to Mick; they had no children, although Lucy claimed she had no intention of having children and spoiling her social life! Katie and Carrie both knew deep down Lucy wanted children, they could just tell. Lucy and Mick both had high-powered jobs and were often jetting off to the sun to 'de-stress' from work.

Katie groaned at the voicemail message. She really didn't feel like going out, and once, again being the one without a partner. Not that they ever left her out, and it always ended up being a fun night when she did go round there. However, Katie still couldn't help feeling very 'single' on such nights. She really just wanted to stay in at home, eat chocolate, drink wine and watch a soppy film that would no doubt make her cry.

Katie reluctantly dialled Carries number "Hi is your Mum there Toby? Its Aunty Katie" she said to Carries eldest son who always eagerly answered the phone. Toby passed the phone to his Mum.

"Carrie, thanks for the offer, but I have plans for tonight" said Katie as convincingly as she could.

"What plans do you have exactly?" mocked Carrie, knowing her friend would have no plans.

"Well...I was going to watch a film that I've been meaning to watch for ages and..."

"So no plans then? See you at eight!" Carrie interrupted.

"Ok – see you at eight" Katie said sighing as she put the phone down. Now she would have to have a bath and get ready. Katie reflected to herself that Carrie was probably right to encourage her to go over; It was quite sweet that they always included her and did not just go out as a cosy foursome. It would be good to see Carrie, but Lucy could be quite hard work, always asking questions like 'met anyone yet?', which really bugged Katie.

Chapter 5

Willow and I were sitting on the beach looking out to the large lapping frothy waves. It was quiet yet noisy as the waves crashed over the rocks on the beach then slowly soaked backwards to the sea.

We were sitting there in silence, I was trying to find some inspiration as to how I was going to tackle Katie; I mean how do you help someone who doesn't really think they need to be helped and certainly wouldn't think of asking an angel for help?

I wondered why I never got the easy cases - to be allocated humans who believed in angels would be a welcome change and would make things so much easier. I guess however that Katie's case should this be seen as a challenge. A challenge that I have to succeed in!

I glanced over at Willow who looked deep in thought, I concentrated hard for a few moments to see if I could read his thoughts but nothing came to me - just blankness, plain white blankness. I so wished I had mastered the skill; everyone else seemed to have it down to a fine art. Well I'm not too sure that Pascolli had, he always said he could read thoughts but personally I think he is bluffing.

I couldn't resist nudging Willow; he looked over at me with an expression that showed no emotion.

"You ok Will?" I asked

"Yes just a bit tired, I think maybe I have too many cases to deal with at the moment, Hibissa seems to think I am some sort of 'super angel', but I'm worried I am being spread to thinly and will not be able to give 100% to all the cases. If I can't give my best then I would rather not do it" sighed Willow.

It was totally unlike Willow to moan, in fact I cannot recall the last time I ever heard him moan (well except about Pascolli and me and how messy the Chamber is), but no, this was different. It was unlike Willow to even talk about his caseload let alone moan about it.

"Any thing I could do to help?" I asked, genuinely wanting to help my good friend.

Willow laughed and shook his head. I felt a pang of sadness run through my heart as I realised that no matter how overworked Willow was, he would never pass work over to me because he knew I was not up to it!

I really wanted to be a good angel. One who, like Willow, could command respect. I felt really sad; even though Willow had not said a thing I just knew what he felt about me, and my capabilites. I looked back out at the sea, the waves crashing even louder, dulling my thoughts temporarily.

Suddenly at that precise moment I decided that I really was going to be a success and Katie was going to be my first real success story, a springboard for lots more cases. Yes, I would help her to become more assertive, more confidants and more in control of her life. It's all very good being 'nice' but to be walked all over again and again and by family and friends who supposedly should love you really does show a distinct lack of self respect and that is what she needs to gain, self respect. She needs to learn to love herself and have faith in what she does and I guess to stand her ground. I laughed out loud thinking I could also be talking about myself because I needed to earn respect. My laugh startled Willow from his pained deep thoughts.

"You ok, what's funny?" Willow asked with a puzzled expression

"Well, I think you should be honest with Hibissa and, tell him that in order for you to provide the best customer care that he's always on about, you need less cases. Tell him it is a matter of quality and not quantity!" I said very assertively and proudly.

"I'm not sure Hibissa sees it like that, he has targets and statistics to complete you know!" Willow replied.

"Targets and statistics - tosh!" I retaliated. "He is a Guardian Angel for goodness sake. Customers are King are they not? If you don't get results it looks bad on him; he trained you. That's why he's always on my case - he doesn't want me to let him down because it comes back on him!"

"Well yes, put like that I suppose that does make sense...did you bang your head or something Nicoise?" Willow asked wondering if he was really talking to me.

"Listen Willow, I have a sunrise slot with Hibissa. Why don't you take my slot to save you waiting and, I'll have your next slot. I'm sure you will feel better if you speak with him sooner rather than later."

"Thanks Nicoice" responded Willow. That would be useful. But, hang on a minute, are you sure you're not just offering to swap your slot because you have nothing to report yet?" Willow was not far off the truth as, it would be useful for me to have a later slot, but that was not why I offered. I genuinely wanted to help Willow. Like I said earlier, he never moans or gets stressy so he obviously needs to sort it out.

Willow looked directly at me and stared into my eyes, scanning my thoughts. I hate it when he does that and Hibissa too, it makes you feel kind of unsettled - like you want to be able to close your mind to their beady eyes staring into your soul.

"It's a deal. How is your case going?" Willow asked, genuinely interested.
"Erm, its all right I suppose" I replied, unconvincingly.

"What do you mean 'alright'?" he probed. I looked around the beach and understood why Willow often came down here to sort out his cases; it was so peaceful, so endless, just miles and miles of white sand.

"Well, I've been down a few times and had a look at her life patterns. She seems very nice, but she doesn't believe in angels, and I really have no idea as to how I start to get through to such an unbeliever. She is nice but also annoying ...... I can't really explain it. I have the urge to shake her and tell her to wake up and deal with life properly. Any ideas Willow?" I asked.

"Well you can't shake her, that is for sure; what have you done so far?" Willow enquired

"Made notes?" I answered not knowing what else I could add.

"Yes but what is your strategic plan?" Willow asked.

"My what plan?" I responded quietly as I really did not have a plan.

"OK - what do you plan to do next?" said Willow, obviously trying to help.

"I don't know, usually I just kind of see what happens and try and help"

"Goodness, didn't you learn any thing at Canes?" tutted Willow

(Canes - in case your wondering, is probably equivalent to your college or university. We have to attend for three seasons, then on the fourth season we go out and gain our work experience, which is where you have found us now).

"Do you remember the 'corner of wings' theory?" Willow continued.

I shook my head, I really had been a bit of a daydreamer during the more boring Canes lessons and, unfortunately, it looks like my lack of attention is now going to effect my performance because I really can't remember anything about 'corners of wings'!

Willow explained "On one wing you have feathers, dreams and light and on the other wing your have colour, voice and presence. Work through these themes one by one and you will get through" Willow said very knowingly as I nodded pretending to understand but feeling a little puzzled.

"You need to be really close to Katie. Even when humans are not religious or believers, they can sense a presence or guiding force. Listen to her dreams, desires, thoughts; Leave her signs, maybe even direct her to a believer, they can sometimes help. Hearing someone else can channel the thought chain across sometimes" Willow said excitedly. He was so into all this guardian stuff!

"Like someone who reads Angel Cards?" I asked quietly not wanting to sound silly.

"Well yes that could be one way, you're starting to get it! Keep positive at all times when dealing with humans because they need to sense joy, love, hope, healing and peace. If you are negative that negativity will pass through to them and it will not work, they will not ask for help. Do you understand?" Willow asked again looking almost scary. He was such a positive influence even though he was a little geeky round the edges sometimes. It would be good to be positive in order to help someone make a difference. Yes I think I get it.

"Good" Willow said, reading my thoughts.

"Thanks Willow, you are a star a shining star" I smiled

"It's nothing, you just should've paid attention at Canes! Do you want to borrow my books? No doubt you don't have yours now...and thanks for the slot" Willow said kindly.

"What part of the corners do you do first?" I asked, going back to the corner of wings theory.

"That's for you to work out Nicoise, I have said enough. You'll need to read up " Willow said, and I knew that these were his final words on the matter; he had been a big help, or at least it felt like he had!

We sat still in silence, Willow obviously planning his session with Hibissa tomorrow and I was pondering over what Willow had said. I have to admit that I did not fully understand it but, I would read up, and maybe have a word with Pascolli too as, he occasionally has a more down to earth approach to the teachings.

Willow suddenly turned to me with a deadly serious face. "Nicoise, you are going to do really well with this

Katie. I've just seen it! Just calm your mind, settle your thoughts concentrate and go for the first three point wing"

"You mean the feathers, dreams and light?" I asked hoping that I had got this right way round.

Willow smiled. I had got it the right way round! He was a good friend and I appreciated our chat today. Even though he had his own problems and really I should be helping him, here he was selflessly sorting out my starting point. I made a vow to succeed and to always be a good and loyal friend to Willow.

"Lets fly," said Willow suddenly "Enough of this serious stuff"

"Thought you would never ask" I grinned, desperate to stop being serious and to fly with the cool breeze in my wings.

With that we flew. Initially my mind was pre-occupied with *feathers, dreams and light'* but after a while soaring through the heavens my mind was still and empty of thought. I was engrossed in a euphoric feeling of freedom.

Chapter 6

Katie arrived at Carrie's a little late, well probably quite a lot late; she had spent too long in the bath, too long doing her hair, too long debating what to wear and then going with her original choice. All this because she was worried that it would be one of those evenings when Lucy would interrogate her with hundreds of questions about her personal life. Whilst she was worrying she had driven to to Lucy's house rather that Carrie's; when no one answered the door, she panicked realising she should be at Carrie's and drove back like a lunatic. She knocked at the door.

Carrie answered with her youngest child, Sophie, stuck to her hip. Katie smiled at Sophie; she was an adorable child, all blond and angel like, not dis-similar to Carrie who still had her 'cheeky' schoolgirl grin - when it suited her.

"Hi, we were starting to get worried, you ok?" said Carrie as she almost pulled Katie in and slammed the door behind her.

A crying young Toby came up to Katie he looked so upset almost hysterical, and Carrie sighed, "He will not go to bed, he is in one of those moods," she said gloomily. Katie looked at Carrie and noticed how tired she looked. It must be hard with young children, Katie thought to herself, although this was something she had no experience of herself. She really admired Carrie for her relentless patience and endurance.

"I want to watch Carboy's" wailed Toby, loudly to his mum.

"No Toby you know it's too late, you can watch them tomorrow, come on up to bed" Carrie held out her hand to him as he started to cry looking over at Katie for some back up. His face was all red and puffy, and tears were dripping down his chubby little face.

"Can Auntie Katie read to me then?" he asked hopefully

Katie looked over to Carrie not wanting to tread on her toes, but she quite welcomed the thought of delaying joining the 'diner' party. Carrie nodded her agreement, desperate for Toby to stop wailing.

"Come on then, what shall we read?" asked Katie.

"Thomas!" smiled Toby "that's my favourite"

"Thomas it is then, come on" said Katie as she led him up the stairs to his very 'blue' room full of pictures of trains and cars, the floor covered with toys and hundreds of teddies staring right at them from the shelf in the corner. Toby ran into the room and found a huge book, and smiled as he handed the book to Katie.

"Read that!" he demanded

"Please" reminded Katie

"Sorry, peas" he said, ever so sweetly.

Katie read three very long chapters to a very excited Toby, who did eventually fall asleep. Katie kissed the top of his head, pulled his duvet up over his tiny body, and put the book down, job accomplished.

Katie quietly left the room and joined the others who were happily tucking into the buffet that Carrie and Tony had prepared. As always there was way too much food, but Tony did this on purpose just so he could eat lots!

Tony and Carrie had been together forever, they were well suited and seemed happy. Tony was a postman (which Lucy and Mick seemed to think was funny), he always helped around the house and was a real 'hands-on' Dad, and the kids adored him.

He also did most of the cooking too, much to Carrie's relief as she, was about as good a cook, as Katie (pretty darn poor). However, Katie knew there was another side to Tony that she never saw; it was the side that Carrie moaned about constantly - his sulky moods and terrible politically incorrect jokes.

"Katie, come and eat. And you've have just missed my brilliant joke" laughed Tony welcoming her into the room. Katie winced praying he would not repeat the joke for her benefit. As his jokes always went beyond her, she just was not very good at understanding jokes. Embarrassing really, she never knew whether to laugh and pretend she 'got it' or to just ask him to explain it, which then always made everyone laugh at her.

"No point in telling Katie, she never gets them, do you Katie?" laughed Lucy, coming over to Katie and kissing her on the cheek.

Katie laughed nervously. She loved Lucy but she always made Katie feel as though she was the village idiot, not quite the full ticket. Lucy's husband Mike laughed and waved across at Katie. Deep down though Katie knew they meant no real malice, they loved her too.

"How are those two cows in the office these days? Sara and Jayne I mean" asked Carrie.

"Oh same as ever" replied Katie sheepishly, not really wanting to talk about work.

"You really should put them in their place one of these days, that would teach them!" said Tony, who had finally stopped telling awful jokes.

"They're ok," said Katie "They don't mean any real harm, they are just young and..."

"Bitchy!"Shouted Lucy, finishing Katie's sentence.

"No – they are not that bad Lucy. Its just their age, they just think life is one big party" said Katie

"Nowt wrong in that theory" chipped in Mick with a mouthful of sausage roll. Lucy threw him one of her legendary disdainful stares.

"Any developments with Mr Darcy?" asked Tony

"Mr who...who is Mr Darcy? Lucy hasn't said anything about a Mr Darcy" said Mick all puzzled.

"He's not really called Mr Darcy you donut!" said Lucy to her husband. "Its that Accountant that Katie has the hots for...John isn't it?"

"James, not John" corrected Carrie winking at Katie who was now blushing a deep crimson colour not unlike the colour of Carrie's settee.

Katie felt all eyes on her. She was cross with herself for having told Lucy and Carrie, on one of their girly nights in, that she quite fancied James; they had not let it go since and, she would never hear the end of it now. She thought briefly about James, and admitted to herself that, yes, she did fancy him but he had no interest in her, in that way. Of course he was kind and courteous, but he was like that to everyone. Anyway in Katie's experience it wasn't good to date bosses or colleagues.

"How is Toby liking playschool?" Katie asked Carrie changing the subject in the hope of some sort of reprieve. Mick and Tony laughed, and Lucy looked up from the other side of the room.

"Don't change the subject Katie. You need to pursue this. James bloke, I mean how old are you now...nearly 37? If you like him bloody well make a move and ask him out for lunch or something," Lucy said.

"I am only just 36!" snorted Katie, always quite age sensitive

"Oh what's a year between friends?" Lucy said

"Quite a lot actually" Carrie said, seeing that Katie was not enjoying the interrogation. "Tuck in everyone there's plenty here. Any more drinks?"

"Think I'll have some more of that tomato pasta" said Mick getting up to refill his plate.

"I don't think you should fattie," laughed Lucy poking his protruding belly. Mick pulled a face back at her and went a bit quiet for a while. He didn't like it that he had recently put some weight on round his middle.

The mood of the gathering went a little serious for a short while. Everyone got on with eating and Carrie was busy refilling all the drinks.

Eventually, Lucy broke the silence (she could never stay quiet for long).

"Why don't you go and see one of those Medium's, get a reading, and see whats in store; see if James is the one?" she suggested.

"What a load of old rubbish!" said Tony to Lucy 'Those 'mediums' just see vulnerable people and just take their money. I'm surprised you would even suggest such a thing to Katie"

"You're wrong Tony" said Lucy, really seriously now "It can really help some people. There was this girl at work and she was told by a medium that she was going to get promoted, then get married and get a cat and it all come true, well nearly"

"What do you mean 'nearly'?" asked Carrie

"Well, she already had a cat and she's just got divorced, but she did get a new job" Lucy said.

Tony snorted out loud "I rest my case. And how much did she pay to be told that?" he asked. "Don't you agree Mick?" he turned to his friend, who had not been following the conversation at all, for moral support. Mick gave his friend a blank look.

"Whilst, I don't believe in that sort of thing, and I think it's just a laugh, and I can see how some people may get comfort from it" Katie said, adding "But I think it's quite expensive though"

"No, its only about £20, that's not too much, I would go" Lucy said

"Katie don't listen to Lucy, you just need to get out more. I mean you're not a bad looking bird," Tony said winking at her.

Katie smiled, but inside she sighed. She hated the way they always seemed to get onto the subject of her relationship status. Surely there was more to life than just having a boyfriend or partner. And now this looking into the future business was really getting on her nerves. She wanted to shout out at them but she could not do that - it just was not her.

"Just ask him for a lunch time drink, he can only say 'no'; what have you got to lose? I think blokes like a bit of directness from a woman" piped up Mick from somewhere

"'Blokes like directness'…where do you get that from?" Carrie asked curiously "Anyway, where have you been sleeping? We've moved on from James"

"Yes, do keep up!" laughed Lucy "We're talking about mediums, readings and knowing the future now"

"What?" Mick asked puzzled

"Readings you know. Like Sue had," Carrie reminded him.

"Angel cards? Oh I like them, can be very positive. Very good" Mick said shocking everyone in the room.

"Who said anything about Angels?" Tony asked, "That's completely different, I mean Angels?? Come on, don't say you believe in Angels," he mocked, and flapped his arms imitating wings, making the girls giggle.

"Piss off. Course not, but they did seem to help Sue" Mick said and Carrie nodded in agreement.

Katie stood up assertively. She had had enough of this and really didn't want to be the centre of the conversation all night so she decided to leave. She picked up her bag off the floor.

"Going to have to fly" she said

"Very good, quite funny for you, almost a joke!" Tony said to Katie as she stood up.

"Do you believe in Angels Katie?" Mick asked quite seriously

"They look cute on Christmas cards," replied Katie. "Listen I must go, thanks so much. The food was lovely, good to see you all, I guess it will have to be round mine next time eh?" She kissed everyone and left before anyone could persuade her to stay longer.

Finally, Katie was back at home in her flat with nobody to keep on at her. No questions. It was bliss. She loved her friends, but every time it was the same; she always was the source of their conversation and the butt of their jokes. Sometimes it really got her down.

She made her way to her bathroom, which was one of her favourite rooms. It had a bath that you had to step down into. She looked longingly to the bath and decided she would have a lovely bubbly soak, and surround the bath with candles.

Katie started running the bath and took off her make up and cleaned her teeth. She felt safe again now back in her comfort zone of home. She slipped into the bath and went into a state of complete relaxation almost falling asleep in the hot bubbly water.

Katie finished her bath and, climbing into bed she noticed a white feather on her pillow. She picked it up and inspected it. The feather was large, very white and quite shiny not an average feather. Then she panicked, how an earth could it have got there? She looked over to the window, which was open; surely a bird would not have got in and out again. She shut the window, and returned to the feather. Inspecting it further she found it very captivating, very beautiful. She stared at it for a while then discarded it. She told herself it was just a feather from a dirty bird. She placed it on her bedside cabinet and thought no more of it.

Katie slept really well that night. This was unusual for her as she was bit of an insomniac, which she blamed on her active mind. But that night she slept a deep, uninterrupted sleep. Although she did not dream, she had the sensation of being surrounded by white, white feathers, which for some reason seemed comforting and supportive.

Chapter 7

"Some bird!" I mocked out loud to myself.

How could Katie possibly think my beautiful feather, left with such hope and care, could be confused with the feather of a common bird – after all no bird's feather (as beautiful as some are) could be in the same league as an Angel feather. And such a perfect, white, pristine, sparkling specimen!

Oh well perhaps I should try leaving another one, maybe at her office? No on second thoughts, perhaps I should try the 'colour vision' that Willow suggested. Yes, that sounded like a plan, but when and how?

There was so much to think about. It would be so much easier if humans just all believed in us and asked us for help, but then I guess then we would be inundated with requests. Perhaps it is right the way it has always been?

I reached high up on to the top of my shelves and pulled down my old Angel textbooks, and with them came a flurry of thick white dust making me sneeze several times (yes Angels do sneeze!). These books had not seen the light of day for many a season and the dust clearly demonstrated this. I thumbed through the pages until I found the section on light rays, and read the very small text on the page:

'You can source different lights, seemingly making them appear from nowhere before the chosen human; these lights may appear in full down streams of colour or glimpses of light gleaming back at them. To administer such rays it is a good plan to first ascertain what colours the human in question prefers. You also need to have a good knowledge of the humans' needs/worries. Think about this and meditate before commencing in order that the light rays are administered safely and to the correct subject. Also take into account that this could scare some humans...'

I closed the book, having read enough. Pretty boring stuff really, shame it did not have pictures to illustrate the technique, I much prefer visual learning. Oh well I guess I'll have to go with what I have. Yes, I will give this a go; don't know when exactly, but soon, and I think that Katie's colour is green. Yes green, lets go with green!

"Green, green, green" I chanted out loud then closed my eyes and visualised green fields, green leaves, green plants, green moss, waves of green leaves scattered on the pathways of woods, (I stopped there; if they had fallen they probably would not be green anymore!) Continuing, I thought of green eyes. Giving green! Yes green is the giving colour, pleasing, calming, easy on the eyes.

I opened my eyes and was amazed to find myself surrounded in emerald green transparent rays of light, beaming down from above and dancing around the chamber in joy. I have to admit I was seriously shocked, I mean this was something created by me! Come on!

Pascolli suddenly came crashing into the room, energetic as ever. He stood in the doorway with his mouth open "Wow! How have these rays got here?" he asked.

'Sssh, I am concentrating on green" I said

"Think blue now. Come on; see if you can change them. Think of azure blue sky" encouraged Pascolli.

Thought hard about blue, lovely cool, fresh, still blue.

"Cool! Nicoise, open your eyes mate. You have changed the colours, that's bloomin' amazing...especially for you!" exclaimed Pascolli.

"Hey don't you know colour is my thing?" I laughed

"Obviously" said Pascolli "Sorry to burst the colour bubble thingy mate, but Hibissa is really cross that you changed your appointment with Willow"

"Who told you?" I asked.

"Willow" replied Pascolli, "I just saw him come out of his meeting. He said that Hibissa thinks you're avoiding him because maybe your case is going badly?"

"Well he is wrong, I'm not avoiding him. I was trying to help Willow out. Honestly, this is the thanks you get for helping a friend. And for the record the case is going fine, hence the practice on rays here" I looked around the chamber at the fading rays which had almost disappeared now.

"I'm just the messenger" Pascolli pulled a funny face at me.

"I know, but I am trying Pascolli really I am, I'll go and see Hibissa and explain"

"You can't go without an invitation, you know that?" advised Pascolli.

"I swapped with Willow, so I'll see him then, I never seem to do anything right" I said feeling a little sorry for myself. A few moments ago I was so happy in the knowledge I had created rays.

"Don't be down, those rays were fantastic, you just have to put it in to practise now" Pascolli said as he patted my back in a friendly comforting gesture.

"Were you reading my thoughts? I didn't know you could yet?" I exclaimed.

"It's a cool skill to learn," grinned Pascolli. I nodded in agreement, feeling a little jealous. Another skill I had to practice no doubt.

"Think I might go for a fly" I said

"Do you want company?" Pascolli asked knowing my reply before I spoke.

"No, not today thanks, I need to do some thinking and planning" I said seriously.

"Happy planning," grinned Pascolli

I left the chamber, went down the winding corridor and out into the air, which was cold, but that was probably good I thought to myself as I shivered. It would keep me from dilly-dallying; I needed to think, and get back and log the plan.

Chapter 8

After a restless night and strange dreams of feathers the last thing Katie wanted to do when she got to work was run errands for Carla – she felt tired and exhausted, and just wanted to sit at her desk but no Carla had other ideas. Running errands was a regular occurrence, as Carla was incredibly lazy, and liked to use her authority, with Katie. This time it was toothpaste. She was going out with an important client and although she had brought her toothbrush she had forgotten her toothpaste. She could not possibly go to a meeting without brushing her pearly white teeth.

Katie brushed past Sara's desk in her hurry to Carla's office and her bag accidently knocked off her pot of pencils which went rolling across the tatty wooden floor, clattering loudly and making Sara and Jayne look up in disgust.

"Hey you should be more careful with that bag," exclaimed Sara, adding, "Where did you get it from?" Katie was could not tell if she was asking because she liked it or, more probably because she thought it was awful. Still Katie needed to see if she could sell some for her brother.

"Erm, my brother, do you like it?" Katie asked tentatively

"Like it? You must be kidding! Where on earth did he get it?" Sara said.

Jayne now looked up and screwed up her rather long nose, saying

"Totally last season or no last decade even" laughing at her own joke and Sara joined in.

Katie sighed, but luckily, her phone started ringing, which she dutifully went and answered, leaving the two laughing hyennas to amuse them at her expense.

After the call, Katie continued with her work, not wanting to get involved any further with the conversation about bags. She sighed to herself again and guessed that she would now end up buying all the bags from Nick because she just could never say no to him.

After reconsidering, Katie decided to rise above it all and act as if nothing had upset her. So in good spirit she offered to make the tea, which of course went down well with Sara and Jayne.

Katie made tea for everyone, took one into Carla, and then popped to James' room with one too; after all it would have been rude to leave him out. Katie knocked quietly on his door.

"Come in" James called

"Tea?" Katie smiled and handed him the mug of hot steaming strong tea, James liked strong tea with one sugar.

"What a star, thank you" he smiled warmly. As he spoke something glistened and caught Katie's eye - a large white, sparkling feather practically identical to the one she found mysteriously in her room last night. There on James desk the very same feather. Katie was totally mesmersised and stood there in a trance staring at the glistening feather.

James suddenly jumped up yelping. Katie realised that in her distraction with the feather, she had placed the mug of tea down on the desk slightly at an angle; it had tipped up and the tea was now flowing across James work, off the desk and onto his smart brown trousers, causing him to jump up in shock. It was just a misjudgement but James looked angry, like he was going to shout at Katie. All of a sudden, Carla was by his side, glaring ...

"What the hell happened here?" Carla yelled looking directly at Katie.

Katie wanted to say, " What an earth does it look like you bloody idiot" but instead said, "I am so so, sorry James, please forgive me."

"Why did you spill his tea? You are so damned clumsy sometimes" interjected Carla

"It was an accident", James said, "My desk is such a tip, there was nowhere to put the tea". He tried to take the blame, but Carla seemed intent on having a go at Katie.

"No James, she should watch what she is doing for goodness sake. Isn't that right Katie?" Carla asked, but Katie was not listening. She was still mesmerised by the white feather on James' desk; it seemed to have a white aura surrounding it. She just stood and stared at it, really wanting to pick it up.

Carla was waiting for a reply, but she then too spotted the feather glistening proudly at them all.

"Goodness what is that?" Carla asked

"A feather!" James said not really understanding the importance of this feather or why both women were now totally mesmerised by its beauty.

"I know it's a feather", Carla replied. "I mean what is it doing on your desk? How did it get here?"

"I don't know, it just appeared" James replied

"Its so pretty!" Carla said in a softer and kinder voice, quite unlike her normal voice.

"Here, keep it" said James as he handed Carla the feather. As she took it, a white transparent light seemed to shine over James, Katie was dazzled and wondered what on earth it was.

'Thank you" Carla said to James fluttering, her eyelashes at him.

Katie felt disappointed and sad. She didn't really know why, but she knew that the feather should not be in Carla's hands. It was wrong - she felt it was bad.

Katie stopped her thoughts and told herself that for goodness sake it was just a feather, an everyday run of the mill feather. She suddenly wondered why she had been getting so wound up about it. Katie looked over at James and Carla, who were standing in an almost a slow motion trance, it was sickening to see.

However, the new 'fluffy' version of Carla only lasted momentarily, she suddenly snapped back into good old ruthless, tactless Carla.

"Katie!" she barked "Once you have cleared up this mess, make James a fresh tea, and then you need to go back and change my toothpaste. You got just plain toothpaste but I need one for sensitive teeth. You know I have sensitive teeth!"

"Sorry" Katie said but was thinking "Sensitive, my arse!"

Carla stormed out of James' office with her usual dramatic air, causing Sara and Jayne to try and appear like they were busy, rather than sitting there chatting. They did not want to get on to the wrong side of Carla; they liked to leave that to Katie, who seemed to do a good job of winding Carla up, much to their amusement.

"I hope you two have been working and not chatting as per normal," Carla shouted at them, as she rushed passed them.

"Yes of course" they muttered feebly together

"Good, job too don't want any more staff slacking" Carla grumbled, clearly directing her ire at Katie's misfortune.

James looked up at Katie as she rapidly tried to clear up the soggy mess from the spilt tea. He smiled at Katie causing her to blush; she thought he was so nice, so kind, and just so suitable.

"Wow, Carla is an amazing woman, so feisty. I like that in a woman" James said, nodding his head. Katie felt her heart sink, it really was the last thing she wanted to hear, and that James thought Carla was 'amazing'.

"I wonder if she is still dating that Anthony chap. Do you know if she is Katie?" James inquired casually.

"I really don't know James, I should get on" Katie replied. She couldn't wait to get out of the office her head was spinning. She was devastated that he – her lovely James - liked Carla or that he was remotely interested in her. Why oh why? Katie wondered why nice people always seemed to be attracted to totally mean and nasty people? Was it the challenge? Was she too boring a person?

"It a confidence thing" a voice said in Katie's head making her stop and stand still, wondering where the hell the voice came from. It certainly was not her voice.

"Confidence is something I'm lacking in" she said back to the voice. James calling out interrupted Katie's exchange with the mysterious inner voice.

"Can you bring a damp cloth in Katie"

"Sure" she replied walking past the sniggering Jayne and Sara. She really did seem to be their sole source of entertainment that day.

Having cleared up the mess in James' office Katie, somewhat thankful for the opportunity to leave the building walked back to the chemist to get Carla's 'senistive' toothpaste. There was a queue of three elderly ladies and a mother with a toddler who was throwing a temper tantrum. The mother was shouting loudly at the whingeing child, whilst the three ladies where tutting and raising their eyebrows at her parenting skills, almost clucking like a group of brown scrawny chickens. Katie stood quietly, people watching as she patiently waited her turn to be served.

Katie felt a presence of someone behind her, the presence of someone different. She slowly turned her head to see who was standing behind her, and was not expecting what she saw – a tall, very tall, thin man with quite a nice face, although most of it was covered with long, wavy ginger hair. Katie suddenly realised she was staring as the man smiled at her, making her blush with embarrassment.

"Cheer up, it may never happen?" the man said
Katie smiled lamely at the man. She really was not in the mood for a conversation with a stranger, even a quite intriguing one who was wearing a corduroy jacket (so last year). She giggled inwardly thinking of Sara and Jayne and what they would make of this man's odd dress sense.

"It already has" Katie replied quietly

"Can't be too bad or you would be crying and you look like you need to laugh" he said, which made Katie feel a little uneasy since she had been laughing to herself about his jacket. She suddenly noticed his amazing piercing green eyes; they were truly beautiful - if a man's eyes could be called beautiful. She had never seen eyes like it before. The man smiled and his eyes looked happy.

"That comes later I guess" Katie said. The man was about to reply, but Katie was now at the front of the queue.

"Can I help?" demanded a very stern shop assistant
"Can I ..." Katie felt embarrassed but continued "Can I change this toothpaste I brought earlier to Sensitive one?"

"Sure Madam. But what did your last slave die of? Go and get one from the shelf, I can't leave the counter," the shop assistant growled

"Goodness love, what charm school did you come from" the ginger man said making Katie laugh, but the shop assistant scowled. Katie changed the toothpaste and turned and smiled at the ginger man.

"Keep smiling, you have a lovely smile" he said then turned to the Sales Assistant to whom Katie imagined he said, "Unlike you love - you need to practice on yours!" Of course he didn't say such a thing, but he did give the assistant a funny grin getting a 'weirdo' grin back as she served him.

Katie smiled. It was funny how a stranger could cheer you up. He was funny, and she wondered who he was and where he came from. He was a little odd. She looked at her watch and realised she had been quite some time out of the office so she quickened her pace and made her way back to the office with Carla's sensitive toothpaste!

Chapter 9

I am feeling a little worried right now sitting here outside the almighty Hibissa's chamber, waiting to be summonsed to his presence. I know he will be unhappy with my progress so far on this case. To be totally frank he would be right to be concerned, but he should realise that I really am trying.

After what felt like an age "Come Nicoise" called Hibissa. I nervously entered. "Sit" he commanded pointing to the large white leather chair directly opposite his ridiculously large desk. Like a puppy responding to its master, I sat as ordered, I certainly didn't have to be told twice. I sat on the extremely comfy, squishy chair almost disappearing from sight as I sunk into the softness of the chair. I pulled myself away from the centre and sat upright on the edge to face Hibissa.

"Tell me Nicoise, how is case 4126999 coming along?" Hibissa stared intensely at me as he asked this question, scrutinising me, observing my body language and no doubt reading my thoughts before I could even utter them.

I barely had a chance to think let alone speak before Hibissa cut in "I am guessing you think not too good? Am I right?" he asked.

"Well, I am trying some new tactics, that I've not experimented with before" I replied as confidently as I could.

"Like?" continued Hibissa.

"Well, you know the techniques including lights, feather, voice..." I explained.

"These are not new ideas" interrupted Hibissa clearly agitated now. " You should have been experimenting with these from third grade Nicoise.... anyway, do you think these new tactics are working?"

"Well ..." I stopped and cleared my throat nervously as Hibissa continued to stare at me. "Well, it has been a bit of trial and error and I have had some successful and some not quite so successful attempts, but I am learning all the time from my errors Sir.... Katie really liked the feather I left her and was totally taken with it, even though she was a little freaked out initially. And yes, she liked the other feather too"

"Other feather?" asked Hibissa

"Yes Sir, the feather that belonged to James" I replied.

"James is who?" enquired Hibissa, seeming surprised that I had some progress to report.

"James is one of the partners at Katie's place of work. She has a soft spot for him, but unfortunately the matching feather left for him ....erm.... well kind of got taken by the wrong person" I paused and looked directly up at Hibissa.

Hibissa continued with his probing "Who was the wrong person and why would this person take the feather"

"Carla" I replied, "She is Katie's boss, quite a fearsome woman who James unfortunately, now seems to be quite taken with"

"Because Carla received the love feather instead of Katie. Is that right?" asked Hibissa, accurate as ever.

"I guess so" I replied, looking down at the floor, knowing I was now on a downward slope here with Hibissa.

"So what do you plan to do now Nicoise?" he asked.

"Well, I think it's a question of confidence with Katie. I believe she needs the 'voice within tactic' to help her overcome her insecurities" I said, feeling quite chuffed with what I just said very confidently.

"Going back to this James person" Hibissa continued "do you feel he is the right one for your Katie, or is it just convenient? Have you explored other avenues, other humans she may meet along her path?"

"Well I guess put like that yes it might be a little to convenient, but Katie rarely goes out, she doesn't really have a social life other than with her two friends both of whom have partners" I informed Hibissa, my confidence growing.

"Well sometimes you have to look a little further 'outside the box' Nicoise" Hibissa advised. "Someone who is not quite the standard model can often be a better match. Katie sounds like she needs someone who can channel the energy you are trying to create into the right direction" Hibissa nodded continually as he spoke as though he thought everything he said was totally correct. I too then joined him in the 'nodding' - it seemed to help, almost making one believe that I was saying or listening to the right answer.

"Somebody different to channel the energy" I said aloud, nodding even more. Hibissa nodded back, as though we were in some sort of competition, it was actually quite funny (well to me at least). Even though I was nodding in agreement, my mind was going back to James and Katie; surely they were both right for each other?

"Keep trying those tactics Nicoise" said HIbissa, breaking my thoughts.
"I will" I stood up thinking he was finished with me.
"Sit down, we are not finished" Hibissa ordered. "Thank you for swapping your appointment slot with Willow; I understand you did it to help a friend, but, I'll make the appointments in future Nicoise, not you. Do you understand?"
"Yes Sir, sorry Sir" I replied nervously.
"Don't look so glum Nicoise. Have a fair day tomorrow and then get back on the case with a vigour that I'm sure is within you". Hibissa said sort of smiling.

"A fair day off?" I asked, totally gobsmacked with this statement. For Hibissa to let me have a day off I must have been doing something right!

"You are" smiled Hibissa, reading my thoughts again "You are trying Nicoise and thats what counts. You are working on it I know. Now go before I change my mind!" laughed Hibissa. This made me a little uneasy; you don't often see Hibissa laugh unless he is with his cronie friends from the Upper Council.

"Thank you Sir" I said getting up again, yet struggling, as the soft chair seemed to want to keep me sitting down.

"Reflect on what we have said today, Nicoise" advised Hibissa.
"I will Sir," I said, leaving the room with a smile on my face, but slightly puzzled as to whether Hibissa had reprimanded me or praised me. I was not totally sure.

Chapter 10

Carla sat seductively on the bar stool at the tiny wine bar, not more than a stones throw from the office. She fiddled with her hair, checked her phone and applied more cerise pink glittery lip-gloss. Every now and again she looked slyly around to see who was checking her out.

Finally, James made his way back from the crowded bar to Carla with two large glasses of rose wine. Carla smiled widely at James as he approached, and he smiled an almost embarrassed smile in return, looking not unlike a cute puppy, totally smitten. James felt like the luckiest man on the planet. He still could not understand why, the wonderful Carla had agreed to go for a drink with him. He sneaked a glance at her and decided, whatever her reason for being here with him tonight it was cool with him. She was so incredibly hot in his eyes.

Carla looked over at James and she could tell he was over the moon to be out with her. So he should be, she thought after all he was totally not in her league, and she felt it was embarrassing to be seen out with such a geek. However, he had clients she wanted, and if Carla wanted something she got it. Nobody said 'no' to her, well apart from her boyfriend Anthony, occasionally. Carla sighed for a moment as James passed her the glass of wine (hand shaking and wobbling everywhere; she prayed he did not spill any on her fantastic new dress). She thought of Anthony and wished he was here and not this freak of a man, but hey work was work and James could be useful, very useful, in her master plan.

She needed to get the Baker-John account from him, it was the most lucrative account the Company had ever sealed, and Carla should be dealing with it, not James. Carla smiled sweetly at James, flicked her hair behind her ears and moved her chair just a little closer to James, so that her toned leg gently rubbed against his.

James nearly jumped out of his skin when Carla's leg touched his, he couldn't concentrate, he felt tongue tied and had no idea what to talk about other than work, and music. Carla only wanted to talk about work, prying and smiling seductively as she listened to James blab on and on.

Meanwhile, Katie had agreed to meet up with Lucy and Mick for a drink after work. This was actually a rare occurrence, but for some reason Lucy had been particularly persistent, and had badgered Katie until she had agreed.

Katie, Lucy and Mick were meeting in the Blue Swan Pub, just up the road from the office. Katie felt a little uneasy and for some reason had a bad feeling about the whole evening right from the offset. Strangely enough she always felt like this when she went out with Lucy, mainly because she was always trying to fix her up with a friend of a friend or a cousin of a cousin!

Katie walked into the pub and glanced around nervously. She hated walking into such places, it felt so unnatural to her and imagined everyone was staring at her and wondering why she was there, and why she was on her own. Of course no one cared, no one stared, no one wondered why she was on her own, it was always just in her head.

Through the dark, dingy and crowded wine bar Katie spotted Lucy and Mick but froze in horror as she suddenly realised that standing next to them was a man, a short (very short!) man. Katie realised that she had been set up; she had the urge to turn and run, but Lucy had spotted her and was waving furiously. Lucy pushed her way through the crowd and smiled a silly grin at Katie, a perfect smile that stretched right across her perfect little face.

"Katie" said Lucy hugging her as though they were long lost friends just reunited. "Great to see you, what are you drinking?"

"Who is Mike with?" Katie asked grumpily knowing all too well what the answer would be.

"Oh, that's Stan, he works with Mike. He…he is really nice, come over and meet him"

"You know I don't like being set up" Katie hissed at her friend

"Chill out Katie, its not a set up. Stan just happens to be out with Mick, and I am with you. But hey, Stan is nice, you never know you might even like him" she said hopefully.

"Yeah right!" Katie moaned, but as she approached Mick and Stan she smiled, even though she really felt cross.

"Hi, I'm Stan, pleased to meet you" Stan said to Katie holding his hand out for her to shake. Katie went to shake his hand but instead Stan caught her hand and planted a wet kiss on it. Katie shuddered inwardly and retracted her hand back as quick as was comfortably acceptable. Feeling quite repulsed she tucked her hands into her jean pockets, Katie turned her head away from Stan, who seemed to be giving her some 'cute' look to face Mick.

"Hi Mick, how are you?" she asked.

"We work together" interrupted Stan rudely. "Well when I say work I mean I am one of his bosses, isn't that right my boy!" he patted Mick on the back making him spill some of his beer. Mick gave him a slightly irritated look but said nothing.

Katie could tell that they had been drinking for some time, and she cursed for letting herself be talked into coming along. She should know better, she must learn for the future, she really must. However, no matter how bad she felt she managed to be polite and make intelligent conversation. Stan, oblivious to her feeling of repulsion towards him, continued to chat away merrily, telling her in no uncertain terms how great he was, what prospects he had, what a fantastic car he owned and what a total bitch his ex wife was... déjà vu, same old same old Katie thought to herself.

"Excuse me for just a moment" Katie said to Stan very politely, and then wandered over to Lucy.

"You too seem to be getting on quite dandy" Lucy nudged Katie as she spoke "He is single you know and loaded" she smiled like the cat with the cream.

"He is boring me, and he so conceited" Katie said

"Ah he is probably nervous, its difficult for him getting back on the single circuit no doubt, give him a chance"

"He's short as well," Katie added

"So what, don't wear heels" she grinned, "You never give anyone a chance – not everyone is Richard you know" she said, regretting that last comment knowing that any mention of Katie's ex would upset her.

Katie saw red at Lucy's insenstivity, and she felt even more infuriated when she caught Stan's eye and he blew her a kiss (like a creepy stalker). She looked around at everyone laughing and having a good time, but she just wanted to get out of this place, to run, to be away from creepy Stan, away from interfering friends and back into the safety of her comfy little home.

The main door suddenly and unexpectedly opened and a flash of daylight filtered into the dark bar. The light was dancing and enticing, it beckoned and teased Katie's eyes. Strangely no one came in through the door and no one left, but it stayed open and the light shone through brightly and proudly. It seemed to Katie to be getting brighter and brighter, but no one else seemed bothered by it, in fact no one else could see it.

Like a moth to a light Katie started to back away from Lucy, picked up her jacket and then ran quickly out of the door through the light and into the street. The daylight was so strong it made Katie squint; she stopped dead in the street and felt a little panicky and lost. Katie felt she should go back, it was rude to just walk out on friends but something said no, she kept walking away.

Katie heard a voice - a very loud screeching voice, it was Lucy! "God Katie what are you doing?"
    "I am going home...I don't feel too good"
    "Rubbish! I can't believe you walked out like that. Mick will be really upset. He thought you would like Stan, he's ok"
    "You said it wasn't a set up!" said Katie angrily.
    "It wasn't" retorted Lucy.
    "Well it seemed that way to me. I'm not interested Lucy, please don't do it again. I'm happy with my life, happy with being single thank you very much"

"Are you really happy Katie? I don't think I've seen you really happy for such a long time, I'm sorry, I just want you to be happy and not on your own" Lucy said sadly, looking down at her shoes.

Katie peered up at her friend. She felt mean as Lucy really did have a good heart even though she was a pain in the arse at times, well most of the time really, and she knew she wanted Katie to leave singlehood. Katie felt a single tear escape from her eye; it rolled slowly down her cheek, then another tear escaped then another and then before she could compose herself she was sobbing loudly in the street, not caring what anyone thought as they walked past. Lucy then also started to cry and they both stood on the narrow pavement hugging and crying.

"I'm sorry," sobbed Katie, hugging her friend.
"No I'm the one who should be sorry, I shouldn't have brought you here. I should have listened to you and to Carrie, she warned me it would end in tears" said Lucy now breaking away from the hug.
"It's not really Stan, I just feel so useless, so different" said Katie.
"Different?" questioned Lucy.
"Yes, I can't explain. It's weird. It's almost like I don't exist but I do, I'm just here doing but not really enjoying. I'm sorry it sounds like gobbledegook I know, and I feel bad moaning because really I have nothing to moan about do I?"

"We all have 'stuff' to moan about babe. Here wipe your eyes you're starting to look like a panda" Lucy laughed, Katie then laughed noting how image conscious Lucy remained even at such a time.

They walked down the road together in silence, not uncomfortable silence just stillness and thinking time. Eventually they reached the little wine bar called the Cobbles, it really was the tiniest wine bar ever.

"Let me buy you a quick drink before you go home. You can't go home feeling so ghastly. Come on, you like it in here usually" Lucy said.
"Ok, but only one mind" replied Katie.
"That's my girl" said Lucy as she patted her arm and whispered into Katie's ear "Still think a good shag would do you good though, I would lend you Mick but best not!" she laughed. This made Katie giggle and as they walked in the Cobbles together they looked like two happy ladies out for a girly night out.

Katie's 'happy moment' came to an abrupt end as she saw Carla and James sitting at the window seat in the corner, looking a little more than work colleagues, a little too cosy. Katie felt hot and sick; she just had to get out!

"I've got to go," she screamed at Lucy
"What? We've just got here ..."Lucy was puzzled and a bit fed up with Katie's erratic behaviour. Before Lucy

knew what was happening, Katie had once again about faced and ran out though the door. Lucy chased after her.

At the precise moment that Katie and Lucy were hastily leaving, Mick and Stan were trying to get in. Lucy literally bumped into Mick.

"Babe are you alright?" Stan called over to Katie who ignored him, and kept running. Lucy continued to chase, or rather totter after Katie.

Mick looked really puzzled "What the hell is going on?" he shouted over to Lucy everyone in the Wine Bar seemed to stop drinking and look over.

"Sorry'" he said out loud to everyone "Come on Stan, lets get a drink. God only knows what's up with those two!"

"PMT?" Stan suggested smugly.

"Yeah you're probably right, women huh?" agreed Mick as they proceeded to the bar.

Carla looked up when she heard the loud man's voice swearing in the doorway, James didn't really take much notice, he just continued looking at Carla and admiring her beautiful face, her beautiful legs, boobs...he didn't care one bit what was going on. Right now he was with Carla and that was amazing.

"Looks like some sort of domestic going on. Wonder what caused that?" Carla said looking at James feeling a bit nauseous of his constant leering at her.

"Well what do you think?" she asked again

"About what Carla? About you, I think you're...."

"Not about me" interrupted Carla "What do you think caused the commotion?"

"Dunno" James mumbled, wondering if he would be lucky enough to get her into bed. Then he felt a bit worried, what the hell would he do in bed with a woman like Carla?"

Carla looked at him and tutted.

Chapter 11

I'm feeling so happy, excited and almost, yes, empowered. The light rays I sent to Katie really worked, she was totally mesmerised by their beauty and enchantment and they drew her to them away from that awkward situation in the bar. On a slight down side, it was a shame she then went straight into another bar, and not just any bar, but the one that her lovely James and Carla happened to be in!

However, on the whole my plan worked, well at least I can muster up the light rays in such a situation. Can't wait to tell Willow and Pascolli!

I thought about poor Katie and how she must have felt when she saw James and Carla all cosy together in the corner, all smiles and flirting. I wished I could tell Katie that it was not what it seemed, but I can imagine how sad she felt coming across them like that. If only I could tell her, but I can't; us Angels can only guide, not interfere. Our cases have to sort themselves out, albeit with a little guidance from us. Very frustrating sometimes and surely it would be a heck of a lot easier all round if we could tell or warn people. It would stop all that upset. But, no it was not allowed.

I thought about the feather; if only James hadn't given Carla the feather, things would have been different. Maybe it would have been Katie and James in the bar in the cosy corner, which is just how it should have been.

I needed to see Pascolli to talk about his case, James. As soon as I had thought this, Pascolli, followed by Willow, strangely entered the room. Impeccable timing if they're ever was such a thing.

"No cross casing!" Willow said sternly looking at me, whom freaked me out a little; he was just too blooming good at this mind reading thing. I mean, he was hardly even in the same room when he must have read my thoughts!

Surely cross casing can't be that bad if it helps solve problems; the humans get what they need to make them happy, we get the results and keep out of trouble with Hibissa and the other Highers. I really believe that teamwork is the way forward.

"It's not allowed you know the rules. Whatever you may believe," Willow added, now not quite so sternly.

"Come on guys, we're wasting valuable sparkles time. You need to enjoy your fair day now you have one, come on let's go" Pascolli said urgently.

"He has had quite a few today" whispered Willow in my ear.

"Lets go" I said, thinking this would be a good opportunity to speak with Pascolli once of course goody two shoes Willow was out of ear shot.

"Yippee" shouted Pascolli looking decidedly the worst for wear.

"Are you sure he is going to be ok flying there?" I asked Willow

"Of course, you know I have awards for my flying?" said Pascolli.

"You do?" I questioned

"He does actually" added Willow "Surprisingly!"

"Hey don't be so cheeky...come on the others will be wondering where I am"

The three of us flew quickly to the Sparkles Bar. Pascolli looked a little doddery as he flew and certainly didn't look like he'd ever won any awards; I guess it was before he had discovered twinkles! We spent a nice few hours the three of us, joined by a few of Pascolli's friends. I was desperate however to speak with Pascolli about James but Willow who seemed to be superglued to his side, probably knew my plan. So for a while I gave up and just enjoyed the time with my friends. It was good to hang out sometimes; I had been so busy watching Katie lately I had almost forgotton how nice it was just to come here.

Eventually, everyone started to leave and luckily Willow suddenly realised he was supposed to be viewing a case and dashed off. I joined Pascolli as he got up and left his other friends who were now very merry and even singing. Oh dear headaches all round tomorrow! As we hit the night, the air struck very cold and bitter, we would have to fly quickly or we would freeze. I flew right up beside Pascolli, feeling a little out of breath because he did actually fly a lot faster than me, probably because he was a lot stronger than me.

"Can we talk?" I asked, panting

"Not sure you can talk and fly at the same time," laughed Pascolli "Gosh the air is cold, but I think I need a dose of cold air to sober me up"

"Can we stop then?" I asked, expecting Pascolli to say no.

"Ok over there" he pointed to a cloud clearing "not for long though or we will really freeze"

We stopped at the clearing, and where the clouds were heaped up they gave us quite a wind shelter so it did not seem so chilly.

I looked at Pascolli, my good friend, crazy angel that he was, but he was such a good Angel. He was a kind of cheeky angel student at school, who used to be naughty all the time. He never got caught though, he was naturally clever and could talk himself out of almost any situation, and so if there was any trouble he always came out ok. Unlike me, who was always the one caught and unfortunately not clever enough to get out of situations, not then back at school and not now. No, Pascolli was pretty cool, and had the most wicked sense of humour. He loved playing pranks especially on poor Willow, who fell for them every time.

"Listen Pascolli, I have two things I need to ask you," I said.

"Two things? Steady on, not sure I can manage two things! Are you ok? You seem very serious?"

"First, how is your case with James going? I need to know how things are progressing with the human Carla. What do you think is going to happen, what is on his mind?"

"Not sure Carla is human," joked Pascolli, I laughed getting his drift, and also acknowledged the fact he knew who Carla was, so he must know something.

"I need to get a feather back from Carla" I said, "She took it. No, it was given to her by James, but it's not hers, I need to give it to the rightful owner"

"A feather?" Pascolli asked puzzled

"Yes Pascolli a feather. You know, a love feather. I need to get it back. Your case James has given it too the wrong person, if its not returned I fear there will be bad repercussions from this Carla woman, she really can't have the feather ...are you ok, can you hear me" I glanced over to Pascolli who looked weary and his eyes were trying to close.

"Yes" Pascolli nodded. I looked at him reflecting that only a moment ago I was thinking how clever he was. Well, he certainly didn't seem very clever now, too many twinkles no doubt! I wondered how many he'd had. Pascolli straightened himself up and looked very sombre. He looked around as if too check no one was in earshot and leant slightly forwards towards me.

"James is totally smitten with Carla, he worships the ground she walks on. They've been out a few times, but it's totally one sided. She has other plans; poor chap has even arranged a surprise trip for her that is so clearly not going to happen. Carla has a very and rich powerful boyfriend, who has been away for a week, but he'll be back tomorrow.

If you think Carla is scheming you haven't seen anything yet. This boyfriend of hers is really a scheming and knifing sort of chap that would sell his mother to the devil to save his skin" Pascolli shuddered as he spoke.

I interrupted as Pascolli paused for breath. "Have they done the love thing that humans do?"

Pascolli laughed. "Oh yes, she is quite the minx, and I don't think James has ever experienced anything like it before"

"Oh no, that makes everything more complicated" I groaned "Why would she do that with James, she has a boyfriend she loves right?"

"Your so naïve Nicoise. She's a player. She like a black widow spider having her wicked way, entrapping her prey making him believe he is special, giving him a false sense of security then BANG she goes for the kill!"

"Your saying she is going to kill James, oh goodness...why?"

"No, you donut, it's an expression Nicoise. It means she uses him and gets what she wants from him in any way she can and then drops him"

"Oh of course, you mean the account she wants that James has"

"Account, that's interesting" Pascolli said "He is going to be so devasted when she leaves him, and its not going to be long until it happens"

"And you're sure she won't kill him?" I asked quietly

"Well as sure as I can be, but who knows with humans, especially women ones they're so unpredictable" he laughed. We both sat there quietly, not speaking just thinking.

"Katie would be much better for James" Pascolli stated after a while.

"How do you know of Katie?" I asked

"I see her of course, plus I know she is your case. She is a drip though don't you think? Needs to liven up and get a grip I think"

"Hey don't call her a drip, she's actually a totally decent human being in my opinion. She just lacks self confidence and doesn't seem to have much luck!" I said.

"The luck part is down to you Nicoise you have to look after her!" Pascolli exclaimed.

I felt a little sad. I could tell from what Pascolli said that I was not doing my job well enough. I was not looking after Katie well enough - I was letting her down. I promised myself I would try harder.

"Do you know where Carla lives?" I asked changing the subject.

"Sure, she has some fancy penthouse in the city with a roof garden. Pretty cool place actually, think it actually belongs to that Anthony chap though and she just lives there. He travels alot.

"We need to go there and soon," I said

"Ok, probably best to go in the daylight when she is at the office. We'll leave at sunrise. Hopefully I'll be feeling a little more Angel like by then. Feel a bit rough now mate. I think we need to make tracks, I'm feeling cold" said Pascolli.

We flew back, and I was happy with Pascolli flying by my side. I felt positive that especially with Pascolli's help I would now succeed in this case.

I knew one thing now and that was that I really wanted to help Katie and I really wanted her to ask me for help.

Chapter 12

Katie awoke in a fright. She felt hot, very hot, and momentarily was unsure of her surroundings. She peered around her room, her lovely cream and pink coloured room, her safe room, her little retreat.

Katie was relieved as she realised she had just had a bad dream, not real, just a dream. Or more accurateley it could be classed as a nightmare, because Carla was in it! Katie snuggled back down under her cosy duvet, quickly glancing at the clock, the light from which shone brightly making Katie turn her head away quickly with a little groan.

The clock said 5.30am, too early too get up, yet not enough time to really get back to sleep for any length of time before the alarm would go off. Katie lay still and quiet in her bed looking up to the swirly patterns on the dated ceiling. She thought about her dream.

She had been at a wedding, an outside wedding, where everything was grey; the chairs were grey, the ribbons on the chairs were grey, the people sitting on the chairs were grey, and they all had very angry features on their grey faces with long protruding teeth and black eyes...they were not nice, ordinary, friendly people.

At the altar were the bride and groom. The groom was dressed in grey, but the bride, Carla, was dressed in black. As she held the grooms' hand to exchange rings, he started to also turn black, first the sleeve of his jacket, then the back of his jacket, then one leg of his trousers, then the other. A slow creeping blackness was taking him over.

Carla, the bride turned around to face the grey people sitting neatly behind her in rows of five each side of the aisle. She looked stern, determined and evil. The groom then slowly turned around to greet the audience of greyness. He was James! His face looked pale and sad. He looked desperate as he glanced down at his clothes, which were slowly but surely turning black. Katie felt sad for James and thought momentarily about the cosy wine bar scenario and gasped as she realised that now in this dream Carla and James were an item together in .... marriage!

Her thoughts returned to the dream. Katie could see clearly the black veil that Carla wore perched on her fancy hairstyle. Everything was black apart from one thing – a very white and gleaming feather, in the corner of the veil near her perfectly made up face (including black lipstick and black eye pencil heavily drawn around her eyes).

Katie recognised the feather immediately; it was the white feather, the lovely mesmerising feather - James' feather. The feather that was identical to her own feather that she had mysteriously received.

All of a sudden the man who was presiding over the marriage of James and Carla plucked the white feather from the veil and threw it out into the grey, miserable, threatening crowd. Katie suddenly realised she was strangely familiar with this man, yet could not remember how or where she knew him from. He was also dressed in grey, but he had wild red unruly hair and such a kind, smiling and welcoming face. A breath of fresh, air amongst all the surrounding greyness.

"Catch" the man shouted as he threw the feather towards Katie, who was standing at the very back of the grey miserable crowd, watching very quietly the wedding proceedings.

As the feather flew up high into the sky, the grey crowd started scrambling out of their chairs to claim the special almost magical feather. To her amazement Katie caught the feather, but soon was surrounded by the mis-hog greys, grunting, pulling at her clothes, scraping and spitting. Katie was crying out to the man with the ginger hair who was trying his hardest to get through the mass of the grey mis-hogs.

Suddenly, everything changed from grey to white and there was calmness, stillness. And that was all Katie could remember. She sat up and looked around telling herself if was just a dream admittedly a weird one, but what did it mean?

She sighed and pondered on why she had had such a strange and vivid dream, and how detailed it was even down to the fine lace on Carla's veil. Katie usually never remembered such dream; they were just vague bits and pieces of odd dreams, but this one was so real. She felt she had actually been there, but what did it mean?

Katie looked once more at the annoying alarm clock, which was eagerly waiting to chime. She reached over and switched it off. It was 5.45am.

"Get up" a demanding voice said in her head.
"Nice cup of tea" she said out loud, speaking as though somebody was in the room with her.

Katie wandered downstairs and put her orange kettle on. It leaked slightly and she made a mental note to get a new one at the weekend. She felt a little shakey and very tired, and groaned at the thought of going to work. She needed to talk to someone, so she phoned her Dad.

"Hello?" answered a sleepy voice
"Hello Dad, it's Katie"
"Is everything ok love? Its only six in the morning!"
"I couldn't sleep. Thought I would just check you were ok?"
"Well, erm, yes I'm fine. Just a little tired now that's all" said her Dad.

Katie could hear her Mother's voice in the background "Who is it? What do they want at this unearthly hour?"

"Its our Katie" said a muffled voice (he was obviously holding the mouthpiece in a failed attempt to prevent Katie hear her mothers voice).

"For Pete's sake" she moaned. Katie's Dad ignored her moans and returned to Katie.

"It's just I had an awful dream Dad, I'm sorry" apologised Katie.

"Don't worry love, it's just a dream" he replied softly trying to comfort her.

"Well it was more like a nightmare Dad, everyone was miserable, grey and grumpy and they were trying to stop me getting a feather – the special feather"

"A feather?" her Dad asked inquisitively.

"Yes, it should have been my feather ....." Katie stopped mid sentence, suddenly realising how early it was to have called her Dad and how everything she was saying would soundi totally ridiculous to anyone but herself.

"I'm sorry Dad, I shouldn't have called so early! Just wanted to say 'hello' really"

"It's not a problem love. I'm always happy to hear from you, I needed to get up early anyway so you have done me a favour. Are you sure that you're ok?" he asked kindly. "You didn't eat cheese before going to bed did you?" he asked randomly, making Katie giggle.

"Cheese?" laughed Katie

"Yes cheese. Your mother tells me that, apparently, it can make you dream if you eat it late at night, close to bedtime" he replied knowingly.

"It must have been the cheese then. Thanks Dad" Katie said, now eager to get off the subject especially as she could hear her Mother moaning at her Dad again.

"What on earth is this talk of cheese?" Katie heard the mother asked in the background, sitting herself up in the bed.

"Dad I'd better go. Bye ...and thanks" Katie put the phone down wishing she hadn't phoned and worried her Dad. But sometimes she so hated living alone; she needed to talk to someone.

Despite being up so early, Katie arrived at work ten minutes late. Surprisingly and most unusually, both Sara and Jayne were already in, chatting and laughing away. Even though they were in early it was pretty clear that neitherof them had done any work; they had not even switched their PC's on.

Katie got to her desk and sat down with a heavy bump. She threw her bag down a little too clumsily causing the unopened bag to flip off the desk causing the contents to then topple out onto the floor.

"Someone get out the wrong side of the bed today did they?" Sara taunted.

"You look really rough Katie. Are you ok?" Jayne added with a sarcastic tone in her voice.

Before she could answer, a loud shout from Carla calling Katie's name filled the office. Katie got up and quickly made her way to Carla's office. Jayne and Sara smirked at her as she passed their desks.

"Sit down Katie, please" Carla asked politely, pointing to the chair opposite.

Katie sat down pensively wondering what she had done wrong now; she only ever got to sit down when something was wrong.

"Katie, I have left something at my apartment which I need for my meeting on the Baker-John case. I really need it but I have no time to pop home. So I would like you to go and pick it up for me and bring it back here as soon as possible. It's a pink folder and I think I left it on the coffee table in the lounge, after I was working on it last night. You need to be back before 11.30am, before that appointment," Carla said in one big breath.

"Yes of course, Carla," said Katie thinking what a strange request it was. "What's your address?"

Carla handed Katie a neatly folded piece of paper. "You'll find the address and directions on there. Shouldn't take you too long now the rush hour is over."

"I'll go now" Katie replied standing up. Carla stopped her as she reached the door.

"The file is confidential Katie," she added sternly. "On no account should you open it. And make sure you lock the door properly when you leave, it has a bit of funny lock as it keeps sticking"

"Yes, of course Carla. Understood. No problem," said Katie finally leaving the room, worrying about the task she had just been given. 'Confidential' she thought to herself wondering what it was about. It would have been better if Carla hadn't mentioned that fact, she thought, as now she was curious. She was also worried about the lock - what if she couldn't lock the door properly?

"Where are you going?" quizzed Jayne as Katie walked back past her desk.

"Out!" replied Katie bluntly."

"Secret mission, or has Carla run out of hairspray today?" teased Sara making Jayne laugh out loud.

Katie ignored their comments, and quickly gathered up the contents of her bag, stuffing them back in no particular order. As she walked through the door to leave, in walked James who was positively beaming. Obviously a good night with Carla thought Katie sadly.

James obviously was not looking where he was going and bumped straight into Katie, this unfortunately caused her to drop her bag, and, once again, all the contents spilled out over the floor. Jayne and Sara shrieked with laughter.

"Its not your morning is it babe?" laughed Jayne. Katie inwardly agreed it certainly was not her morning, and it seemed to be going from bad to worse.

"So sorry" said James, helping Katie pick up the contents of her bag.

"No, it was my fault. Sorry. Don't worry, I'll get these bits," she said a little embarrassed that James could see everything in her bag, which was a total mess.

"Can I make you a cuppa" smiled James "You look like you could do with one, you look a bit tired"

Katie felt dreadful especially with everyone reminding her of how tired and awful she looked this morning, why do people have to mention that? "No" she said, "I have to go out, thank you"

"Out where?" asked James.

"She's on a secret mission to Carla's flat" interrupted Jayne. Katie glanced at James and he looked slightly flushed which made him look quite cute yet vulnerable.

"I've just got to pick up an account folder for Carla's meeting with Baker-John later this morning" explained Katie.

James stood up and looked strangely puzzled. Katie suddenly panicked as she realised she maybe shouldn't have said anything as Carla had been very specific about how confidential it was. And now she had just blurted it out in front of the whole office. She looked over at Sara and Jayne who luckily now looked preoccupied and were actually typing away.

It suddenly dawned on Katie that the Baker-John account belonged to James, not Carla, and that is probably why he had given her a puzzled look. However she knew that James would not question Carla and Katie herself certainly would not.

She quickly made her way back to the door, but before she could actually leave Carla came into the main office and looked over to James and then Katie.

"Well good morning James" she said in a sickly sexy put on voice. This even made Jayne look up in surprise. Carla then turned to Katie. "I thought you had left!"

"Just going" Katie replied; she did not have to be told twice.

Katie found Carla's flat quite easily which was pretty good in itself, as she was usually very poor with directions. She climbed the stairs to the fourth floor. She could have taken the lift but she wasn't a lover of lifts ever since getting stuck in one in Spain several years ago whilst on holiday.

Katie found Carla's flat and put the key in the lock, which seemed fine. She entered the flat, which on first impressions was pretty amazing; really spacious and light with massive windows looking out on to the street scene below. There were some pretty abstract paintings on the wall, including one of Carla herself, semi-naked, leaning over a load of brightly coloured metal tins. This made Katie chuckle, thinking that only Carla would want such a photo - so vain!

Katie's eyes scanned the room for the pink folder, and sure enough there it was as Carla had said on the glass-topped coffee table in the lounge amongst the glossy fashion magazines placed neatly on the table.

Katie picked up the folder and as she did, a white piece of paper, a letter, slipped from the folder. She picked it up but the temptation to read it was too strong (just human nature). She sat down on the leather settee beside the coffee table and read the letter.

'Dear Ms Red,
I look forward to meeting you on Friday to discuss the transferring of the Baker-John account to you as discussed last week. I am sorry to hear that your partner James is unwell and unable to continue looking after the case. I also agree to your transfer terms involving a slightly higher fee rate in recognition of your particular expertise on such accounts and look forward to working with you on this ...'

"Shit!" Katie exclaimed out loud "What is going on?" She remembered the look on James' face earlier when she had mentioned the Baker-John account. It came to her that moment that Carla was only interested in James for one reason and this was it!

Taking the lucrative Baker-John Account from James for her benefit. The Bitch! Katie felt really angry, but was at a loss as to what to do now she had this knowledge. James would not believe her; he was like a little puppy dog where Carla was concerned. She started to feel even more cross, but then noticed white prisms of light trying to escape from the sides of the door to her left. She walked towards the light.

She stood mesmerised for what seemed like ages, her anger fading. She edged closer to the light, and slowly turned the handle of the door, which opened exposing Carla's bedroom. She entered the huge beautiful room in the centre of which was a massive bed, with a blackhead board and white lacy covers. Sitting right in the centre of the bed was a huge fluffy cat with piercing green eyes looking directly at Katie.

The white prisms of light continued to dance before her. They were concentrated on the dressing table by the window. Katie followed the lights, towards to the dressing table, which was full of expensive creams and potions (probably more than an airport outlet here!). There, amongst the creams was the white feather, James' feather. She reached out and picked it up. At that precise moment the lights stopped and Katie heard a key turn in a lock the door open and then a very heavy footed person march across the wooden floor of the hall way!

Katie was scared, very scared. Still clutching the pink folder and the feather, she quickly scrambled under the bed, not daring to breathe.

Chapter 13

Pascolli and I were at Carla's apartment too. We had seen the feather in the bedroom and were trying our best to guide Katie to the feather, and to get her to take back the feather, which should not be with Carla.

We needed to try and break the infatuation James had for Carla, and the only way we could see to stop this was to get Katie to pick the feather up. Admittedly this was a little dangerous, but up to now the plan was going well, especially when Carla asked Katie to go to her apartment. This was a total dream scenario, but now things had got a little complicated, a little out of hand.

Anthony, Carla's bad boy boyfriend had unexpectedly returned to the apartment for reasons we could not work out. He sounded loud and large as he stomped across the wooden floor as he entered the apartment.

"Oh boy! Oh boy!" exclaimed Pascolli
"Ssh" I pleaded with him to be quiet.
"Its ok Nicoise. Read my mind rather than hear me talk. Stop the light! You need to stop the light now! .... he'll freak out if you don't stop the light" exclaimed Pascolli
I concentrated, and somehow managed to stop the light rays. "It's done"
"Nicoise, you need to get Katie to ask for your help so you can protect her from this situation" said Pascolli.

"But she doesn't believe. She doesn't know I or we exist" I replied.

"She needs to start believing right now! If this Anthony bloke finds her under his bed, snooping about she is going to be in big trouble. And believe me I mean 'big' trouble"

"Katie ask me for help. You need my help. Please, I'm here to help" I pleaded.

Nothing happened.

Pascolli and I looked at each other not quite knowing what to do next.

"Try again" urged Pascolli looking a little more worried now.

I closed my eyes and willed Katie to ask me for help, but my thoughts were interrupted by the loud and cumbersome Anthony who to my horror came marching into the bedroom, sat down with a bump on the bed leaving only inches between him and Katie hiding underneath. I could sense Katie trembling not daring to breathe. He chucked off his very large brown boots, making an even louder clatter as they flew across the room.

Suddenly, his mobile phoned started singing some awful song, which made both Pascolli and me jump. Honestly we were as nervous as poor Katie trembling under the bed.

"Hi sexy" he replied to the voice on the phone "You missed me?" ......"Of course I have missed you, I'm waiting now on our bed. Come home now. I need you!"

Pascolli pulled a horrified face at me "She can't come home!"

"Call Me," I urged Katie through my thought waves I was urgently trying to send her, slightly desperately now.

"I can't get there until after lunch honey. You know I have that meeting with Baker-John" we heard Carla say down the phone.

"Oh yes of course...nice little earner that's going to be... .How is the 'dating' going with that wet weasel James?"

Carla laughed, "Good, I have the information I need now. Once I have clinched this deal this morning, dating with James will be history"

"Good, not sure I really like the whole idea of it. I mean kissing you, touching you... he hasn't tried anything else has he?"

"Oh Ant don't be silly honey, of course he hasn't. He's a true gentleman!" Carla laughed meanly.

Pascolli looked across at me and I read his thoughts "Not true! They slept together every night this week. Try harder with Katie!"

"God help me, if there is a god please help" Katie's whispered scared voice said, making Pascolli and I look at each other in a confused state.

"That's good enough don't you think?" said Pascolli

"But I am not God!" I exclaimed.

"No, you're not" laughed Pascolli "But it's near enough a call to you as an angel don't you think? She needs your help Nicoise"

"How though. What should I do?" I asked.

At this point Pascolli tutted loudly, maybe a touch too loudly as Anthony glanced around the room obviously hearing a strange noise.

"You really are quite useless sometimes Nicoise. Put a protective shield around her, so this numpty man can't see or hear her... Do it now!"

"Yes" I interrupted "That's what I was thinking of doing"

"Well hurry up then!" said Pascolli with a disapproving look on his face. We both looked back at Anthony who was still on the phone to Carla.

"Ok sexy. See you back here after the meeting"

"Meow" purred Carla down the phone causing Pascolli and me to both giggle. I was pleased that Pascolli had not stayed grumpy with me for too long.

The protective shield was in place. Now Anthony would not be able to hear or see Katie, and she would now feel calmer, and she would feel like she had someone helping her, calming her.

"Good luck with the meeting then babe. I'll go and have a bath now and prepare myself for you!" Anthony continued. They said goodbye (finally) and Anthony put the phone down, took all his clothes off just dropping them on floor and leaving them where they landed. He then trekked off to the bathroom naked apart from his designer boxer shorts. On the way he flicked on the stereo, which then filled the room with a loud banging sort of music (human music – a disturbing racket to an angels sensitive ear, nothing like the angel chorus music we are accumstomed too!).

"Now is Katie's chance to get up and get out" whispered Pascolli

"Yes I know you don't have to tell me everything you know!" I said mildly irritated.

"Really, could have fooled me!" Pascolli said in a slightly sarcastic tone, but there was no malice in his voice.

I waited until Katie had scrambled out from under the bed, she then tip toed quietly through the bedroom, back through the lounge and out of the front door. Thank goodness for the loud human music, which for once had a useful purpose, I thought.

"Has she got the feather?" Pascolli asked urgently.

"Yes, she has" I smiled.

"Excellent...job done. Let's get the hell out of here, and quick, I certainly don't want to be here with that

Carla and Anthony together" Pascolli said, and I agreed that was a sight I would rather miss.

We left through the lounge window, laughing together.

Chapter 14

Katie was confused. She could not understand how one minute she was as scared as scared could be, trembling uncontrollably, not daring to even breathe, lying under a bed with some man sitting on it above her, talking on the phone to her boss. Then all of a sudden, as if a switch had been clicked off, she felt calm, safe yet a little angry.

Thoughts danced around her mind. She was puzzled, confused and thankful. "Why did I go into the bedroom in the first place? If I had stayed in the lounge there would have been no problem...The light was so beautiful, so welcoming, almost calling me...What made me hide under the bed, what was I thinking...What should I tell James? Should I warn James?"

Slowly and quietly Katie had crept across the lounge, confident in the knowledge that Carla's boyfriend was happily singing badly (very badly) in the bath accompanied by the loud rock music booming out of the speakers from the lounge. Katie clasped the pink folder tightly to her chest alongside the white feather.

Once she had left the apartment, she flew down the four flights of stairs and almost leapt into her car. Her heart was beating uncontrollably fast. She paused before starting the ignition, not knowing whether to laugh or cry. She wanted to phone someone but yet she had nothing to say.

Spookily, just as she thought of her phone it started to ring out the quirky ring tone she had unfortunately chosen. She glanced at the name of the caller – Carla!

"Where the heck are you?" Carla screeched down the phone. "Its nearly 11.15 and the appointment is at 11.30!" Katie froze momentarily not quite knowing how she should reply. She didn't want Carla to have the folder, and she certainly did not want to be any part of the plan to bring James down.

"I couldn't find the folder." Said Katie. "I searched but just couldn't find it, I'm so sorry, Carla" Katie said, crossing her fingers as she lied though her teeth - something very alien to her.

"What?" screamed Carla "It was there this morning! You can't have missed it surely?"

"Well…I"

"Go back and look again you stupid idiot! I need that file and I need it now!" screamed Carla.

"I'm not going back actually. I know I searched and its just not there!" stated Katie remarkably calmly considering who she was speaking to.

"What! …If you don't go back right now you will not have a job to come back to!" shouted Carla

"That's blackmail – you can't do that!" Katie said.

"Call it what you like! I need you to go back. Look we're wasting time as we speak! You heard what I said Katie, now go back"

"No" Katie barked back.

"Do you not value your job? Go back and you will still have a job" Carla said.

"I quit. I'm not coming back!" shouted Katie, the words leaving her lips before she really had time to comprehend what she had said or done.

"Fine. I'll call Anthony; he's at the apartment now...yes... Well good luck at the Job Centre Katie. I'll send you a month's pay so don't bother coming back to the office" with that statement Carla hung up the phone.

Katie took a deep breath in and tried to comprehend what had just happened.

"Shit! Shit! Shit!" she exclaimed out loud and then proceeded to cry. She did not know what to do, she needed someone to help her, make things better.

She wondered whom she could go and see, she thought suddenly of Carrie and looking at her watch knew that Carrie should be home, so she decided to go and see her.

Katie glanced in her mirror and groaned as she saw how red and puffy her eyes looked; she then looked across to the passenger seat, the white feather gleamed out proudly as it sat on top of the pink folder - the pink folder that had lost Katie her job. She sighed and then proceeded to start up the car and drive off rather erratically until she reached Carrie's house.

Carrie opened the door reluctantly, thinking it was probably one of those really annoying sales people, or worse, some religious people trying to convert her to their 'better' way of life after finding the light.

She was surprised to find her friend Katie, a very sad and sorry looking Katie standing meekly on her doorstep.

"Katie?"

"Can I come in? Or are you busy?"

"Of course you can come in. I have to collect Toby from Pre-school shortly, but other than that...."

Katie started to cry and Carrie just hugged her not having a clue what she was crying about. Carrie had seen Katie cry alot especially after the break up of her last relationship, but Katie seemed different this time. Katie stopped crying abruptly and pulled herself away from Carrie's comforting arms.

She looked at her watch."I'm going to have to go!" Katie said to a puzzled Carrie.

"But you've only just arrived?" stated Carrie now worried about her friend.

"I know, but I really need to get back to the office. Could I come back this afternoon? Would it be ok if I quickly washed my face?" asked Katie.

"Of course. You know where the bathroom is...but Katie what's wrong?"

"Oh it's really complicated. And I lost my job!" she blurted out.

"Oh my god, Katie, how? I mean I am so sorry. How will you cope?" asked Carrie.

"Dunno, but I hated it, so maybe this is my chance, new start and all that"

"They say things happen for a reason, but not sure really" Carrie said grimly.

Katie ran upstairs and into Carrie's bathroom, which was full of bubble bath, bath toys and wet towels all over the floor. Katie smiled a meek smile at her friends' bathroom then looked in the mirror at her red blotchy face. She quickly washed her face, and then reapplied her eye makeup and a little lip-gloss for good measure. As she came down the stairs, Tony had just come home after his morning shift of delivering mail; he looked surprised as he noticed Katie coming down the stairs. He mouthed across to Carrie asking what was wrong but Carrie just shrugged her shoulders back at him.

"You ok Katie?" he asked kindly

"Yes, well no actually, I quit my job" said Katie.

"You quit?" asked Carrie "I thought you said you'd lost your job?"

"Well I did. It's really complicated, I'll explain later. I must go" Katie looked at Carrie's worried expression. "Actually I am happy that I have lost my job. Yes, happy. It could be the making of me!"

"You don't look very happy," Carrie said gloomily

"Well, it's just that it was unexpected. Once I get used to it I'll be fine. I must go now, I need to get into the office when everyone's at lunch to get my bits, I'll call or pop back later, promise"

"Katie" Tony called as she was opening the door, and handed her a card. "It's the name of that medium lady I was telling you about the other night. She runs workshops as well as assertiveness courses... might be worth a call?"

"Tony?" Carrie gave Tony a stern look "What on earth..."

"It might help that's all. She's at a crossroads," said Tony.

"I thought you didn't believe in that 'stuff'!" said Carrie.

"Hey guys. I'm really going now before you two have a domestic. Thanks Tony, I'll bear it in mind." With that Katie left, leaving Tony and Carrie bickering on the doorstep.

Katie arrived at the office. She stuffed the pink folder into a shopping bag she had in her car, and then took the bag into the office with her. She quietly slipped in.

Jayne was the only one about, obviously on lunch cover. She glanced up at Katie but did not pay any attention; she obviously had no idea of what had occurred between Katie and Carla that morning, thankfully.

Katie could hear voices in Carla's room - the Baker-John meeting she presumed. She walked casually over to the stationery cupboard and took out a large brown envelope. She slipped the pink folder inside the brown envelope and then entered James' office and placed the brown envelope underneath some of his current work cases on his desk. Hopefully he would read the contents and come to his senses, and then put a stop to Carla?

As she was leaving his room she remembered the feather. She took it from her handbag, admired it briefly, her mouth breaking into a very small smile. She looked over James' desk and wondered where she could leave the feather. It belonged to James not Carla and she certainly didn't want Carla to see the feather. She decided on putting it safely in the draw of James' desk under his leave card. And then made a quick exit from his room and back to her own desk. She quickly popped a few of her own bits and bobs in her handbag conscious that Jayne may wonder what she was doing. Jayne looked up.

"You off to lunch too?" Jayne asked.
"Yep" Katie nodded not wanting to get into a conversation with Jayne who was obviously bored. "See you"

As she skipped down the stairs to the ground floor, Anthony passed her on the stairs; he was as always on his mobile.

Katie heard his side of the conversation he was obviously having with Carla "It's not there babe. You must have brought it to work, it must be in the office…"

"You think who has it!" he asked

"Oh shit" thought Katie, Carla obviously had an idea that she had the file. Katie started running and once again jumped into her car in a mad dash, the getaway car! Katie drove, not really knowing where she was going but she drove as far away from Anthony and Carla as she could.

Chapter 15

Pascolli and I knew we were in trouble. Willow had tried to warn us that 'cross casing' was strictly forbidden, and, as usual, he was right. Hibissa was not happy, in fact he was very angry.

"So, let's run through this again...first you discussed each other's cases and realised that you were dealing with two people in the same circle that have a direct affect on each other. Secondly, you were both present in this human 'Carla's' apartment when Katie was there, and you used special effects namely light prisms, which I am not sure you have licence's for to entice her into a forbidden room that she would probably not have entered on her own accord. Furthermore you encouraged her to take a feather from Carla's dressing table...."

"Hibissa, Sir it was not like that...." interrupted Pascolli, but soon stopped in his tracks when Hibissa threw him a stony stare.

"Do not interrupt me Pascolli! Remember etiquette and wait until I ask you a question!" ordered Hibissa.

"Yes Sir" Pascolli looked at the floor miserably. I felt bad because I knew this was my entire fault.

"So, then you willed her to ask for help, which she did, but she asked God for help...I am just wondering when you thought you became God young Nicoise! For goodness sake this is outrageous!" Hibissa barked.

"I did it to help Katie!" I exclaimed, trying to explain.

"I can see why you did it Nicoise, but you broke the rules. The rules, as you well know, are there for a reason. Imagine if all guardians allowed this to happen, what sort of state would we be in? Dear dear" he tutted loudly.

"I put the protective shield on to help. I believed it was the right thing to do to help my case Sir," I said bravely.

"I know, I know, but you interfered with the natural course of fate Nicoise. Katie needs to ask for help from you Nicoise no one else. Then and only then can you intervene and help. Is that clear?"

"Yes" I nodded sadly.

"So lets re-cap shall we? Katie has lost her job, stolen a case folder from her ex boss, stolen a feather that she was willed to do against her better judgement, and told lies!"

"Not lies, your honour. Carla has to be stopped. Katie did what she did in the circumstances to protect James," I said protectively.

"And James needs to wake up and get away from Carla before she totally destroys him. She is planning to steal his cases, his share in the partnership, and make a stack of money for herself and for her boyfriend. It will lose him; James, his job, and that will destroy him. He is weak and needs that job, Carla is evil," Pascolli added.

"That is as it may be, but I am afraid your job as guardians is not to play god. The quicker you realise this the quicker you will succeed, you cannot write the script." Said Hibissa.

"But Sir, surely we can't stand by and watch people destroy each other. What is our purpose if we just watch?" I asked

"As I just said, you do not write the script. Katie has her own story to write. You are merely there for when she needs your help, when she knows you are there. You can only help her when she specifically asks for you Nicoise...am I now making myself clear to you both?"

"Perfectly" I almost growled forgetting myself, making Hibissa now look up from his papers on his huge desk and stare directly at me scanning my thoughts no doubt. Very unsettling when mentors do that I can assure you.

"Please, I understand your reasoning for your actions, but you need to conduct yourselves in the correct way following the correct rules. Take this as a verbal warning for your mis-conduct of rule 66219(i). If either of you do anything like this again you will be in front of the High Order. Am I now making myself crystal clear, or do you wish to ask any questions?" said Hibissa almost with a glint of evil in his eyes.

"Yes, yes" we both replied very sheepishly and desperate to leave his chamber.

Hibissa then beckoned us to leave pointing to the door; we did not need telling twice and flew quickly out of the chamber, down the corridors and back into the safety of our own chamber. We found Willow pacing up and down, looking worried and very pale, if that was possible.

"How did it go?" Willow asked gently, knowing the answer before he spoke.

"Don't ask" Pascolli said gloomily "For helping a friend, I am now in trouble, my copybook is blotted. It means I am going to have to work even harder now to redeem myself. Thanks Nicoise!"

I felt bad. I had indeed encouraged Pascolli to help me, yet it was in his interest as much as mine. Honestly I felt that I had made progress; I mean who would have thought that Katie would have stood her ground on this matter?

"Actually, I'm very proud of Katie. I think, on balance, the outcome was desirable, despite what Hibissa says," I said.

"Really? How do you figure that one out? We just got a verbal warning for conduct?" Pascolli said sarcastically.

"She stood up to Carla. She did the right thing. She was courageous, which is what we need to be I think. Yes, we need to be courageous and inspire new guardians. All these rules make me sick, you cant do anything. And, can't you see that once James realises Carla and Anthony's scheme, it will help him too?"

"I agree" Willow said randomly, surprising both of us. "I think she did the right thing not giving the case folder to Carla, and it sounds like she is best out of it, that office sounds ghastly"

I smiled, grateful for Willow's contribution. Everybody always respected what Willow said, he was quite frankly a perfect model of a trainee guardian, and we all aspired to be like him. Well he is sometimes a little nerdy, which I probably would not want to be. Pascolli scowled at me, he seemed to think that he was in the same league as Willow, which he clearly was not. Gosh even I have more common sense, well maybe.

"Well at least it was just a verbal warning," said Pascolli slowly coming out of his grumpy mood. He could never stay grumpy for long; he was too much of a happy go lucky soul.

"Exactly" I smiled "Friends?" Pascolli and Willow laughed and I laughed. How I loved my friends, they are simply the best.

"So shall we schedule a meeting to cross case next week?" I joked cheekily; both Pascolli and Willow threw me a look. "Only joking!"

Chapter 16

It was Saturday. Not that this was now of much significance to Katie given that she had joined the unemployed! Katie felt miserable, and was running through the events of earlier in the day.

It all happened so quickly, like a whirlwind, rapidly changing every part of her life.

She glanced at her mobile phone. There were no messages. She sighed with relief as she had half expected some screaming message from Carla. Then she felt sad that there were no messages from James. She wondered if he had come across the folder yet, and if so, if he would act on the findings or bury his head in the sand as usual? She went to dial his number then stopped and changed her mind. On reflection she thought it was probably better to do nothing today, well nothing more than her usual 'fun-packed' Saturdays.

Katie started to feel sorry for herself, she just wanted to be happy and loved. A hot wet tear slowly trickled down her cheek, and then a few more followed. She wiped her eyes on her sleeve and told herself to stop feeling so sorry for herself, she knew she was pitiful.

Katie thought about when Richard had left her, when he told her that he did not love her any more, that she was boring, that she wasn't fun and that she had let herself go. His words had cut into her heart like a hot knife. She hadn't understood, and did not feel she deserved those words, those very cold and negative words that haunted her frequently, mainly on days like today when she felt small and very alone.

Their sex life admittedly had dwindled down to barely anything, but she questionened whether that was normal in long term partnerships. Perhaps not, maybe she should have tried harder. She remembered then how she had cried and cried, unashamedly crying in front of anyone who may have shown her an ounce of sympathy, but had this helped? No. People had just started to avoid her after a few weeks of hearing her woes; they had their own lives their own worries to contend with.

Katie sniffed her tears back, and then thought back to when her Nan had died. How she had cried then. How she missed her little Nan, who had always been there for her, encouraging her, singing to her, telling her amazing stories about the past, being a child in the war, evacuation, hardship; it was all amazing. Yet had her endless tears brought her Nan back or made her feel better? No of course not. And her Nan would not have wanted her to keep on crying.

Katie thought further back to when she was a young child, playing in the playground at Primary School, which she had to admit was a regular occurrence. She had been a bit of a crybaby back then, but the girls in her class could be pretty mean to her. Some days they would include her in their games of French skipping, catch, conkers or whatever the current game was, but other days they would not and Katie would never stand up to them however mean they were. She would just cry and that just encouraged them to tease her more.... see, she told herself, crying certainly didn't help then and it certainly won't help now.

Katie's indulgence in feeling sorry for herself came to an abrupt end when her mobile phone bleeped at her loudly, making her turn and pick the pink mobile up off the table and check the message.

"Hey you, are you ok? Tony and me worried! Please call or pop in. I am around all weekend. Ps – told Lucy, hope you don't mind. Hugs xxx"

Katie gave a little smile, but didn't feel like talking to Carrie or Lucy as lovely as they were, so she just sent a little text back saying she would call later. Then she switched her phone to silent, and put it back down. She decided she would pop and see Mrs Hogan who didn't have a clue what day it was, let alone noticing if someone was upset; she would not judge, or even realise. Yes that's what she would do.

Mrs Hogan was in the garden, a garden that was almost as cluttered as her house, full of bushes, roses, pansies in terracotta pots and of course lots of weeds, some quite pretty but nevertheless weeds everywhere.

"Oh you made me jump deary," giggled Mrs Hogan who continued to break the bread crusts into tiny crumbs for the birds, placing the crumbs carefully on the wobbly wooden bird table that had seen better days.

"Sorry" smiled Katie.

"Nice sunny day" nodded Mrs Hogan

"Yes" acknowledged Katie staring up to the clouds in the sky, and noticing some pretty fierce looking ones on their way over, so not really too sunny.

"Looks like it could change soon though" Katie said still looking up.

"Things always change, nothing ever stands still for long" Mrs Hogan said, not really realising how apt her words were to Katie.

Katie thought about what Mrs Hogan had just said, realising of course that she was referring to the weather, but so apt ...or maybe Mrs Hogan did know?

Things change she thought, they certainly do.

"For the better" a voice said in Katie's head, slightly taking her by surprise.

"Need to dead the heads" tutted Mrs Hogan interrupting Katie's thoughts. Katie looked across to Mrs Hogan and smiled.

"Would you like me to help you, and perhaps weed the beds?"

"Have you got time deary, that would be so kind" beamed Mrs Hogan, she looked so happy that it made Katie feel happier too.

"I have plenty of time"

"Lovely, lets get busy ... the gloves and secatuers are in the potting shed," she said excitedly, pointing to the small wooden shed, which was only just about standing.

"So many weeds. My Tom used to say they were demons and that you need to clear the blooming demons before the flowers could breath and thrive ...yes get rid of the demons and things will blossom"

Katie repeated the words in her head *'get rid of the demons and things will blossom'...* How very true, the voice returned in her head.

"Get rid of the demons, deal with the demons in your life, then you will feel free to flourish in your life, to move on in your life" the voice said cheerily.

Katie did not know whether she was going mad, or her brain was playing tricks on her, but she felt somehow calm now. The words had made sense - more than sense, they were the way forward. She looked around the messy garden and thought of it as her messy life and now she was going to make a start on clearing the mess up! She almost skipped across to the potting shed, as she opened the door the door handle came off in her hand, she laughed and held it up to show Mrs Hogan.

"Whoops!" she said

"Oh dear, don't worry, just push the door" said Mrs Hogan laughing.

They spent the morning tiding up, clearing the demons from the garden and mind. The sun did actually stay out, and those threatening grey clouds moved on and away. Katie had a nice morning, and for the first time felt positive.

Chapter 17

Pascolli, myself and even dear Willow are now watching Carla with delight as she attempts to conduct the meeting with Baker-John without the file and case notes that she had so wanted.

"Not so impressive now, is she?" I said

"She has no idea, is she even qualified I wonder?" responded Pascolli.

"Did you see his face, he can tell she's bluffing – I'm sure, " I said.

"Oh my goodness they are asking where James is ...good for him, this will be interesting to hear" Pascolli said.

"What do you think she will say?" I asked.

"Sshh and listen!" Willow interrupted.

"Okay, okay keep your wings on!" Pascolli hissed back at Willow.

"Oh my goodness, did she really say that?" I said intrigued.

"Poor James" Pascolli sighed.

"We need to see that folder..." I said

"Where is he? He is not at his desk?" Pascolli asked.

"At lunch?" suggested Willow.

"Let's go, seen as much as I can stomach," I said gloomily.

We spotted James, sitting on a bench facing out on to the busy main road, staring out to the cars driving past and munching on a huge baguette (always amazes me where the food goes in humans, I mean that baguette is seriously almost as long as his arm – well almost!).

"He knows," observed Pascolli

"He knows what?" I asked

"He knows… he has seen the case notes, I can just tell by his body language"

"Oh dear!" added Willow

"Oh yes!" I said loudly "Game on!"

"He looks really sad" Willow said

"Yes I can see, but once he gets over it, he can sort it out, cant he?" I asked Pascolli who obviously knew his case better than me.

"I really can't say for sure, he's not that strong a character and I don't know how he is going to cope with the fact that Carla was 'using' him. I just don't know I really can't tell how it will turn out," said Pascolli quite sadly.

"You need to intervene," I said

"No way guys, remember you both already have a verbal over your heads" said Willow quickly.

"Oh yes how could we forget?" commented Pascolli.

"Oh come on, have a heart. We can't just leave this situation, I don't care about the rules, they're out of date and stink if you ask me. I mean just look at the feeble guy" I said crossly, amazed my friends felt differently to me.

"He'll sort if out" winked Pascolli to me so that Willow could not see.

"Pascolli, don't think I didn't see that?" said Willow

"Got to shoot, catch you later" with that Pascolli was gone, leaving me and Willow watching the colourful parade of cars speed past James as he sat motionless watching them but yet not really watching them.

"Should we follow?" I asked

"No" Willow replied firmly.

"Why?" I asked.

"You know why. Pascolli has to deal with James and it is not your case. You can't interfere, anyway should you not be watching Katie now?" Willow asked wisely as always.

"Yes, yes ...I guess... I was there earlier you know" I answered defensively

"What was she doing then?" Willow enquired.

"Not sure, she spoke about cleaning demons from her thoughts and was pulling up plant things from the garden.

"Erm, sounds cool," said Willow "Shall we fly?"

We left James with his cars and crumbs from his baguette as we took to the sky to fly away from earth back home.

Chapter 18

Katie dialled the number on the card that Tony had given her. She had told herself that she had nothing to lose, and wondered what else could be possibly be in store for her. Perhaps it would be better to see if she could find out? To maybe prepare herself? Katie knew this could not really be the case, but nevertheless she was curious and continued making the call.

"Hello" a small child's voice answered.

"Hi can I speak to your mum please?" Katie asked politely

"Mum!" Shouted the small voice, which was not so small now!

"Hello?" An older voice now spoke "Can I help you?"

"Hi, I have been given your card and recommended by a friend and wondered if you could fit me in for a reading sometime soon?" Katie blurted out all in one go.

"Sorry honey, I am not able to help" the voice said quite abruptly making Katie feel bad for calling.

"Oh ... sorry to have bothered you"

"Don't apologise honey, it's not your fault or problem is it? So never apologise when you do not need to ok?" The voice replied, taking Katie a little by surprise.

"Well no, I just ..."

"Look honey if it's a reading your after why don't you go down to the Psychic Fair at the Tavern on the corner of the High Street, next Tuesday. There will be lots of mediums there who will be only too pleased to help you".

"Oh – ok thank you, I will"

"Split up with your boyfriend honey?" replied the voice.

"No!"

"Not sure whether to go travelling?" Laughed the voice. In the background the small voice that wasn't so small was yelling out.

"No!"

"Usually is"

"Thank you. What time does the Psychic Fair start?" Katie asked.

"I don't know. Check with the Tavern. Bye honey, hope you find what you're looking for, but don't expect to receive all the answers; some you have to find for yourself!" the voice said and then clicked off the phone, leaving Katie to ponder over the strange conversation. She was not sure whether the lady was being helpful or taking the micky. She stopped thinking about it telling herself she was becoming paranoid and that it was probably just as well the lady could not see her, she sounded a little weird in truth. She returned to scanning the local paper for jobs.

Later, Katie had asked Carrie who had in turn asked Lucy to come to the Psychic Fair with her. They had both agreed, each claiming that it was just to help Katie and they certainly did not believe in such stuff (yet secretly both quite excited at the prospect of having a reading and asking those all important questions about what the future may hold for them).

Tuesday soon came round (the days just seemed to fly by for Katie now that she was not working, she found it hard to keep track of the days). Katie picked up Carrie and Lucy in her little old car that unfortunately had seen better days, however it served the purpose. Lucy as usual was first in, and went marching though the large tatty blue door of the Tavern and walked straight past an odd looking woman sitting at a small wooden desk by the entrance door.

"Excuse me" called the odd looking woman to Lucy

"Yes?" Lucy replied looking cross to be stopped

"You need to buy your entrance tickets here. £6 each please!" the woman said curtly.

"Does that include a reading" Lucy asked

"No! You pay whomever you chose to do your reading direct. The entrance fee does include refreshments though" the grumpy lady tutted.

"Should think so!" grunted Lucy, who always acted like this when out, Carrie looked at Katie and raised an eyebrow making Katie grin slightly.

"How much are the readings please?" Carrie asked the lady kindly

"Varies, from £20 to £40" the lady replied very matter of factly.

"Goodness, I'll just come in with you, but I can't afford that, Tony would have a fit if he knew I'd spent that!" Carrie said to Katie and Lucy.

Lucy handed the odd lady the money and paid for all three "My treat" she told Carrie and Katie.

The three of them entered the dimly lit pub function room, which was now brimming with people, mainly ladies it had to be said, some sitting having readings done in little booths, some just wandering about, some chatting and telling their friends about their readings. It was very noisy and seemed a little scary to Katie.

"What do we do?" whispered Katie to Carrie
"Not really sure, Lucy will know" Carrie said "What do we do Lucy?"
"How the heck should I know?" She replied.
"Lets just look around first then" Carrie said always the logical one out of the three of them.

Katie suddenly felt a pat on her left shoulder making her jump, and turned around to see who had patted her. Standing there behind her was the red-haired man who she had met in the chemist a few weeks ago (though it seemed much longer). She also felt she had also seen him somewhere else, but could not quite remember where.

"Howdy" he grinned at Katie "Sorry if I startled you, how are you doing?"
"I am fine thanks. And you?" Katie replied politely.
"Who the hell is he?" Lucy whispered to Carrie

"How should I know?" Carrie replied looking the man up and down.

Lucy pushed herself forward directly in between this red haired stranger and Katie and extended her hand out to shake his hand.

"Hi, I'm Lucy, this is Carrie, and we are friends of Katie. And you are?" she asked somewhat protectively.

"I'm Blaze," he laughed as he shook Lucy's hand "Nice to meet you all" he then turned back to Katie "Did you get the right toothpaste for your boss in the end?"

"Well she didn't send me out to change it!" Laughed Katie.

"Who are you here with?" Interrupted Lucy

"Oh my Mum, I've come to help her with all her stuff," said Blaze.

"Does she do readings then?" Lucy asked. Katie threw her a look thinking how rude and abrupt Lucy could sometimes appear.

"Yep, she sure does. That's her over there in the corner" he pointed to an auburn haired lady wearing almost every colour possible - an orange flowery blouse, a purple shawl, a silky pink floral scarf round her neck and a lavender flower in her hair, it wasn't possible to see the bottom half as she was sitting down, but no doubt it was just as colourful!

"Is she any good?" Carrie asked timidly, not wanting to seem too keen to the others.

"Of course. She is ace; top of the pack is Mum. Been doing the whole thing for years - crystals, tarot, angel cards, whatever you want really" said Blaze rather proudly.

"How much?" Lucy enquired very directly. "Do we get a 'friends' discount?"

Katie blushed and looked down at the floor embarrassed by the directness of her friend, yet kind of admiring her at the same time - how wonderful to be so confident.

"Just mention my name and say you're friends and she will give you a discount I am sure" Blaze grinned.

"Thank you" said Carrie and Lucy together and with that they wondered over to 'Mrs Blaze' as they named her.

"Do you fancy a cuppa before you have a reading?" Blaze turned to Katie who was left standing alone as her friends had scuttled away "They do a mean carrot cake here too"

"Sure, that would be nice" Katie said slightly apprehensively, not really knowing this guy but feeling as though she did.

They sat down together on the very hard wooden chairs which had certainly seen better days in the cornered off 'refreshment area'. That's where they stayed for the next two hours, chatting, laughing and indulging in a second cuppa and cake, this time some scrummy flapjack.

For some reason unknown to her, Katie felt she could have told Blaze her whole life story including all her problems; there was something about him, something kind, calming. He listened to her as she poured her heart out to him, including the whole story of losing her job, about the set up on James, how awful Sara and Jayne were, and of course all about Carla. Oh yes, and on a positive point how lovely Mrs Hogan's pansies now looked since weeding the garden. Blaze never spoke, but just listened, his green emerald eyes sparkling as he focused on Katie's expressive face.

Katie suddenly stopped, and wondered why on earth she was telling this total stranger all this information about her and realised that only she was speaking. She looked him up and down briefly; his face was kindly and boyish. He was, she thought, quite good-looking in a non-conventional sort of way; his clothes were strange, dark and clearly un-ironed.

"What?" Blaze asked aware that she was scanning him.

"Nothing I just ..."

"Go on, spit it out" encouraged Blaze.

"Well, here I am blubbing on about my problems, and well I don't know you, I know nothing about you. You must think me very rude, I am sorry" said Katie.

"No need to be sorry. Anyway you needed to talk and, as you have gathered, I am a good listener" Blaze smiled warmly at Katie as he spoke.

"Yes you are a very good listener and actually I feel a lot better for saying it all out loud to someone. It sounds crazy, but it makes me realise I need to deal with it all now" Katie replied.

"Good, glad to be of service. What is your plan of action now then?"

"Plan?" Katie asked somewhat surprised.

"Yes, what are you going to do?" Blaze continued.

"Well, firstly I guess I should meet up with James and tell him"

"Tell him everything?" Blaze raised one of his eyebrows as he spoke.

"Well, erm, yes everything he needs to know, yes" said Katie.

"What about your feelings for him?'

Katie blushed, thinking that she had made no reference to the fact she liked James to her new unofficial 'Counsellor Blaze'.

"Feelings ... No, it's men that have to ask ... No. Anyway, I'm not looking for a relationship, I have not long come out a long-term relationship, which was not good for me! Need to be me for now - don't think relationships are for me" Katie stuttered out.

"Why not? Perhaps he was the wrong person for you?"

Katie thought about Richard. She had loved Richard dearly, or thought she had at the time, but looking back he never really made her happy. Their relationship was fine as long as it was all going Richard's way. He was pretty damn controlling if the truth were told.

"I couldn't be myself" admitted Katie, surprising herself. God, this Blaze should do this for a profession, he was good she thought. "It was always about Richard, and what he wanted. I think part of me resented that but for a quiet life I went with the flow, and it was not my flow. I guess I should have spoken up before ... oh well whatever!"

"Always be yourself, be true to yourself Katie" Blaze said looking directly into Katie's eyes. Katie looked down but smiled to herself, she looked at her watch.

"Oh goodness, we have been talking for almost two hours ... I'd better find my friends; too late to have a reading now" Katie said scanning the room for sight of Lucy and Carrie.

"You needed to talk Katie, that's what you needed to do today" Blaze said almost in a tone that you would use to speak to a young child. "I'll let you be" he stood up, and for the first time Katie realised how incredibly tall and lanky he was. At that moment Lucy and Carrie bounced back full of chat and giggles.

"Your mum is amazing" smiled Lucy (smiling for the first time that day!)

"She is so sweet," added Carrie

"What have you been doing Kats?" asked Lucy knowing only too well that she had been chatting to this odd chap all the time.

"Talking" replied Katie quite non-committal "Did you both have readings then?'

"Yes" Carrie replied all excited and looking like her own child Toby when he gets excited. Carrie and Lucy then went on to fill Katie in on every last detail that Mrs Blaze had told them, they started to walk off, and then Katie remembered Blaze and turned and smiled at him.

"Thank you," she said, genuinely grateful to him.

"I'll be seeing you" and with that he walked off into the crowd heading towards his Mother, Mrs Blaze.

"Well? Fill us in," said Lucy

"With what?" asked Katie?

"What happened? Are you seeing him again? Where does he work? What music does he like?' Lucy asked as if reading from a questionnaire.

"Oh it's not like that, he just listened, and that's all"

"Just listened?" Carrie chirped in.

"Did he say he would meet up again?" asked Lucy.

"No" Katie looked across to where Blaze was, and had a feeling she would indeed be seeing him again and quite soon she felt. "Not all men are prospective boyfriends you know!" she added

"No I guess not, and he's not really your type" Lucy said, pulling her button nose up slightly as she looked across at his scruffy clothes.

"Don't judge someone by their clothes" said Carrie (although she also thought he looked a little odd and wasn't sure about the ginger unruly hair)

"What is my type then?" Asked Katie.

"Control freaks" laughed Lucy. Katie pulled a pretend angry face and Carrie laughed.

"So you never had a reading?" asked Carrie

"No, but I feel better" Katie replied feeling quite positive for a change.

"Apparently, I will be pregnant soon" Lucy announced proudly

"Wow" Carrie exclaimed.

"We'll see" smiled Lucy "Shall we have a quick glass of wine at Cobbles?'

"Why not, be rude not too" giggled Carrie "I'd better phone Tony though and see if he minds baby sitting a little longer"

"He won't mind. Come on Carrie, it will do you good" Lucy said

"Lets go," said Katie feeling happy "A drink will be good, mine's a large white wine!"

They walked down a few roads from the Tavern to Cobbles where they stayed for quite some time!

Chapter 19

I'm feeling so happy, maybe just a little smug too, as I realise that the worm is starting to turn ... the worm being Katie here, in the nice sense of the word.

The last few times that I have viewed her she has been appearing more in control and has got those tears out of her system, well hopefully. Looking stronger, more confident ... yippee my skills are working, or are they? Perhaps Katie does not need me? No of course she does, everyone needs his or her Guardian Angel. The best bit of all is that she has now met Blaze; many angels know him, and he believes, he understands, he can channel energy - he will help heal Katie, happy days!

I feel like flying, flying as high as an angel can fly, but alas I have work to do and have no time for such a luxury, I have to complete stage 1 of the assessments ready to hand to Hibissa. I've been putting this off, but now with such good news I feel the time is right to complete. Who knows, Hibissa may even be impressed? Well maybe just a little? Pascolli and Willow came into our chamber stopping my chain of thought.

"Goodness you ok Nicoise? You're looking very serious!" exclaimed Willow being unusually cheeky.

"He's just pretending, he's probably reading some book on how to play practical jokes on guardian mentors!" laughed Pascolli

"Very funny guys, I'm actually working on writing up my Stage 1 assessment" I said grumpily.

"You won't want to come and have some sparkles with us them?" asked Pascolli

I groaned inwardly. I was always in the mood to bask in the cloud sparkles, to chill and spend time with friends, but I really did need to crack on with this assessment work. I would have to decline, which was a first.

"No thanks" I said seriously.

"Gee, are you ill or sickening for something Nicoise?" Pascolli genuinely looking slightly worried for me.

"Come on Nicoise" urged Willow, who seemed in a particularly jovial mood today, it was usually me trying to persuade him to leave his work and join us.

"No honestly, I need to do this while its fresh in my mind, perhaps I could join you later?" I added hopefully.

"Really must be poorly" said Pascolli.

"Must be!" agreed Willow.

"Look if you're going to go could you go and leave me to work?" I said hoping they would hurry up before I changed my mind.

"Ok we're going, no need to get your wings in a twist!" said Pascolli

"Look, sorry don't mean to be grouchy. Its just that Katie has met Blaze, which is a great stroke of luck. Well of course you guys know Blaze, he is a gem, is he not?"

"He is!" smiled Willow looking suspiciously smug.

"Good man, Blaze" agreed Pascolli looking at Willow as he spoke.

"Look do you guys want to tell me something or what?" I asked.

Pascolli and Willow looked at each other and then looked at me, answering together in unison tune "No".

"Lets go Willow, we know when we're not wanted" laughed Pascolli nudging Willow.

"Sure lets go and get sparkled!" said Willow joyfully.

I so wanted to go, and it had been a real achievement for me to be so responsible and say 'no' - believe me, but once they had gone I felt better in my solace of quietness I was able to get on with the work in hand. I worked solidly for hours and finally finished the assessment. Gosh, I was so proud of myself, and I was positively glowing from where I was beaming so much. I decided that I would now treat myself to a quick Sparkle if the others were still there.

I flew quickly down the corridor and unfortunately for me I flew straight into a very startled Hibissa and one of his High Court friends, as I was totally whizzing at top level speed round the corner of the corridor just past the Great Hall.

" Nicoise" scolded Hibissa

"Sorry Sir" I replied thinking 'shit'.

"Is he one of yours?" asked Hibissa's colleague as though I was some awful creature.

"Erm ..." grunted Hibissa staring right at me, obviously not wanting to admit that I was indeed one of his students. Damn, I wish I could read his mind at this moment. "Yes, this is Nicoise"

"I have finished the Stage 1 Assessment Sir, which is why I was in such a hurry," I blurted out.

"Excellent, I will take it now, I have a free period this afternoon"

"Oh, I don't seem to have it" I said lamely not expecting that Hibissa would ask to see right now.

"You did say you were on you way to me with the assessment Nicoise or did I not hear you correctly when you mumbled?"

"I think I must have left it as I was in such a hurry, I will go back now Sir" I replied lamely.

"Good idea Nicoise, I will be waiting in my Chamber," he grinned at his colleague that wicked glint that he sometimes does, very unsettling! I nodded and turned away and set off back to my chamber, I heard Hibissa and his colleague laughing, probably laughing at me. I'll show them all I vowed to myself.

"I don't know how you put up with those young ones Hibissa, I know I couldn't do that job any more"

"Oh I don't know its quite satisfying really shaping them up, seeing them squirm and all that," he laughed.

"Yes I guess that bit can be fun, but still … do you think he has done the work?"

"Lets hope so for his sake, or he will be in trouble" Hibissa said.

"Think I'll stick to the legal side, sounds like too much hassle to me," said the pompous colleague.

I could no longer hear their voices, as I got closer to my own chamber. I wish I had not bumped into Hibissa literally, as now I would never get to the sparkles, but on the other hand I was a little excited that Hibissa would expect me to be lying about the assessment being complete, so I quite looked forward to handing over the work and seeing his face!

I returned to Hibissa with the assessment just as his grumpy High Court friend was leaving. He glared at me, as he passed looking as if some muck had stuck on my wing. I glared back and brushed past him as quick as I could. On arriving at Hibissa's desk, I handed him the assessment. I watched his face for any clue of what he was thinking, but his face remained unchanged and no raised eyebrow or twitch of an eye could be noted. I felt slightly disappointed at his lack of facial expression. I shuffled from side to side nervously, waiting for a response.

"Nicoise be still," Hibissa said without even looking up. "Ground yourself angel" he ordered.

How can you ground yourself when you feel so worried, excited, puzzled and happy all mixed up together. I tried to keep still but found it almost impossible. It took all my energy to keep quiet whilst Hibissa read my work.

It seemed to take forever, and he is a very slow and careful reader, sometimes reading back over what he had already read. My 'grounding' was not working very well and I could feel myself swaying very gently like a tall tree in the breeze of an autumn wind as Hibissa continued to read on. Finally, he put the case notes down.

"Right" he sighed. I felt my heart slowly sink - he didn't like it. Something was wrong. He obviously did not feel the same enthusiasm that I felt when I read it back earlier.

"This is coming along, and I can see you have put some good work in and taken heed of some of my earlier comments to you, but ..." he paused at the 'but' before he continued with the other side of a 'but' "reading between the lines I need a few answers to be sure"

I was puzzled and not sure of what he meant so I asked him to explain further.

"How did you manage to get Blaze into Katie's life?" he asked, his eyes piercing through my soul.

"He met her in a chemist a few weeks ago. He just happened to be there at the same time I guess. Then he appeared in a dream of hers and then ..."

"No, no. Not what I meant. Who put him in the dream for instance, did you?" Hibissa asked.

"No Sir" I replied honestly.

"Curious – Blaze is quite a unique human. He can channel and shape thoughts from other humans towards us here, but he has to be called and I am wondering who called him?" Hibissa said. He had totally lost me; I had no idea of what he was talking about. I had not planned anything; I just thought it was luck. Obviously Hibissa didn't' agree.

"I just don't know Sir, really I don't," I answered truthfully.

"Well, I need to know. You need to find out. Did anyone else help you?"

"No Sir" I replied, Hibissa nodded and handed back the assessment to me.

"Do not look so worried young Nicoise, you have presented some good sound work in that assessment, and I am particularly pleased to see references to your studies, such as the three corners of the feather ..." Hibissa paused and looked at me, I smiled nervously back at him. Then he continued "However, you know the rules of cross-casing and interfering, and I know we spoke in detail on this matter recently so I won't go on again, but just be aware, if it happens again it will not just be a verbal warning!"

"Yes Sir, I understand Sir"

"Good, you have nothing to worry about if you continue with the good work that you have shown me today. Now run along and catch some sparkles or two with your friends who are no doubt already there. Good day Nicoise" with that Hibissa beckoned me to leave the chamber I bowed my head and flew out pretty quick.

Once I had left I felt somewhat puzzled. Was Hibissa happy or was he warning me? Warning me about what? Who is this Blaze? Did someone purposely place him in Katie's life, as Hibissa seemed to be implying. I suddenly had a flash back to Willow and his very smug face when he and Pascolli were speaking about Blaze. It was Willow ... Willow had broken rules to help me? I quickened my haste to make sure I caught up with Willow at the Sparkles Bar.

Chapter 20

Katie felt as though it was a Saturday morning as she sat at the kitchen table at her parents house, but in fact it was only Wednesday, a wet, dull and dreary Wednesday. The atmosphere was a little tense, Katie's Father was pretending to be interested in what the local paper had to say, her Mother was busy making tea, and her brother was standing in the door way, texting.

Mum gave everyone a mug of tea, each mug was different, and they all had their own special mugs. Katie glanced at each mug and wondered why her Mum still did that separate mug thing after all these years. It was a tradition continued on from her childhood, when almost every Christmas or Easter they would each get a new mug, indicating something that they liked at that time. With her Dad it was usually something related to gardening or trains; with her Mum it was usually flowers or some symmetrical pattern; her brother Mick's was usually a West Ham football mug although in later years they had been more jokey cups.

Katie's used to be fairies and princesses but now they seemed to be more like her Mum's flowery, sensible mugs. Katie shuddered at the thought of being 'sensible' like her Mother, and made a mental note to buy herself a mug with a fairy on it when she went shopping next.

"So you got the sack?" Mick said tactlessly "What are you going to do for money?"

Katie looked over to her weaseley brother, angry that money was his main concern, as he would no longer be able to borrow from his soft sister if she had no money coming in. Well that's no bad thing, Katie thought, he will have to go somewhere else!

"Are you looking for a new job now then?" Katie's Mum enquired.

"Of course, I have an appointment at an employment agency tomorrow" Katie lied.

"That's good," her Dad said kindly.

"You won't get much there, they never have anything worth getting out of bed for!" said Mick

"Like you would know!" Katie snapped back at her brother causing her Mum to look up from what she was doing and stare directly at Katie.

"Why do you say that?" Mick asked.

"He does have a degree in Physics Katie, remember that please. He should't have to take any old job with his intelligence" Katie's Mum said, robustly defending her precious little boy.

"How could I forget ...so I should just take any old job then because I'm not intelligent. Is that right?"

"Katie," her Mum barked back. "It's not Mick's fault that you've lost your job so please don't start on him. You know that's not what we mean. Lets close the matter shall we? Biscuits anyone?'

Katie sighed. She could not be bothered to argue and, in any event, if her Mum and Mick were siding up together as they usually did, there was absolutely no chance of winning an argument. She looked over to her Dad for support, but he was trying to keep out of it as always, being impartial, invisible. That was always his ploy. He was hidden behind the pages of the paper, but no doubt he was not reading a word.

Katie's mobile phone bleeped, and she looked to see whom the message was from. She was relieved that it was not Carla; sad (again) that it was not James - she really thought he would have contacted her by now. No, the message was from Blaze, which surprised Katie, as she did not recall giving him her number.

She read the short message. *'Hi Katie, Blaze here, do you fancy meeting up for a coffee today?"*

She checked the time - it was nearly 12 noon. At least it would give her an excuse to leave this tense family meeting. She stood up and put her jacket on.

"You going love?" Her Dad enquired surprised she was leaving so soon.
"Yes, I'm going to meet up with a friend," replied Katie, buttoning up her jacket.
"Ladies that lunch huh. Alright for some" jibed Mick
Her Mother made no comment, and just continued to clatter about and look busy in the kitchen as she

collected all the mugs ready to pop into the dishwasher.

As she left Katie dialled Blaze's number.

"Hi" Blaze replied cheerily as he picked up the phone.

"Blaze, it's Katie. Thanks for the text. I could met up now'ish if you'd like?" Katie suggested.

"Cool" responded Blaze.

"By the way, how did you know my number?" Katie asked.

"Your friends put your number down on Mum's database to receive newsletters ... hey hope you don't mind, but thought it'd be nice to meet up again as we got on so well last time?" responded Blaze enthusiastically.

"Oh that's fine. Where should we meet?"

"Curiosity Bella" Blaze offered.

"Where is that?" Katie asked. She had never heard of the place despite having lived in the town for a long time now.

"At the back of the Art shop round the small arcade road leading off the High Street. There's a side door. Ring the bell and then go up the stairs to the shop come tea room" replied Blaze "Mum runs it, you'll love it I'm sure" he added.

"Ok see you in about 25 minutes then" said Katie.

Katie put her phone away and wondered why she had never seen that shop, but then on reflection she remembered she did not really go round the back of the High Street, so she probably would not have noticed it.

She decided to walk thinking that the exercise would do her good and there was never anywhere to park easily anyway. Katie walked briskly until she arrived at the entrance where she saw Blaze waiting outside. She felt a little hot and flustered, and made a note to try and get back to the gym, her fitness level was worse than ever.

"Hello. Sorry I'm a little late. I walked and it was longer than I thought" Katie apologised
"No worries. Come on let's get a cuppa" Blaze replied as he held the door open for Katie.

They ascended the wooden stairs, which really echoed with each step. It almost sounded like a herd of elephants rather than two people! At the top of the stairs, Katie gasped with amazement as she entered the shop. It was a strange shaped room on two levels. On the second slightly higher level there was a serving counter with cups, plates and tea bags of every description. Scattered around the counter were several odd coloured stools. On the lower level there was what could only be described as a cave of sparkly goodies; it was crammed full (a tad untidily Katie noted) with crystals, wind charms, colourful bags and colourful clothes, candles, pictures of American

Indians, Buddha's of all sizes and loads more bits and bobs – all very intriguing but very messy.

Blaze led Katie away from the treasures to the tea counter and then promptly rang a small brass pixie bell. Very promptly Mrs Blaze appeared from one of the three doors behind the counter (office and treatment rooms Katie was later informed).

"Hello" beamed Mrs Blaze "What can I get you?"

"I don't know, there are so many teas, ... " Katie said staring at the shelf full of herbal teas. "Do you just have 'normal' tea?"

"Yes of course. Would you like some cake with it?" asked Mrs Blaze "I have lemon drizzle, date and walnut loaf or scones with butter and jam"

"Lemon Drizzle please" interrupted Blaze "You should try it Katie"

"Ok, make that two please" Katie replied. Immediately Mrs Blaze started preparing the tea using the cutest spotty mugs with a little spotty teapot.

Katie and Blaze sat on the stools, which Katie found a little difficult to actually get up on to, as they were quite tall for someone with little legs.

"Have you heard from James or Carla?" asked Blaze.

"No," replied Katie. "I really feel I need to speak to James, but would rather he contacted me first. Silly I know, it's just the way I am"

"Just call him" encouraged Blaze.

"I wouldn't know what to say or how to start" replied Katie.

"The words will just roll out, you'll see. Call him," said Blaze again.

"You mean I have to call him?" asked Katie, a little apprehensively.

"Well, yes, looks like you will have to call him" Blaze nodded.

"Do you think James knows about Carla's scheme?" Katie asked.

"Probably but it sounds like the poor chap's in denial. Just call him as a friend and meet up. Simple huh?"

Blaze's Mum put the teas and lemon drizzle cake on the counter, and smiled. She then stood and waited for Katie to try the cake. Katie wondered why both her and Blaze were just standing watching.

"What?" Katie asked self-consciously.

"What do you think?" Mrs Blaze enquired, whilst Blaze scoffed his down at super greedy speed hoping to get a second portion.

Katie ate some cake, which was superb "Totally scrummy, very nice" she complimented Mrs Blaze.

The shop door suddenly flung open, causing Katie to jump. An elderly lady entered and asked for Bella (who turned out to be Mrs Blaze). Bella greeted her and took her off to the treatment room at the back. More customers came in too, who Blaze promptly served.

Katie had been having such a nice tea and chat that she had forgotten that this was actually a business. The shop became really busy. Blaze was rushing about serving customers and a little queue built up at the counter leaving Katie no option but to help serve. She got stuck in and started making teas/coffees, cutting cake and smiling lots. The afternoon rushed passed by quickly and finally at 5 0'clock Mrs Blaze closed the shop after the last few customers had left. She then joined Katie who had clambered back on to the tall odd stool by the counter.

"Blaze said you'd recently lost your job" Mrs Blaze said "I'm actually looking for an assistant to help me here in the shop and tea room so I can concentrate on the treatments. Fancy a trial?" she asked.

"You mean apply for the job here?" Katie asked a bit shell-shocked at the surprise offer.

"No, I mean if you would like to give it a try the job is yours. You'll be perfect, I was watching you earlier and you have a lovely customer way about you" complimented Mrs Blaze.

"I don't really have experience in..." Katie paused and looked around the room "in retail"

"No need." Said Mrs Blaze "I can tell you're the right person for the job. I'm afraid the money is pretty basic. At this stage of my business I can't really pay out too much at present, but who knows, if the business grows, which I'm hoping you will help with, that is marketing the business, that will make it a little more interesting for you wont it?"

"I don't know what to say!" Said Katie absolutely amazed that somebody thought she was the 'right one for the job.' What a lovely compliment.

"Just say yes," said Blaze pulling up a stool and joining Katie and his Mum.

"Use it as a stop-gap until you decide what you want from life, if you like" added Mrs Blaze.

"What hours, what do I do? Do I need any special clothes, training, sorry lots of questions" blurted out Katie.

"Well just turn up tomorrow and we'll go through it and see if you like it before committing? How does that sound?" Mrs Blaze suggested, helpfully.

"No. I mean yes! I wont just come for a day; I would love to be part of the team. Thank you so much; I just don't know what to say. It's so cool," bubbled Katie hardly able to contain her excitement.

"Excellent. See you tomorrow then" said Mrs Blaze as she got up and left Blaze and Katie sitting on the stools smiling.

"Wow!" exclaimed Katie to Blaze "I can't believe it - that is so nice of your Mum to give me a chance"

"Yep Mum is like that, if she thinks something is right she goes for it – she obviously realises you have potential!" laughs Blaze, pouring out a cup of tea "Quick cuppa before you go? Think you deserve it? You worked pretty hard you know."

'Ok – then I must go, I didn't realise the time, I have been here ages" Katie replied taking the spotty mug fron Blaze.

After finishing her tea and saying goodbye to Blaze, Katie walked home, not believing her luck, thinking how strange it was. Nothing normally happened like this, and it felt like a piece of the puzzle slipping into place, well at least one small piece of the puzzle. Hopefully the others would follow.

Katie arrived at home, kicking off her shoes across the landing floor, clicking on the kettle and then she phoned home, hoping to speak with her Dad. However her Mum answered the phone.

"Is Dad there please Mum?"Katie asked.

"He's in the garden" Mum replied bluntly.

"Oh, well I just called to say I've got a new job" Katie said with excitement.

"Well done. What Accountants is it then?" asked her Mum.

"It's a coffee and ..."

"A coffee shop!" exclaimed Katie's Mum. She could detect the disgust in the tone of her Mothers voice as she spoke.

"Its not any old shop it's a special shop" Katie added.

"Oh well at least you'll be earning I guess. It's just a stepping-stone until something better comes along. I'll tell your Dad when he comes in. See you soon" Katie's Mum hung up the phone abruptly, leaving Katie holding her phone and feeling like a small child that had just been reprimanded.

No matter how hard she tried she could never please her Mother!

Usually a negativity and critisism like this would have brought Katie's mood down, but today she felt really happy, on a buzz almost. She had a good vibe about the Curiosity shop, and about Blaze. He was strange but amazing. Yes, Katie liked him and Mrs Blaze alot.

Chapter 21

Pascolli and I were watching James. He was making us feel dizzy, as he was paced up and down his office, to and fro, his face taunt and pale. He looked lost and alone. I looked over to his extremely messy desk, which even made my chamber look positively tidy. I scanned the top layer of files to see if I could spy the pink folder, but it was nowhere to be seen.

There was a loud knock at the door, a pause, and then Sara entered holding a cup of steaming tea or such other beverage. James barely acknowledged her as she put the mug down on his desk. She waited for a response from the usually polite and thankful James, but then turned and left realising James was still in a sullen mood.

"Did he challenge Carla about the account?" I asked Pascolli

"Well he half-heartedly asked her but she, well lets just say she took his mind off things temporarily" Pascolli replied gloomily.

"How? Oh ...I see," I said realising what he meant, "So he knows?"

"Yes he knows, but he hasn't done anything. In fact he doesn't do anything now, his other cases are all becoming over-due, he can't concentrate and he's making silly mistakes. I think he believes that its his fault and that Carla has taken the prize case to save the

Company, so he is almost thankful to her!" Pascolli sighed.

"Goodness" I responded, "This is not good"

"Goodness indeed, and Carla has also convinced him that he is depressed and is arranging counselling sessions for him with someone she knows in the business!" Pascolli added.

"Is he really depressed, or just being led to believe that? What have you done to help, Pascolli?" I asked.

"Nicoise you know the score. He needs to believe in me, but he's not got a clue. He would never ask for help, so I am pretty helpless in the matter"

"I think he needs to meet up with Katie, she is the key I am sure," I suggested.

"You think so?" asked Pascolli. "She is not a believer either though, so how would that help?"

"She is changing, I really think she could help him, which in turn would help her. I know she wants to see him"

"Has she asked you for help then?" enquired Pascolli.

"Not exactly, but things are starting to take shape. She is becoming ... Well I don't really know, but she is changing and I just have a gut feeling she needs to see James and soon. Carla is going to be on her case soon I can feel it, especially after that disastrous meeting she had with the client, without the case file – heads will roll ... probably Katies!" I said glancing back down at James as he threw a piece of work into the bin, well he actually missed the bin, but he didn't bother to get up and pick up the rubbish. "Think Katie is going to be a

little shocked though when she sees James like this –
shame really"

Pascolli and I both looked down at James and sighed,
what a pitiful sight. At that precise moment Carla came
bowling into the office, the door flying open and
crashing back onto the door (always a dramatic
entrance with that woman). James looked up and for
the first time during our viewing session showed a
remote flicker of interest.

"James, good news darling. Mr Heath can see you
tomorrow at 2.30pm. You're really lucky, usually
people have to wait for weeks but as he knows me, well
… say no more!" she laughed, flicking her mass of black
raven hair behind her as she spoke seductively.

"Thanks, I will check my diary. Who is he?" asked
James, a little unsure of this whole situation. Carla
looked slightly annoyed that James asked this question,
but gave him a fake smile that sent a shiver down my
back.

"Why James don't you remember? We spoke, and we
felt it would be a good idea for you to have some
counselling sessions to understand your break … " she
stopped and then re-worded her sentence " … your bad
patch that you're currently going through. You know
how it pains me to see you like this" she walked behind
him and stroked the back of his hair, James looked up
at her cunning face in complete adoration.

"I'm ok Carla, really. I don't think I need to speak with anyone; I just need to be with you. I feel happy with you, I want us to be close again" said James as he tried to catch one of Carla's hands.

She retracted her hand back very quickly, smiling a sickly sweet smile as she did so. "Poor James, I know it is hard for you, but I really think you need this support. And I think that while you are recovering from your breakdown we should act professionally, and then once you are through it well, who knows" she said carefully.

"Breakdown! My wings!" whispered Pascolli "God I could swear!"

"Don't say it Pascolli, you know we are forbidden, but I know what you mean. What a player she is!" I replied.

James looked directly at Carla and then looked down. Perhaps he was depressed, he certainly felt unhappy, but depressed enough to need counselling? Maybe he should accept this help, she obviously liked him alot to want to bother helping, and it would be rude to not see this counsellor.

"I appreciate your help Carla and the extra work you have taken off me to help me get through this 'bad patch' I seem to be going though" said James.

"It's a pleasure, I know you would do the same for me if the tables were turned" she replied, again flashing her pearly white teeth as she gave him yet another sickly smile (cringy or what!).

"I will take the appointment, what time did you say it was?" James asked reaching for his leather desk diary "With Mr Teeth?"

"Heath not Teeth!" Carla snapped thinking 'what a geek' "Its Mr Heath darling and its at 2.30pm. He will come to your apartment too, so that's easier for you"

"Oh, that unusual," said James "you'd normally go to their practice would you not?'

"No not always," replied Carla "anyway just be there, it will help you darling" she leant forward, now flashing her rather large chest at him and kissed him gently on the cheek.

"Judas kiss" Pascolli whispered "Let's go! I really can't stomach any more of this"

"It is going to be harder for Katie to get though to this bloke than I thought. He's totally lost the plot" I said

"You can see what is occurring here. Carla is going to get him out of the Partnership, she's going to prove that he's unfit for work, then she will run the joint, get all the cream clients, and then ruin the company and pocket the money with that Antony chap by the looks of things" said Pascolli to me quietly in a very sombre tone of voice.

"No, we will not let her, we really do need to act. I think we should get James to the Curiosity Bella shop and soon. Blaze could help too, he could do that listening thing he did for Katie, seemed to help her" I said.

Pascolli did not reply, he just shrugged his shoulders then flew out of the window without any warning to me, leaving me alone watching James, who was now rocking to and fro on his executive office chair. Carla was screaming out for Sara (it made me smile to think that Sara and Jayne probably had to work a lot harder now my Katie had left).

I had one last look around, thinking that there was no option but to intervene, just a little. I then flew out of the window and tried to catch up with Pascolli who seemed to have already flown miles; eventually out of breath I caught him (I made a mental note to start flying more).

As I caught up alongside him Pascolli turned to me and said "Nicoise, we need to get Willow in on this. You know it was Willow that helped you indirectly by bringing Blaze into Katie's life?" This revelation from Pascolli caused me to hover stationary for what seemed like ages but infact was only seconds. I had had my suspicions, but to be actually told that Willow had intervened was quite a shock. I felt a little sad because I had thought it had been all my good work that was helping.

"Well, of course. Who else could have done such a thing, I mean Willow is a straight 'A' student after all, he can do no wrong, unlike me" I said maybe just a tad bitterly.

"He did it to help you Nicoise, don't be mean, he is our friend, and we are both lucky to have such a friend" Pascolli added.

I thought about what Pascolli had said and I knew in my heart of hearts he was right, but I wished Willow had told me he was doing it. However, on further reflection I realised that Willow had compromised his professionalism to help me and indeed I should be grateful, and we really did need him on board to help in this situation now with James.

Pascolli was right, I should not be cross "You're right, we need to work together as a team. Sod the High Court, they are just out of touch, we are the future not them!" I exclaimed.

"Yes it is dated, its time for radical change!" Agreed Pascolli

"Lets go and find Willow" I said. Pascolli nodded and we took to the sky once more.

Chapter 22

Carrie was sitting with Katie, who was working; Carrie was wide-eyed, as she looked around at all the goodies to buy in the shop, whilst Katie sorted out a tea and cake for her. The shop was pretty quiet at that time, so they were able to catch up.

"Wow this is just lovely Katie, it really suits you being here. You look loads happier already"

"It's really nice yes. Actually it's a pleasure to be here after the hassle of the office. It's a little quiet, but one of my jobs is to market the place," replied Katie, happy that her friend liked her new work place.

"Well, I could hand out flyers at Toby's school, lots of those mums go out for lunch and this place would be perfect. While they're lunching they might buy some bits huh?" Carrie paused "Or what about starting some sort of breakfast club? Lots of the mums go and get breakfast together straight after the school run. This place would be perfect … no fry ups though, not really a fry up sort of place is it really?"

"That's not a bad idea Carrie, cheers I'll give it some thought, and if you could hand some flyers out once they're printed that would be really helpful."

"No problem, what's my commission?" Carrie joked.

"Your commission is seeing your friend happy," laughed Katie.

"Aw its just so good to see you smile" agreed Carrie.

"Still need to sort out the James and Carla thing though. It's worrying me, and I keep having weird dreams about it."

"He can sort himself out surely!" Carrie said a bit hard faced.

"No, you're wrong. He actually needs me to help, you don't know Carla like I do" Katie replied.

Before Carrie could answer, Blaze came bounding over to them, followed by a couple of customers who started rummaging around the shop.

"Morning ladies" grinned Blaze. His wide smile was deeply infectious, and both Katie and Carrie could not help but give a big wide smile back.

"I'll have a tea and some carrot cake please Katie. Just got to pop back out and make a call. I'll be back in a minute." With that Blaze stomped loudly back down the wooden stairs out onto the street below.

"He likes you," teased Carrie

"He likes everyone Carrie, that's Blaze, it's the way he is"

"No, he sees something in you. Its strange how this all happened don't you think? Things happen for a reason you know" Carrie replied knowingly.

"What are you saying - that I only got the job because he fancied me?" with that Katie poked her friend on the arm.

"Ouch! No and, well, yes maybe"

"It really isn't like that, you're wrong," said Katie.

"We'll see," said Carrie knowingly again. She then shut up as she noticed Blaze coming back towards them. She certainly did not want to embarrass anyone, unlike Lucy who, if she had been here would be full of questions to this new person in Katie's life.

Blaze sat on the stool opposite Carrie, and Katie passed him his tea and cake from the other side of the tall counter. "Nice to see you here, what do you think of the place then?" Blaze asked Carrie

"Its great, just great and the cake is to die for" she replied politely looking him up and down.

"Yep Mum certainly knows how to make a mean cake or two. Where is the old girl anyway?" he turned to Katie.

"Doing a reading, she should be out soon" Katie passed Blaze a second helping of cake and he grinned back at her.

"What are we talking about then?" Blaze asked "Clothes, men, kids?"

"No" Katie said sternly "This and that" she added vaguely not wanting him to know that he had been their source of conversation.

"So when are you going to met up with James?" Asked Blaze changing the subject.

"Soon" replied Katie not really wanting to get on that subject again.

"I think she should just leave that part of her life behind, and move on, it's gone. Live for now I say, she doesn't need the hassle," commented Carrie.

"No" Blaze replied firmly "I disagree, I think to move on Katie needs to address it now" he looked across at Katie, who caught his eye as he spoke she knew he was right.

Carrie looked away; she was a little hurt by Blaze's firm dismissal of her opinion. The awkwardness was broken by one of the customers requesting some assistance. Blaze instantly got up smiling and went across to help the lady in the green spotted Mac and the older lady with her. He eventually returned to the till with loads of items that he had charmed them into buying. He was a pretty persuasive person when he wanted to be, however charming.

Carrie suddenly screamed out, making everyone in the shop jump, as she read a message on her phone.

"Sorry" she apologised to everyone "Katie quick look at your messages!"

Katie went to her bag and found her phone and checked her messages, she also then screamed out, causing the customers to give odd looks to these two screaming women wondering what was causing all the commotion.

"Lucy's pregnant!" Katie said excitedly jumping up and down on the spot.

"That was on the cards," said Blaze calmly.

"What cards?" Katie asked wondering what he was talking about.

"Oh yes, Mrs Blaze said at the reading that Lucy would soon be pregnant. Oh my God, how exciting!" Carrie said joining, Katie in her jumping up and down dance. She glanced at her watch "Oh no, I have to go. Can't wait to tell Tony; got to be a playschool in ten minutes; shit I'll be late! See you!" Carrie made a speedy retreat. Blaze then sat on her stool; it was not as uncomfortable as the one he had been sitting on.

"I must call Lucy," said Katie excitedly.

"Yes then call James," said Blaze. Katie pretended not to hear and started collecting up the cups and plates from the counter. Blaze screwed a paper serviette up and threw it at her, making her stop and turn to him.

"Did you hear what I just said or have you selective hearing today?" he asked.

"What?" Katie asked as she picked up the serviette Blaze had thrown at her.

"You heard, you need to call James. Do it TODAY!"

"I know, I will. Promise"

"When?" continued Blaze like a dog with a bone?

"For goodness sake Blaze, I will do it today, I've promised haven't I?" she answered, a little flustered that he was intent on hassling her on the matter. "I will call this evening"

"Good, let me know how it goes" Blaze said kindly then turned to his Mum who was coming out of the treatment room with a client. The lady came over to Katie to pay, Blaze went over to his Mum and gave her a kiss on the cheek and handed her a package; she smiled adoringly at her son.

"See you tomorrow" Blaze called to Katie as he left.

"Bella" Katie called to Mrs Blaze (she never called her Mrs Blaze but always thought of her as that) "I was thinking. Perhaps we should have an official 'Open Day' with special offers, free samples and delicious refreshments. What do you think?"

"Splendid idea" responded Mrs Blaze "Just sort out and let me know the details. You're more than capable"

"Thank you, I will. I'll need a budget from you though ... oh and by the way, my friend Lucy is pregnant," blurted out Katie.

"Yes I know," replied Mrs Blaze, to Katie's surprise. "Twins will be a handful for your friend though I fear ... spend what you need within reason"

"Twins!" exclaimed Katie. "Does Lucy know?"

"Not yet, but she will soon enough!" laughed Mrs Blaze. "Come on, let's lock up. You need to get away sharp tonight, you have things to do"

"I do?" questioned Katie

"You do. A call has to be made hasn't it?" Bella said firmly

Katie looked puzzled and then nodded, thinking that this woman was very spooky sometimes "Yes you're right, I have a call to make." With that they locked up and all left the shop and made their separate ways home.

Chapter 23

Pascolli and I had had a long fly this morning. Admittedly our time could have been better used on working, but hey, occasionally, a bit of recreation time helps clear your mind, and creates space for further thoughts. Well that's my theory and I'm sticking to it!

We arrived at James' small apartment. Not a bad place really for a single chap. Very neutral colours - creams, beiges with a splash of coffee colourings here and there; leather settees and a huge flat screen TV, sort of place I wouldn't mind if I was a human. We looked down at James laying aimlessly on one of his settees, doing nothing, looking very glum and a little vacant! Sad really.

"Looks like we're in for a fun session of viewing today" I said quietly to Pascolli.

"Shut up Nicoise! Spare some feelings for the poor chap will you" Pascolli replied curtly.

"Touchy ...sorry, but I mean look at him all this lounging about feeling sorry for himself. He needs to get a grip; he never seems to do anything. Do you ever see him do anything or see anyone?" I asked.

"Not much" agreed Pascolli.

"Surely this is not just because of Carla; it'd be pretty poor if it was"

"No .. He's always been pretty quiet and introvert really. He lost his parents when he was quite young, it doesn't take much to bring him down. He is a clever chap - very studious. I think as a teenager studying was everything to him, so he pretty much missed out on the 'fun' side of being a student. He always falls in love too quickly too and with the wrong sort of woman. He gets very serious and intense too quickly which scares them off usually"

"Gee, he needs to lighten up. Sounds like he could do with some sparkles," I added.

"Yes, you're right he certainly needs something, but not Carla! We need to get her out of his mind and life. She's trying to bring him down. I worry for his sanity, she knows how vulnerable he is"

"She is a..." I stopped myself from swearing, remembering just in time that as angels we're not allowed to swear or curse out loud, or really even have such thoughts.

Willow suddenly appeared from nowhere, startling Pascolli and I.

"Found you at last, been looking for you both all morning. Where have you been?" Willow asked with a worried expression on his pale face.

"Well, we were just ...." Started Pascolli but seemed distracted watching James lightly move on the settee.

"Flying" I finished Pascolli's sentence for him.

"Flying all morning and you didn't ask if I wanted to come along? Anyway I've been looking for you to tell you that I've been doing some research. It appears that Mr Heath who is about to arrive here any minute now is not actually what he seems," announced Willow proudly.

Pascolli and I looked at each other and Willow continued, "No, he's not a Counsellor at all. He is actually an Actor!"

"An Actor? What like in plays? There is no play!" I stated puzzled with what I had just heard Willow say.

"Well yes. But he's not in a play, he's here to 'play' a part for Carla and bring James closer to downfall, meltdown even. He is pretending to be a Counsellor, he ...."

Willow was interrupted by the doorbell, which rudely rang out once then twice and then three times, James slowly got up to answer the door.

"Alright I heard, on my way," he mumbled, irritated with the ringing of the bell; once would be enough - he was not deaf. He opened the door to a tall, geeky looking man with a wide grin planted over his angular face.

"John Heath. Nice to meet you, Carla arranged for me to meet with you?" he held his hand out and James reluctantly returned this man's limp handshake.

"Come in" James said, "Go through. Would you like a drink; tea, coffee or a cold drink?"

"Black coffee with three sugars would be great, thanks," the man said as he marched past James into the lounge, not even bothering to wipe his slightly muddy shoes on the doormat. James looked at the trail of mud on his beige carpet and sighed, he disliked inconsiderate people.

"He hates mess" whispered Pascolli "so perhaps it's a good sign that he's a bit hacked off" I nodded thinking that sounded feasible. I don't think I'd like mud over my nice beige carpet if I was a human either.

"He's very nosy, look at him scanning the place," I said to Pascolli.

"James, Carla tells me you've been very down at work lately and, shall I say, your ability or your professionalism has suffered due to this slip in your usual impeccable record. Carla is worried about you and said she has had to take some of your cases to help you out at no extra pay to her, and she's doing this to help you until you get back on your feet. Nice lady huh?" Mr Heath said, and then preceded to slurp his coffee in a very loud manner "Any biscuits" he asked cheekily.

"Sorry no, I'm out of biscuits. I've not been shopping recently" replied James, looking a little embarrassed that he had no biscuits to offer, but why this should matter was anyone's guess.

Mr Heath then said he was going to start the counselling session. He got out a black notebook and pen and proceeded to ask James lots of probing questions. Questions that he could no doubt use for Carla. James however was not that forthcoming, and was quite reluctant to answer such personal questions, but he was trying to be helpful because he knew that Carla was trying to help him.

Mr Heath just kept on and on at him in a very unprofessional way. We had all seen Counsellors on earth, work before and he certainly was not acting as these had. We could tell that James was struggling. He really wanted to tell Mr Heath to get lost, but he was much too nice to do that.

Suddenly Pascolli nudged me and whispered in my ear. "Listen to James thoughts – he's asking for help!"
I listened but, as you may recall, mind reading is not one of my strong points, I concentrated, trying to block out the endless questions from Mr Heath, then I too heard a faint voice.

"Please help me ....if there is an angel please take this man away, I want him to leave me alone. No more questions please"

"That's it," said Pascolli "That's the cue, lets act"
"Lets act then" I agreed, I looked over to Willow who was looking increasingly worried, and this teamwork was not for him at all.
"Do you feel that life has been unfair to you James, especially with you parents dying so ..."
Before Mr Heath could finish the sentence, which was clearly going to upset James, Pascolli threw two cushions from the opposite settee across at Mr Heath,

causing him to spill his hot coffee all over his naff shiny grey suit, (which was also a bit short in the sleeves). He jumped up yelping like a dog.

"Shit, that was hot!" He yelled, "Where the heck did those cushions come from???"

James continued to sit still almost in a daze and very stressed that there was now coffee as well as mud on his beige carpet!

"A cloth would be good" Mr Heath shouted at James

"Yes of course, sorry" James got up and returned with a cloth, which unfortunately he had forgot to wring out so it was dripping wet. As James plopped the cloth onto Mr Heath's lap the water seeped out everywhere over his trousers (making it look like he had wet himself, we angels had to giggle).

"You bloody idiot" shouted Mr Heath obviously deeply upset about coffee and water stains on his suit.

"I think you should leave" James said very matter of fact; he must had a moment of inner strength filter through.

"What?" said a very agitated Mr Heath.

"I would like you to leave now please" James repeated.

"Fine with me. Pretty strange set up all round if you ask me!" moaned Mr Heath

"What just spilling coffee?" asked James.

"No. The whole bloody situation, I tell you what, Carla can pay my Agent extra for this to cover my suit-cleaning bill. Look at it ... its ruined" said Mr Heath angrily.

"What do you mean, Counsellors don't usually have agents. I'm paying anyway, Carla just set up the session to help!" James said, luckily on the ball for once.

"Wrong" we all shouted from above

"Look you seem like a decent chap, I'm not happy with this situation," Mr Heath said worriedly.

"What?" asked a puzzled James scratching his head. "I'm not really getting this – coffee does come out, look if it's the cleaning bill, sure I will pay, its no big deal ..."

"Oh Shit!" exclaimed Mr Heath who was now pacing up down "look I need to clean up and get out of here mate"

"Sure" said a confused James wondering what on earth was stressing this Counsellor out so much besides the coffee. "Bathroom is down the corridor"

Mr Heath started to walk down the corridor then turnt round and came back to James "Mate, sorry I can't screw people over, this is wrong ... look I'm no Counsellor, I am a ..."

"What? A fraud?" James interrupted.

"Don't be bloody daft, no I'm an actor!" Mr Heath confessed, not really understanding why he had just blown his cover, and realising he had probably just blown any chance of getting paid for this strange job.

Pascolli nudged me and winked happily at me. I wondered what he had done to get this man to suddenly confess?

"An actor? What are you on about mate?" James asked getting really confused now and looking at the dripping coffee falling onto his carpet. "If you are an actor what are you doing here ... oh I see .." James paused as the penny dropped "You are playing the part of a Counsellor today?"

"You got it, Carla sent me to pretend to be a Counsellor. Pretty weird if you ask me, but hey I needed the money, so don't hold it against me buddy. Hey, I really think I should leave, I've said too much – but had a bad vibe about that woman, I mean it's weird, don't you think? I'd watch your back with that woman, nasty" Mr Heath said now in a calmer tone of voice.

James almost started to shake, Mr Heath could see the fear in his eyes, he felt sorry for him, and patted him on the shoulder in a friendly sort of way.

"You'll be ok mate, hey I really better clean up now, I'll pop in your bathroom now, if that's ok?"

"Yeah, it's still straight down the hall" James said still in a total trance.

"Shit man, looks like I've pee'd myself," said Mr Heath as he came back to the lounge "What size are you mate? Don't suppose I could borrow a pair of trousers from you?"

"34" waist"

"I'm 32. Guess that's near enough"

"Sure, I'll get you a pair, sorry" said James.

"No, I am sorry mate, putting you through this, I shouldn't have taken the job, didn't like the sound of it, but you know if someone wants to pay you then well who am I to argue - stupid of me, its just not my sort of thing" explained Mr Heath. "I am not going to pass the information on to Carla, shall I tell her you were out and I now can't do the job?"

"You're sure you're an Actor and not a. ...Oh don't worry" said James still not quite comprehending why Carla had set this strange scenerio up. "Oh Yeah, do that, thanks".

"Look, I'm in a play at the Princes Theatre for the next two weeks, come along with a friend as my guest if you like! Feel like we've got off on the wrong footing because of that 'woman'. How about it, might cheer you up, it's a comedy" said Mr Heath, who clearly was not cut out to lie to people – a good quality. We now liked Mr Heath!

"Erm, ok cheers" replied James.

"He should take Carla," whispered Willow "that could be interesting"

"Wouldn't it just?" I giggled at the thought of it.

James opened the front door for Mr Heath to finally leave, now as sort of friend. They shook hands, and Mr Heath turned back and looked seriously at James. "Watch her – I'll pop the trousers back, mate"
"Thanks"

"I mean it, watch your back! See you at the Princes. I left the tickets on your side-board" said Mr Heath as he finally left.

James closed the door and walked over to his desk. He searched about though the drawers, and eventually found what he was looking for - the pink case file. He sat down and opened the file up and he sat there until he had carefully read every word in the file.

We left James reading, feeling that our trip and viewing had been a real success and quite amusing – humans, very strange at times, very strange!

Chapter 24

The shop was quiet, so Katie had taken the opportunity to start work on her marketing plan for the open day. She was surfing the Internet to identify potential suppliers she could approach for giveaways, prizes in return for some marketing for the companies that provided these.

Katie was really enjoying her new job, and she still couldn't believe her luck. Admittedly the pay was less than she was used to, but she could just about manage if she was careful, and maybe if this open day paid off and brought in more custom she could see about a modest rise. However, the main thing was she felt so much better in herself, getting up each day and coming to work was nothing like the chore it used to be, sometimes she actually couldn't wait to get to work!

Her only niggling problem was James, or more to the point what Carla was intending to do to James!

She had promised Blaze she would call James the previous night, she had tried but there had been no reply. She hadn't wanted to leave a voice message, as she did not really know what to say. Katie therefore took the opportunity while the shop was so quiet to try and ring him again. She sighed as James' voice mail clicked in again. She was about to leave a message - but changed her mind, she would try again later. She carried on surfing the Internet, and then tried ringing again.

There was still no reply, but she plucked up the courage and left a message:

"Hi James. It's me Katie. You may remember me from the office ... erm ... I haven't heard from you, not that I should hear from you - guess you're busy, but hey I just thought I'd phone to say 'hi' and see how you are ....Erm. ...Maybe you could call me back? Bye"

Katie put the phone down cringing "you may remember me?" what a bloody stupid thing to say she told herself. She didn't hear Blaze come up behind her.

"Talking to yourself is the first sign of madness, they say" Blaze said cheekily.

"Not sure about first sign of madness, pretty certain I am already mad and it's not the first time it's been said to me!" Katie laughed "Tea?"

"Yes please sweetie pie, and hey lets go mad and have some carrot cake too"

"You'll look like carrot cake soon! By the way before you ask, I tried to call James several times, left a message"

"Good, hopefully he'll call back soon then" Blaze replied taking the large slab of cake from Katie as she passed it across the counter. "Been busy?" he asked.

"No, it's been really quiet actually. What do you think about this wording for the open day flyer?" Katie asked Blaze as she passed him a typed sheet of ideas. He scanned the words super quick with his extremely green eyes, but just as he was about to reply, the phone rang. Katie answered with her polite customer care voice.

"Curiosity Bella. Katie speaking, how may I help you today?" Blaze winked at her as she spoke, impressed with her impeccable telephone manner.

"Katie, is that you?" a man's voice asked quietly

"Yes, this is Katie speaking" she said thinking didn't he hear what I said when I answered the phone?

"It's James," the voice announced.

"Oh James!" she exclaimed looking across at Blaze, covering the hand piece mouthing to him "Its James!" Blaze nodded and smiled already guessing that.

"Hi James how are you?" she asked.

"Good, and you?"

"I'm good thanks, how is everyone back at the office?" Katie asked making the customery 'expected' polite conversation.

"I've been on leave" James lied "So I've not really been in much lately"

"Oh, leave that's nice." Katie said, which was followed by an awkward silence, neither really knowing what to say.

"Did you call for a reason?" asked James, quite bluntly and breaking the awkward silence.

"Well ..." Katie started looking over at Blaze and shrugging her shoulders, she didn't know what to say. Blaze indicated the word 'lunch' to her. "I wondered if you fancied meeting up soon for some lunch. I wondered if you could bring my P45 rather than posting? And it would be good to see you." she said and Blaze nodded approvingly.

"Ok, of course. I would be pleased to help. When and where? I am pretty free this week, so what suits you?" James asked politely.

"What about tomorrow, its my day off, in Berties Café down Queens Road at say 12.30?" suggested Katie.

"Sounds like a date!" James said "See you there"

"Ok. See you then. I'm looking forward to it." Said Katie as they ended the conversation.

"Well done girl!" Blaze exclaimed pretending to clap.

"That was really difficult, how did I sound?" she asked hoping she had come across quite casual. Blaze put his thumb up indicating 'good'. "He said he's good and he sounded ok"

"He was lying!" said Blaze "Everyone says they're ok when really they're not. So tomorrow huh, you really need to get to the bottom of it then"

"But how? I can hardly blurt out that Carla only slept with him to get his prime cases for herself, can I?" Katie said, esasperated.

"Yes you can, but maybe not quite as blunt as that. He probably suspects it any way, he's not stupid, and he's an accountant for Christ sake. Didn't think they took risks though!" said Blaze.

"Just don't know what I'm going to say to him – or where to start?" Katie said with a worried expression on her face.

"Just say what comes out of those lips. Be you, be true, and don't even worry about it until tomorrow. Now can I have another piece of that cake?" Blaze said greedily licking his lips in anticipation.

"You'll get fat" Katie scolded

"No chance. I'm a lanky bean and need feeding up, look at that flat stomach!" he laughed pointing to his dead flat stomach making Katie moan.

"It's so unfair, I would be the size of a house if I ate like you" she laughed.

All of sudden about five customers entered the shop, all wanting teas. Katie set to work, and Blaze smiled and said quietly to Katie as she was pouring the teas "Happy days."

Chapter 25

I was on my way to Hibissa's chamber, as always slightly nervous, not really knowing what to expect. I entered the room quietly and waited to be spoken too. Hibissa looked up very slowly, in fact so slow it seemed like an eternity as his head gradually moved upwards until he was looking directly at me, scanning my thoughts, I tried to keep my mind blank, but little thoughts kept darting about through my brain, but still I waited until he spoke. Too many times in the past I had broken this unwritten etiquette rule.

"Relax Nicoise" Hibissa spoke eventually and quite softly. "How is case 4126999 going? Any more reports for me to check?"

"Well Sir, I have been keeping a daily journal of progress and events that occur, and yes I believe there is progress with this case Sir"

"A journal, how very organised. An idea passed on from Willow no doubt?" Hibissa said.

"No Sir, my own doing" I said trying to remember if Willow had advised me to do that, although I couldn't remember such a conversation.

"May I see the journal please?" Hibissa said, stretching out his large white fingers towards me.

"I am afraid I didn't bring the journal with me Sir, I was in a hurry"

Hibissa sighed, "Pity. You're always in a rush, Nicoise you need to pay more attention to your time management. It is I fear one of your weaknesses. When you come to see me I expect you to bring evidence to back up your words in future. Actually, I think I have the very book for you Nicoise, one moment." He reached across and read the binders of several large books on his desk then pulled out one of the fattest books you have ever seen. He blew the dust off, which came floating over my way causing me to sneeze several times.

Hibissa flicked through the pages until he found the chapter he needed. "Here we are, there is a whole section on 'Managing and Creating Time Wisely' for angels who need help in prioritising workloads etc etc. Now this could be a useful read for you this evening" he then handed the extremely heavy and old book across to me.

"Thank you Sir" I said as my heart sank. This looked such a boring book and the last thing I wanted to do was to read it.

"Now back to the case," Hibissa said. "As you have no evidence today please proceed with a short summary of the case?" he sat back into his chair preparing to listen to what I had to say.

"Certainly Sir. Well, I think that since Katie asked for help from."

"God, not you, if I remember correctly" interrupted Hibissa.

I looked down, remembering only too well the episode of when Katie was hiding under Carla's bed with Anthony sitting directly above her. She did indeed call for help from God, but Pascolli and I had helped …. sort of on of God's behalf?

"Yes, well after that Katie lost her job at the Accountancy Firm she worked for, due to … well her old boss actually"

"So it cost Katie her job? Is that what you call progress?" asked Hibissa.

"Ah, but that's the twist Sir. Although initially it seemed bad, it's been the making of her. She's met someone different, oh yes you know Blaze, and through meeting him she's started working in his Mothers shop come tea room establishment. She is really enjoying it and I feel much happier. Admittedly there is still some way to go, but I do feel it was right for her to get away from that office, it was no good for her"

"Is it a suitable job then, working in a tea shop, is it going to 'stretch' her?" asked Hibissa.

"It's a new business. Treatments, angel cards, crystals etc. You would love it, Sir I'm sure"

"You are sure I would are you?" asked Hibissa sarcastically.

"You would Sir, and the owner Bella (Blaze's Mother) is so cool and just lets Katie get on and work on her own initiative"

"Bella – Bella who?" enquired Hibissa stopping me from continuing with my blabbing on.

"Bella Blazier, I think"

"Ah Bella" a big smile came over Hibissa's face as he said her name. I had never seen Hibissa look like that;

he seemed to go all gooey and soft and sort of sparkly, a bit scary actually. I'm just not used to seeing mean old Hibissa look that way.

"Pray continue Nicoise I am waiting," he barked – the softness quickly fading.

"Well Bella ... " I couldn't resist another look at Hibissa's face as I said her name ".. has taken on Katie to help promote the business as well as the everyday running of the place. Katie loves it Sir, she truly does. She has also stuck up a really good relationship with Blaze, who I believe calms Katie and will channel her energy force towards us angels when the time is right."

"Excellent" beamed Hibissa "And?"

"Well Katie does need to help James, who has been manipulated by Carla somewhat and now stands to lose his job"

"Carla?" asked Hibissa

"Yes she was Katie's old boss, the nasty one, Sir"

"Oh yes, the one Katie stole notes from under your supervision?"

I felt a little sick; I don't know why Hibissa even goes through the process of listening to me when he clearly already knows everything anyway.

"I like to hear your version, your take on it" Hibissa said after reading my thoughts at that very moment. "If you want to know where I get my knowledge on cases from Nicoise look over at the wall" he pointed to the very large and white wall to the right of the Chamber, it was very plain, and had no pictures hanging on it, no furniture pushed against it. I wondered why on earth I was looking at this blank boring wall.

The wall altered from being a white wall to a vision tunnel. All of a sudden the whiteness cleared and I could see Katie under the bed clutching the case notes, with that Anthony marching about the bedroom and chucking off his shoes. But worst than that was an image of Pascolli and myself in the room together watching. Then the image cleared to be replaced by a second image of Pascolli, Willow and myself all watching James and the actor chap, and oh goodness, the image of Pascolli chucking a cushion at Mr Heath causing his coffee to spill all over him. The wall abruptly returned to its former plain but dazzling white self. I realised that if he wanted to Hibissa could see everything.

"No Nicoise, I can only tune in every now and then," said Hibissa, again responding to my thoughts. "I don't have the time or patience to watch everything, it makes me despair though that I clearly said no cross casing and there the two times I watch, you are there with your friends colluding together. But I have to admit that occasionally, and I mean occasionally, teamwork can be beneficial I can see that. However as mentor I have a duty to report any mis-interpretation of rules to the High Court, which if you had the misfortune to attend it would be likely that they would stop your trainee guardian angel status" he paused and looked up as I gasped, I really didn't want that to be the case.

"This would mean you would never qualify as a Guardian Angel, which would be a shame, especially as you are know enjoying your work"

"What would I do Sir?" I asked worriedly.

"What would you do? You would likely become a servant angel, a waiter, a messenger boy to Mentors and High Court members," explained Hibissa theatenly.

I gulped loudly, I didn't want to be a servant, and I knew that if Willow didn't get to qualify it would finish him being the straight 'A' student that he was, and Pascolli too … It didn't bear thinking about.

"The choice is yours Nicoise. I'm not actually saying don't work with Pascolli on the James thing as clearly it has advantages, but you need to be very careful young Nicoise"

"Yes Sir," I responded, confused, by what Hibissa had just said. I mean can I or can I not work with friends to solve these cases? I waited for Hibissa to say something after reading my thoughts, but he did not comment. I went to leave.

"There is actually a time management course I have booked you on Nicoise. It is on your next Fair Day, it will help I feel – so I'm sure you feel giving up your Fair day beneficial in this case? Good day" Hibissa said, ending our meeting.

"Great!" I thought sarcastically, forgetting Hibissa could still read your mind if your back was turned

"Yes I thought that would please you" Hibissa said with an evil hint of pleasure in his voice.

Chapter 26

Katie woke up very early, which was annoying because it was her day off and she could have had a few more hours sleep. However, waking up to a day off is always a nice feeling.

Katie remembered that she had her lunch meeting with James, could be interesting she thought. She thought momentarily about Carla, visualising her long black hair, sharp features and deep brown eyes. She was scary but stunning at the same time. She used her good looks to wrap men around her little finger. She was powerful and intriguing to men and she always got her own way, a trait that Katie felt had eluded her. The only person who may let her have her own way was her Dad and that was only if she did not tell her Mother!

Since she was now wide awake, there was no point in just lying there dwelling on what might or might not be, so she decided to get up and go to the gym (she remembered she had not been anywhere near the gym since losing her job – not good, she looked down at her tummy which was arguably a little more wobbly than before). She pulled on her leggings which felt a little too snug for comfort, digging in stubbornly at the waist, Katie made a promise to herself that she would cut back on all the cake she now ate whilst at work.

She was in the gym by 8.00am, feeling pretty pleased with herself. She waited outside the aerobics studio for the first class of the day to start. Gradually the other class attendees turned up and then she didn't feel so good, they were all like size 8 or 10, perfectly made up, with matching outfits. Katie felt a little conspicuous and a little large!

In the corner of her eye she saw Jayne, and panicked for a moment and wondered if she should leave but luckily the Instructor waved Jayne to the front of the class, Katie was right at the back hiding behind several tall beauties.

The loud music began and Katie soon realised how unfit she had become. Everyone else seemed to cope effortlessly including Jayne who was bouncing away at the front, yet Katie felt hot and out of breathe most of the time. The music changed and Jayne looked around and saw Katie, she smirked and gave Katie a half-hearted wave.

After what seemed to Katie like the longest workout ever the class finished. Katie was exhausted and looked as red as a beetroot. She tried to sneak out quickly before Jayne caught her, but alas the Instructor called to all the ladies to put their steps away.
"Damn" thought Katie returning to her spot to pick up her step and put it away in the storage cupboard in the studio.

"Bit inconsiderate of you trying to rush off Katie, leaving the Instructor to put away your stuff!" Jayne said coming straight over to Katie and not looking the least bit red or sweaty.

"I forgot. In a dream world me, sorry" she said, feeling cross with herself that she was again apologising to Jayne who just had that effect on her.

Jayne's face softened "How have you been anyway?"

"I'm ok" Katie replied, "How's things at the office?"

"Not good actually. They're not replacing you, which means more bloody work for me and Sara!" Jayne complained as if it was all Katie's fault.

"Oh dear" Katie smiled inwardly thinking it was about time they actually did some work.

"Carla is totally hypo and working like crazy. She's such a bitch to work for. Actually I just don't know how you put up with it for so long to be honest. She is so rude. Mind you I don't let her speak to me how she spoke to you!" added Jayne.

"What about James, how is he doing?" Katie asked casually.

"He's been off sick for a couple of weeks now" said Jayne

"What's wrong?"

"Don't know for sure but Carla said he's had some sort of break down. It seems a bit odd if you ask me, as I, can't imagine he would have a break down. He seemed fine to me"

"A break down?" Katie asked, incredulously.

"Yes, you know a nervous breakdown, caused by stress ... Carla has had to take on all his cases now, which is causing her to be a total stress head and bitch to work for. I hope James hurries up and comes back," said Jayne.

"Poor James. Have you spoken to him?" Katie asked.

"No, Carla said we're not allowed to contact him as it would be too stressy for him. Apparently it's not good to have contact with any part of what caused you the stress is what she said. So no. Mind you, she's organised stress counselling for him and she's gone through all his outstanding work and gutted his desk. In fact she's actually cleared his office. I think she may move offices as his office is way bigger"

Katie sighed sadly, her suspicions now confirmed by Jayne "So he is not coming back?"

"Doesn't look that way" said Jayne.

"Poor James"

"Yeah he was ok James, bit of a pushover to work, for but ok"

"Is Sara ok?" Katie asked, changing the subject

"Yes, she has a new boyfriend, so she is fluttering about. Anyway must dash, got to shower and get to work. Its alright for you unemployed people!"

Katie was about to say that she had in fact got a job, but then thought better of it. She didn't want anyone there to know her business. She loved her new job, she was part of the team there - something she had never really been with Sara and Jayne. She smiled at Jayne and they said goodbye.

Katie looked at her watch; she didn't have much time now to get ready before meeting up with James. She dashed out and jumped in her car, but was stopped by every red light, every zebra crossing, and then to top it all someone had taken her parking space outside her flat so she had to park what seemed miles up the road.

As she turned the key to her flat she could hear her home phone ringing out loudly, she dashed in and just made it before it stopped.

"Hi, I'm so excited. I've just come back from the hospital and the scan shows twins, and both are fine, and they are girls!" said Lucy clearly so very happy

"That's wonderful news, you must be soooo happy – congratulations" Katie said to her friend.

"I am, I just want to cry"

"Cry? But you're happy right?"

"Very happy" Lucy then started to cry "I never thought I would be a mum, it's just so wonderful, I can't explain how I feel," she said.

"How is Mick?" Katie asked.

"He's so exited, he won't let me lift a finger. He's talking about letting me have a cleaner, which I've wanted for ages. I mean I don't know why I should have to clean, I need to rest"

Katie laughed to herself. That was just so Lucy to think she now needed a cleaner. She could tell Lucy would totally 'exploit' being pregnant, it would cost Mick a fortune, but she knew he would happily pay to keep his Lucy happy, "Are you going to give up work" Katie asked guessing she would.

"I will do, but I have a few months yet. Trouble is I get so tired already"

"You will do," replied Katie knowingly, not that she really had an idea of what it was like to be pregnant.

"How about you? Do you want to meet up with me and Carrie soon?" asked Lucy

"Yes that would be great. I'm meeting James for lunch today" Katie said excitedly.

"Oh yes James, the one you like" teased Lucy

"It's not like that ..."

"I better get off the phone then so you can make yourself beautiful for your date. I'll speak to Carrie and come back with the date. See ya"

"Bye" Katie put the phone down smiling but no sooner had she put it down it started ringing again. 'Damn' she thought I am never going to have time to get ready.

"Just checking you're getting ready to meet James," said Blaze's happy voice

"Well I would be if the phone didn't keep ringing" said Katie, a little stressed.

"Sorry, I'll go then," said Blaze apologetically.

"No, I didn't mean that. It's been one of those mornings already and its not even 11 O'clock yet" moaned Katie

"Yes I know what you mean 'one of those mornings,'" mocked Blaze

"I saw Jayne this morning at the gym, and she said that Carla has completely cleared James office out, and told Jayne and Sara not too contact him and that he has had a nervous breakdown! Its awful she is so scheming I could spit! Do you think he has had a nervous breakdown?" Katie asked.

"No he hasn't. It is what Carla wants people to believe; it will be easier for her if they believe that. Anyway I just phoned to say 'good-luck' with James at lunchtime. Meet me in Curiosity Bella after for tea and cake if you like?"

"Ok but no cake, I'm on a diet."

"Diet?" Blaze laughed, "See you later for tea and cake. Ring James and say you are running a little late"

Katie took Blaze's advice and called up James just to explain she was running late.

"Leave it if it's not convenient today" said James

"No" Katie almost snapped the word out "Its fine, I'm not busy its just been a hectic morning"

"Ok"

"Shall we say 1'0 clock now then?"

"Fine, I am not doing anything" James replied gloomily.

Katie reflected on how quiet, meek and almost uninterested James had sounded. She felt sad this was not the old James she knew. She needed to help him she really did, but didn't really know why. She looked out of the window into the fresh and quite sharp morning air and said, "Help me to help James please"

Chapter 27

The Sparkles felt particularly refreshing and zingy today. I glanced over to Willow, with whom I had come with today to the Sparkles Bar. He grinned a soppy grin; good old Willow I thought as I pulled a face back at him. He is such a good friend.

I looked around the surrounding white peaks and troughs of the clouds. Everything seemed still and calm. All the angels around me seemed free and happy with positive white faces. This place is so good; I am so lucky to live such an existence.

Willow flew to my side "Nicoise, how did the meeting with Hibissa go? Did you get into any more trouble?" he laughed.

"I am not really sure how I got on, to be truthful" I replied

"What do you mean?'

"Well, he showed me the vision screen revealing me and Pascolli working together on a case" I said.

"Oh no, you mean he can see what is going on?" Willow asked, worried.

"Well yes and no! He doesn't watch it all the time, just now and again, so it's a bit of a lottery to see if you've been caught. Then he went on about how sometimes teamwork is useful. It didn't really make sense to me and seems to be a bit of a grey area".

"Odd" nodded Willow "Sounds like he is mellowing in his old age"

"Oh yes, and when I mentioned Blaze's Mum, Bella, he went all white and shimmery" I added.

"Oh, I can help you there", said Willow. "Bella was one of his cases many years ago when he was a trainee guardian like us, and I think Bella was his big success story. Apparently she was an absolute wild child, a lost cause even until she saw the light. I believe they're still in touch. She really believes in Hibissa and he helps her"

"That explains things a bit, small world really huh?" I asked.

"Yes indeed. How is your case Katie coming along then?" Willow asked.

"Not bad, not bad. I'm just waiting for Pascolli and we've then got to fly down to the lunch meeting between his case James and my case Katie. Could be interesting, do you fancy joining us?" I asked knowing only too well that Willow would politely decline.

"Love to, but have my own appointment I am afraid" Willow said.

"Any thing juicy?" I asked, hoping Willow would have something significant to talk about.

"Nah, nothing for you to worry about" he replied quietly.

Pascolli swooped down nearly knocking poor Willow over, bad landing.

"Careful Pascolli!" Willow gasped, recomposing himself after Pascolli bumpedinto him.

"Sorry guys, I'm having a few problems with my landings lately, don't know why" Pascolli said

"Too many sparkles?" I laughed; Pascolli threw me a hurt look. "Are you ready to go then?"

"Sure, you coming Wills?" Pascolli asked

"Sorry, not this time. Good luck and be careful with the landing," replied Willow cheerfully.

The journey down seemed quite chilly as the Earth's winter was fast approaching, and the trees were changing from their vibrant green colours to the pretty rustic and orange colours. Earth is so much more colourful than heaven.

The wind in the air was strong and bracing, making our flight slightly harder than usual and the clouds were dark and bumpy. I sighed, wishing it were still the warm summer - such better flying conditions!

We eventually arrived, first popping into James flat. Pascolli again landed quite heavily and I wondered what was causing this technical problem he was currently experiencing.

James' cat screeched out in fear when Pascolli landed, and when it saw us it arched its back and hissed loudly, making James turn to see what all the commotion was about. But of course all he could see was his bad tempered cat.

"What's wrong Sydney?" James asked his cat, coming across and stoking his black furry neck. Honestly you almost expected the cat to speak and give the game away, but of course he didn't. He just continued hissing at staring at us with his green glassy eyes.

"What a friendly cat!" exclaimed Pascolli sarcastically.

"Very strange how animals see us, but humans don't. Pity Sydney doesn't sense that we are here to help his human though"

"Erm, shame James doesn't realise that we are here to help"

"I should get over to Katie's," I said, impatiently.

"Chill Nicoise" said Pascolli "let's go together, two heads are better than one huh" he nudged me with his wing.

"He looks pale," I said, referring to James

"Probably because he never goes out, never sees the sun" responded Pascolli.

"Where is the file?" I asked.

"How should I know?" Pascolli replied curtly.

"I think he should take it with him to the meeting with Katie" I said.

"You think so?" asked Pascolli "He might lose it"

"Come on, let's look for the folder." I said and Pascolli dutifully followed me to look.

We scouted around each room of the apartment, and each one of them was quite messy; not dirty, just messy and unloved, which we both knew was not really James style. Eventually, in the small spare room or guest room as I think you humans call them, we found the pink case folder.

"Pick it up quick" I said to Pascolli.

"No you!" he complained.

"James is your case not mine!" I said impatiently.

"Yes, but indirectly its helping you too!" We exchanged stubborn looks. I sighed heavily and then picked up the pink folder; it had to be done and there was no point in arguing about who should do it, I brought it back into the lounge.

"Where should I put it?" I asked

"I don't know, somewhere he's bound to see it," replied Pascolli

"Very helpful. Not!" I snorted.

"What about under his door keys then?"

"Yeh good idea Pascolli" I replied looking for his keys "Where are the keys?"

I couldn't find the keys anywhere, so I placed the pink folder at the front door on the doormat, where James couldn't fail to see it.

We heard the phone ring; it was Katie telling James she was running a little late. James nearly cancelled the engagement at which, Pascolli pulled an 'oh no' face, but luckily the lunch was still on, albeit a little later than planned. I glanced over to a solemn James who was still wandering about in his pyjama bottoms.

"You need to get him dressed Pascolli," I urged, looking at James thinking this will never do. He needs to be respectable and look half alive.

"Dress him! I'm not dressing him!" protested Pascolli "That's certainly not in the job description!"

"I don't mean physically dress him! Just help him, encourage him to get dressed, put the clothes under his nose"

"What would he want to wear? I don't know!"

We went into the bedroom and inspected James' clothes, mainly drab suits, white shirts, patterned shirts, loud shirts, all too formal.

"Any of those jeans and t-shirts?" I asked

"Jeans?" replied Pascolli, looking confused "What are Jeans?"

"You know the blue hard cotton material trousers that they all seem to wear at weekends" I explained.

"Oh I know what you mean. Are these any good?" Pascolli held up a beige pair of cotton trousers.

"They're not jeans but hey they look sort of casual and 'lunch time like', so yep go with them and some sort of top, and hurry!" I said aware of the time ticking on. Eventually we agreed on the trousers together with a long sleeved dark brown t-shirt, with a hooded dark brown jacket and some suede effect boots (secretly quite enjoying this matching up of clothes, something us angels never have to worry about, always crisp white gowns for us!)

Pascolli threw the clothes next to James where he was sitting on the settee causing him to jump (not very subtle – I moaned to Pascolli who just shrugged his shoulders at me).

"What the hell!" James exclaimed jumping up and away from the clothes just hurled at him from nowhere. His face was actually quite a picture, he looked puzzled and scratched his head, wondering how an earth that had just happened. I couldn't help but giggle, but Sydney the cat threw me a dirty look and I stopped laughing.

"Oh my god, is that the time!" exclaimed James, "Oh well, these clothes are as good as any." He changed into them there and then without even closing his window curtains. He then walked over to the mirror above the mantelpiece in the lounge and looked at his reflection. He didn't really like what he saw, as a tired and unkempt face look back at him.

"Shave," shouted out Pascolli

"Best shave" said James, a bit spooked that he thought he heard someone tell him to do that. He really felt he was losing it, Carla must be right; he was slowly going mad, being couped up here. It would be good to get out he thought as he ambled slowly, painfully slowly, to the bathroom to shave.

"Will you hurry up?" I shouted after James

"Sshh let him be, he's making an effort to get ready now so let him be. This is a development believe me" Pascolli said.

We waited and waited and eventually the door opened and a cleaner, shaven, dressed version of James came out, he even smelt better!

Pascolli and I exchanged looks and nodded approvingly. James popped his wallet into his trouser pocket and found his keys in the drawer in the kitchen and popped them in his jacket pocket.

"Ah that's where they are!" I said watching James pick his keys up.

"Ready to go" Pascolli said cheerfully.

"Game on" I said, but stopped as I watched James reach the front door. He paused and looked oddly at the pink folder on the mat propped against the door. He scratched his head and gave a puzzled expression, as he knew that he never would have left the folder there. Very curious, he thought. He picked up the file and placed it on the sideboard in the hall.

"No ...take it with you!" I said "Pascolli, tell him to take it with him, he'll hear you" I said urgently.

"Doubt it" replied Pascolli

"Try, " I urged "he really needs to take it with him"

"James, you really need to take that pink folder with you, it could be very useful" Pascolli said to James half-heartedly and pulling a face at me "Good enough?" he asked.

James continued unlocking the door and stepped out into the porch. Pascolli and I looked frantically at each other.

"Try again and this time try and sound like you mean it," I said crossly.

"JAMES, TAKE THE PINK FOLDER WITH YOU FOR GODS SAKE!" shouted Pascolli to my utter astonishment.

It did the trick though because James suddenly turned around and picked up the folder, telling himself he should put it in the car to return it to Carla!!

"Carla! No! Why?" we called in unison.

"No" James said "I will keep it with me!"

"Good man!" Pascolli said "Now go and meet Katie, and hurry"

"Right now to meet Katie" James said out loud, making Pascolli and I smile and nod.

"You're getting through," I said

"Cool, he heard common sense, he heard me" Pascolli said in a daze

"Not sure you and common sense go in the same sentence" I laughed making Pascolli tut in disgust "Come on we need to follow as quick as possible"

We followed James in the cold air hoping that the meeting would be successful.

Chapter 28

Katie had rushed to Berties Bar, and had by the skin of her teeth just made it by one. She sat down feeling stressed as a result of her rushing, then looked around and noticed that James was not yet there. She really hoped that he was going to turn up. She felt slightly conspicuous and wondered if she should go an order a drink or just stay where she was and wait. She hated sitting alone in such places; it always reminded her of how very single she was for some reason. A waiter came over, so she ordered some tea, and then moved across to the table by the window so that James would easily see her. It was a cute table with a red gingham tablecloth and two white carnations in a small glass vase. She waited and waited, she tidied her handbag, sent a few texts and watched the world go by outside. But, still no James.

A waitress came over and startled Katies daydreaming by asking if she was ready to order. Katie told her that she was actually waiting for a friend, but ordered another cup of tea for now. She looked at the time and realised that James was now an hour late. She prayed he would turn up, but how long should she wait? She did not want to call him and look like she was hassling him so she sent Blaze a text.

To which Blaze replied *"He will be there, be patient"*

The waitress returned with the tea almost spilling over into the saucer as she slammed it down, she seemed a bit cross that Katie was sitting in the prime seat by the window and only ordering tea. Katie smiled and thanked the waitress who grumpily scuttled off to the kitchen.

The glass door of Berties squeaked open for the umpteenth time. Katie could hardly be bothered to look up but she did and at last it was James. She smiled and waved him over to her.

Katie felt butterflies in her stomach not really knowing how to start a conversation with James, how to continue it or how to finish it, but she thought of Blaze's words 'just be natural' he had told her. She looked at James as he sat down opposite her. He looked gaunt and his eyes were sad and grey, kind of lost eyes. Her instinct was to get up and hug him and make him feel better, but she remained sitting.

"Hi James. Tea or coffee?" Katie asked politely.

"Do they do Lattes?" he asked

"Probably, I'll see" she caught the eye of the grumpy waitress who came over and finally took a small order, for another tea, a latte and two Danish pastries (sod the diet Katie thought, only about 650 calories in one of these delicious cakes)

"How have you been then? I heard you've been off work" Katie was careful not to say 'off sick'

"Err yeah," replied James "I've not been feeling too well lately, so I've had a little time out"

"Oh dear, I'm sorry to hear that" Katie replied, not wanting to pry any further "I've got a new job, it's only supposed to be a stop gap, but actually I'm really enjoying it. The people I work with are so lovely, and I get to meet lots of new people everyday" she blurted out.

"That's nice" James replied, a bit non-interested Katie felt. He looked up and realised that he must have sounded a little rude thinking to himself that Katie didn't deserve that, as she had always been very nice to him at work. "Where are you working?" he asked.

This served to break the ice, and Katie lunged into a long conversation about Curiosity Bella, her marketing plans, about her best friend having twins and, a little about the weather. But she avoided the 'Carla' topic. James seemed to cheer up and chatted back. They ordered more tea and some Panini's, the waitress returned with the tea and this time she carefully placed it down, happy that at last she was getting some proper orders.

Everything was going swimmingly well, until all of a sudden James pulled his chair in closer to the table and leant across to speak quietly to Katie as though people were listening. He grabbed one of her hands and looked at her intensely.

"I thought she loved me Katie, I thought Carla really loved me. How could I have been so naïve, she just used me!" he said quite pathetically.

Katie saw how distressed he looked; she tried to think of what she could say without directly slagging off Carla.

"I think Carla actually has a boyfriend, but I think she probably really liked you. I mean everyone likes you, James"

"No you're wrong. She used me Katie, used me! I found my notes on my desk, which had gone missing and then just, turned up, and I knew she had used them. She took the Baker-John case off me. She doesn't think I can cope!" James said clearly upset now.

Katie could feel herself blushing, she thought back to the manic day she had left the case file in his office and she hoped that he didn't suspect her. "What sort of notes?" she asked not actually looking up as she spoke.

"All about transferring the Baker-John account. They contained some really confidential information, and amongst my notes I found a letter to Mr Baker saying that Carla would now be dealing with him and not me as I was unable to cope and off suffering from stress and a suspected nervous breakdown! I mean Katie can you imagine me being off with stress??"

Katie looked at James and felt for him. Yes, she could imagine him with stress, he was clearly stressed over the whole thing, and now he knew Carla's plan had sort of worked. Katie was really sad that James felt so depressed, but she considered this was probably the first time he had opened up about the whole situation, so that had to be a positive thing in her opinion.

"She even sent a bloody actor around to my house to pretend to give me counselling for stress, and basically wanted more information out of me!" James said, now getting quite angry.

"That is way out of order!" Katie exclaimed.

"And she got rid of you didn't she?" James asked Katie not really knowing what happened there.

"Well I kind of quit actually. I was not prepared to do what Carla wanted, even though she was my boss and I needed my job." Katie explained.

"Don't you like Carla then?" asked James curiously.

"No. I don't like how she is with people although I don't really know her socially. She is probably really nice when you get to know her" Katie said carefully.

James let go of Katie's hand and started to cry, really cry, in public in front of Katie. She didn't know how to react, this had taken her by total surprise. He had seemed relatively ok a moment ago, a little angry and bitter perhaps, but ok. And now all the tears!

The waitress looked over with a curious expression on her face, wondering what Katie had done to upset him, and worried that it would put customer's off from coming in.

"James, I am so sorry, please don't cry" Katie said gently looking around as all eyes in the bar seemed to be on them.

"I loved my job, but now no one will ever take me on. My reputation is in tatters, and I'll never work again!"

James wailed, a tad too dramatically for Katie's liking. "Women are all the same," he continue "you just take everything and then leave, take and then discard that's what women do!"

"Not all women James, just some.   It's just unfortunate that ..." she stopped herself saying that Carla was such a woman.

James looked up and wiped his eyes on his sleeve. Katie was finding it hard not to cry as well, she always got emotional when she saw people cry, even in films or soaps on telly.

"Please forgive me Katie, I shouldn't have done that" James said apologetically

"No you should. You obviously needed to get it off your chest, so it's good. There's nothing to forgive" Katie smiled kindly.

"But you don't want to hear all my problems surely?" he said

"I do, James," replied Katie, honestly.

"You do?" James asked somewhat incredulously

"Well" laughed Katie "I want to help you, to be a friend"

"Do you know, what I need is a pint of beer. Do you fancy a drink before you go?" James asked.

"Good idea, lets go to the wine bar," suggested Katie.

With that they left the Café, and Katie broke one of her rules of always tipping. She actually didn't leave a tip for Miss Grumpy, she didn't deserve one (usually she tipped everyone just because it was the done thing). She thought she would feel bad about this, but actually she felt rather pleased with herself.

Chapter 29

Pascolli and I were sitting watching James and Katie together, and listening to their conversation almost wanting to interrupt and stop it. We were however pleased that the meeting had taken place and that James had opened up to Katie, a starting place we felt. We followed them from Berties Cafe down the busy High Street, which was full of people coming out of the railway station, people calling taxi's, people doing a little shopping, and some just out for leisurely meetings in bars like James and Katie, (but probably none with such a purpose as ours I thought to myself).

The next Bar was a crowded, strange sort of place. It was very dark inside (not like our Sparkles Bar), and quite grim really. It had little china jugs hanging from every possible place and one wall was completely crammed with bottles of wine for effect. It seemed strange to me, but that's me.

James found a small table for two in a corner whilst Katie struggled through the busy bar to get served, eventually making it back to James with the drink. They chatted away for ages, and for a casual observer they looked like a perfect young couple.

"It's good that he's opening up," said Pascolli, breaking my concentration

"Yes, and Katie makes a very good listener I think, she loves to feel needed, that's very important to her, so it will help her too" I replied.

"So, would you say that our 'team' effort is a success?" Pascolli asked with a wink.

"I think you could say it is a success, yes," I said grinning back.

"You think?" Pascolli nudged me

"Yes, and this is the way forward. The High Court needs to learn" I said.

Pascolli pulled a face at me, which I took to mean 'listen'; we continued to observe as the two of them chatted away. We were quite content to just sit there and let it all just roll, but then from the corner of my eye I saw something, or someone I should say, that made me shudder.

A large, tall dark man was abruptly pushing his way through the crowd of people until he reached the bar where he rudely waved his money about in his quest to be served. I nudged Pascolli who looked across to where my eyes where, then looked back at me with a look of horror across his face.

"Anthony!!" gasped Pascolli

"And you know what that means?" I asked, scanning the bar for sight of Carla his partner in crime. Oh yes, there she was in her full glory, smiling yet looking mean, dressed in the tightest red suit possible with a black patient belt pulling in her already tiny waist. She was standing in a crevice around the corner, not far from where James and Katie were sitting.

I looked back over to James and Katie and realised that James had (on our encouragement) brought the pink folder that Carla so desired; there it was, sitting proudly on the small table in between James and Katie; this was not good!

Pascolli had not seen Carla then he too saw her "Carla is here," he cried.

"I know, and so is the folder!"

"What? Oh yes!" said Pascolli, remembering that James had brought the pink folder "We need to get him out of here, he's not ready to confront those two today, especially with the folder in his possession"

"But they will have to pass right by Carla and Anthony to leave" I replied.

"What should we do now then?" Pascolli asked

"I was going to ask you the same question. Any bright ideas spring to mind?" I asked.

"Bright?" said Pascolli thoughtfully "What about using the light skills to reflect light off Carla's glass giving her a headache and making her want to leave?"

"Eh? We're not supposed to hurt humans in any way are we?" I asked.

"Technically no, but we will not really be hurting her. Anyway I'm not really sure if she is human!" Pascolli said making me giggle. "You keep James and Katie sitting" he continued "Don't let them move, not for another drink, not to go to the toilet, nothing ok?"

"I'll try, but what are you going to do?" I enquired a little nervously.

"I'm going to get Carla and Anthony to leave this place," Pascolli said confidently, though I couldn't see how.

"Pascolli" I called after him as he got up "Remember Hibissa may have that Visual Screen on"

"Yeah, well what else can we do? We're here now, so we'll worry about that later. Anyway you said he said he does'nt have time to always view everything, right?" With that he went.

I glanced over to where Katie and James were still cosily sitting and chatting. I relaxed slightly, but then I thought I heard one of them say 'shall we get another drink?' "No!" I shouted out at them "You don't want another drink"

"Do you want another drink Katie?" repeated James

"No thanks" Katie replied (I let out a sigh of relief) "I really should be making a move to go home," she continued (No. No. No! I thought.)

"Do you have to go so early?" asked James (yes Katie, surely you should stay a little longer I urged willing her to hear my message)

"It's nearly 10 O' clock James and we've been chatting for hours," Katie said.

"Bloody hell, is it really" replied James "I still thought it was the afternoon! I didn't realise. I'm sorry I've taken up so much of your time. It's just that it has been so nice to talk to someone, err to you" James said.

"Its been so nice catching up with you too, its just I am on the early shift tomorrow" Katie smiled "I'll just pop to the ladies first. Do you know where they are?" to my horror she started to look around the room.

I was at a loss to know what to do, one way or another Katie was going to get up and walk past Carla. I wondered how Pascolli was getting on. Unbeknown to me his plan was not working. He had tried to create this light thingy to give Carla a headache, but it wasn't working.

I found Pascolli watching them, both preening themselves glancing around every now and again to see if anyone was admiring them. They're both as bad as each other, so vain!

"It didn't work" Pascolli whispered "What now?"

"James and Katie are about to leave," I said, with increasing urgency.

"Maybe they won't notice?"

"You're joking! They both keep looking around to see if anyone is looking at them!" I exclaimed

"We'll just have to walk in front of our cases, and will have to ensure we keep straight and direct," I said

"What...." Pascolli started, but before he could finish, both James and Katie were on there feet pushing in their chairs under the small table.

I looked over to Katie and then said out loud "Stop for no one, go quick!"

"Sorry what did you say?" Katie asked James as they got up to leave.

"I never said anything?" he replied.

"Strange. I just heard someone say 'stop for no one, go quick'. That keeps happening lately, I think I'm going mad"

"Stop for no one!!" I repeated in Katie's mind.

"There it was again. Are you sure you didn't hear anything?" she asked James, who shook his head and gave her a worried stare.

"Weird ... oh well, lets go" she said, flinging her bag over her shoulder.

"Shit I nearly forgot the folder" James said picking it up, "Could you put it in your bag?" he asked Katie.

"Of course" she said opening her large tan satchel and pushing the folder in, she couldn't quite get the whole folder in, so a little pink showed above the top of the bag.

"There" she laughed "Come, and stop for no one, quick!" she mocked

They pushed their way through the crowd; it was even busier now than it had been earlier. Katie looked like she was on a mission, she really did just focus on getting out of the place, it was quite a feat, James got out and Katie popped to the toilets.

As Katie left the toilet, Carla was coming in through the door. Katie never saw her as she was still on her mission to get out. However, Carla looked across at her. I took a deep breath.

Carla was actually looking at Katie's clothes rather than her face, and laughed inwardly at the awkwardness of this woman before her; she had no idea of fashion obviously, she was wearing a cardigan for goodness sake, and her bag was overloaded with something sticking out the top; something pink. Katie had left, while Carla was still thinking about 'pink'
"Oh my God... Katie!!" she yelled, making two other ladies stare at her as if she had gone mad. Carla just glared back at them, she never apologised to anyone.

Carla ran out into the Bar, looking all around, but she could see nothing but crowds of loud people, laughing and chatting. She hurried past and ran out into the street, but there was no sight of Katie (who, with James, had luckily just got a taxi which had conveniently just been passing).

Carla went back inside the Bar. She was feeling angry and puzzled thinking she needed to contact Katie. It was clear to Carla that Katie had the Pink Case Folder, and was sure that was what was poking out of that hideous tan bag. She went back to Anthony, who was now complaining about a headache and wanting to leave.

"That was close!" Pascolli exclaimed.

"You're not wrong there! I thought Carla was on to Katie then. I really don't want them to meet, well not yet; the time has to be right, it has to be Katie's timing not Carla's," I said

"We need a plan," replied Pascolli.

"Yeah, I can't take too much more of this haphazard working pattern, its stressing me out! Honestly I am a bag of nerves now!" I said.

"Perhaps we should get Willow to help?" sugested Pascolli "He'll come up with a plan"

"Maybe. But hey, I actually spoke to Katie and she heard me. She actually heard me and did what I said. Wow!" I said proudly.

"Cool. That's good," agreed Pascolli. "You did well"

"Thank you. So did you. We did well together," I added.

"Ok. But I know why the light trick with Carla didn't work" said Pascolli "Light can only be seen by humans that you're guarding, and, luckily I'm not guarding Carla!" he laughed thanking his lucky stars.

"You tried. Come on lets go home. I'm in need of sparkles" I said to which Pascolli nodded in agreement.

We left the wet and drizzly street and flew home, feeling quite proud and righteous, but also knowing we had a lot of work ahead on this case!

Chapter 30

Katie was back at work telling Blaze and Bella about her meeting with James. They listened carefully, occasionally glancing at each other in time and raising the odd eyebrow.

Blaze watched Katie, thinking to him self that she had come so far in these last few weeks. He felt like he had always known her, which was a strange feeling. He watched her as her expressive face glowed as she excitedly told the story relaying almost every word she and James has spoken.

Blaze knew Bella would be pleased to know that Katie had heard a guiding voice. He sensed something must have been occurring for her Angel to speak out, and he wondered who her Angel was. He also wondered when Katie would realise she had a guardian; not many people believed, which he knew was a real shame.

Trade in the shop was particulary slow that morning with just the odd curious customer browsing, but no one purchased anything, not a bean. Katie could tell that Bella was worried about the lack of customers and she knew she would have to work harder on the marketing and the open day. Perhaps she should bring it forward but she wanted everything to be right and not rushed.

Katie was deep in thought about her meeting with James, when Carrie came bursting through the door, with Lucy a few steps behind her.

"Hello" beamed Katie, thinking how cool it was to have a job that allowed you to catch up with friends in work time. She did feel a little guilty if she chatted for too long, not that Bella seemed to mind, but she continued to clean or make teas whilst talking.

"I've brought Lucy along to check out this place that you call 'work,'" laughed Carrie. Then turning to Lucy who was busy looking around the shop full of sparkly things she asked "Carrot Cake and tea?"

"What's in the cream on the carrot cake?" asked Lucy "I have to be really careful. There are so many things you can't eat when you're pregnant you know!"

"What, like bottles of wine" asked Katie grinning, knowing her friend would be missing her wine.

"Bloody hell, yes, I miss wine so much, but hey" she patted her very tiny bump (you would hardly know she was pregnant)

"Are you still feeling sick?" Carrie asked

"A bit, but I'm so tired all the time - just want to sleep," moaned Lucy

"That's just natural, you're lucky. I was sick all the way through my pregnancies, especially with Toby" Carrie added.

"Excuse me ladies, but did you want to order something or are you going to compare pregnancy notes all morning?" butted in Katie sarcastically feeling a little left out of the conversation.

"Get you! Feeling left out Katie? You want to speed things up with James if you ask me" Lucy said, but stopped when Katie glared at her "Erm I'll have a tea with no milk, and just a tiny slab of the chocolate cake please. It's so cute here Kats" she added, nodding approvingly

"Have a look around while I sort the teas, what are you having Carrie?"

"Usual" she grinned "and make it large! How did the meeting with James go then?"

"Good, well at least I think so. He opened up but he cried a lot"

"Cried!" Lucy stated horrified "I can't stand men who cry, it's just not right"

"He's been through a bad time Lucy, and why should men not cry?" Katie asked.

"Because...erm ... this cake is delicious," Lucy said.

"Do you still fancy him?" Carrie asked, looking carefully at Katie as she asked.

"Ssh" said Katie "Blaze is in the back office"

"Why should that bother you? Or are you also warming to the charms of red Blaze?" Laughed Lucy, making Carrie laugh too.

"No ... it's not like that with either of them. James needs my help and Blaze is well Blaze. He's a really cool friend to have"

"Did I hear my name ladies?" said Blaze popping his head out of one of the doors behind the counter. "Tea and the usual cake please I think Katie" he pulled a stool up where Lucy and Carrie were sitting.

"May I join you, or is this a ladies exclusive?" he asked, tongue in cheek.

"Be our guest," said Lucy "We were just asking Katie how she got on yesterday"

"She did just grand by the sound of it. She really cheered James up. Just got to sort out that Carla woman now" he said.

"Why don't you just leave it? Seems silly stirring it all up again" said Carrie in a worried voice

"No!" Blaze said firmly "We spoke on this before. That woman needs to be stopped and exposed. She can't just go around destroying people's livelihood's when she pleases, and Katie is the girl to sort it!"

"Why are you so interested in getting even with Carla, you don't even know her, do you?" said Lucy in her usual blunt manner.

All three women looked at Blaze for his reply who seemed momentarily lost for words, but he soon laughed and broke their questioning stares by answering Lucy's question. "I know women like Carla and I know what Katie has told me so that's enough for me" he smiled at Katie who smiled back as she passed his tea and cake across to him.

"Anyway, Katie we just popped in really to see if you can come over for dinner on Saturday – Mick is cooking so that should be interesting!" said Lucy changing the subject. She glanced across to Blaze "Bring a friend if you like" she said mischeviously.

"James or Blaze?" whispered Carrie to Katie, who instantly threw her a disapproving look.

"I'll let you know, if that's ok" Katie replied

"We'd better go Lucy, I've got to get Toby soon"

"Sure, Katie, speak soon" said Lucy kissing Katie on the cheek.

After they left and the shop was once more quiet, Katie got out the marketing folder and scribbled some notes inside. Blaze went downstairs to sort out a delivery, and it was ages before either spoke; the day went quite quickly despite the lack of customers.

Driving home Katie thought about going to the gym but changed her mind after she succumbed to two chocolate bars at the petrol station.

Instead thought she would pop round to see Mrs Hogan, she had not seen her for a couple of days.

Katie knocked a few times but there was no reply. She was just about to turn away and walk back to her own place when the door creaked open, and a small Mrs Hogan popped her head around the door.

"Hello" her little voice said

"Mrs Hogan. Hi it's me, Katie, I wondered if you had time for a quick cup of tea?"

"A cup of tea?" Mrs Hogan looked vague and confused

"Are you alright Mrs Hogan? May I come in?" Katie asked slightly concerned. Mrs Hogan then opened the door wide open exposing her quaint hallway to the street. Katie stepped in and closed the door, thankful to be out to that ghastly rain that had suddenly started falling unexpectedly, weathermen wrong as usual she thought.

She followed Mrs Hogan along the autumn coloured passageway into her tiny cluttered kitchen. Mrs Hogan filled up the kettle with water and popped it onto the gas cooker. This always made Katie smile, as it seemed so very old fashioned; she wondered why she just didn't have an electric kettle like everyone else, it seemed to take ages to heat this way.

"You had a few visitors today" stated Mrs Hogan as she offered Katie the biscuit tin. Katie declined, as she knew the biscuits would probably be stale as they usually were.

"Visitor's? Like who? Who would visit me during the day when they know I'm at work?" Katie asked.

"Maybe they didn't know that you were working," said Mrs Hogan, who had a point.

"I guess ...did you recognise them?"

"No, I don't think so. The first man was youngish, in a green coat and had very messy hair"

"Oh that sounds like Nick my brother. Three guesses what he wants"

'Yes, I think I have seen him before now you mention it" nodded Mrs Hogan slurping loudly on her tea.

"And the second visitor?"

"The second? The second what?" Mrs Hogan seemed confused again.

"Did you recognise the second visitor?"

"A tall, big, dark man. He didn't knock though; I think he may have put something in your letterbox. It wasn't Ben - our usual Postman. No, and he wasn't wearing shorts" Mrs Hogan said.

"A tall dark man eh? I can't think who that would be. A mystery. Oh well, probably just delivering some junk mail" said Katie.

"He didn't put a note in my door, or any other door and he drove off in a loud black sports car" added Mrs Hogan, being a right Miss Marple!

"Oh ... well don't worry I'll check when I get in. How have the meals on wheels been this week?" Katie enquired, wanting to change the subject but slightly concerned about the mystery visitor.

"Very tasty. I had chicken pie today no sorry the chicken pie was yesterday and I had shepherds pie today. Very hot though, burnt my tongue" she stuck her tongue out to show Katie how red it was. Katie smiled.

Katie listened to Mrs Hogan for over an hour, even though she had only popped in for five minutes, but it seemed rude to leave so quickly. All the time she was listening she was thinking about the dark stranger. She had a nagging feeling that it could have been Anthony, Carla's boyfriend, what could he have put through her door?

Eventually, Katie managed to get away, and left Mrs Hogan happy that she had had a nice long chat. When she got home and unlocked her front door she immediately looked for the note or whatever the dark stranger had posted through her door, but there was nothing there, not even junk mail. Katie thought this was odd, perhaps Mrs Hogan had dreamed it all, she was a bit confused. She phoned her brother to check if he had indeed been the one of the visitor's.

"Yowl," answered Nick

"Hi, you ok?" Katie asked politely

"Yep" then there was silence

"Did you pop round to my flat today?"

"Oh yeah I did, how did you know?"

"My neighbour thought she saw you"

"Oh, a curtain twitcher huh!!"

"Is everything alright or was it just a social call?" asked Katie knowing only too well what he probably popped around for.

"Well I needed £20 but you weren't in so I asked Mum, anyway where were you?"

"Working"

"Oh yeah, I forgot you got a waitressing job"

"I am not a waitress Nick!"

"Whatever ... good you're working again. Mind you, your boyfriend nearly knocked me over; he looks loaded, nice car, where did you met him?"

"Boyfriend?" Katie replied shocked "What are you talking about, I don't have a boyfriend"

"Oh well some geezer with a wicked Porsche knocked on your door after me. Thought it was too good too be true. So who was he then?" Nick probed.

"I don't know I wasn't in remember!" Katie replied in a sarcastic tone

"Perhaps your curtain twitcher will know then," laughed Nick "Guess some sales bloke or something then Sis, catch you later" With that he was gone.

Katie put the phone down. Well at least Nick had confirmed that Mrs Hogan was indeed right she had had two visitors, it must have been Anthony on an errand from Carla, but why and what did he want?

Her mobile phone bleeped a text message from James appeared. It simply read, *"Can we talk"*. Katie was intrigued. It all seemed very odd, she texted back *"Yes – when?"* She originally added a few kisses then deleted them. There was no immediate response from James, so Katie decided to see what she could rustle up for diner. She wasn't really in the mood for a big dinner. Something light, soup maybe?

Her phone bleeped again showing the reply from James *"Tonight at mine, 7.30?"* – Katie didn't quite know how to take the message, that's the trouble with text messages she thought, you did not always understand the other person's meaning. She called up Blaze to tell him about the strange caller and the urgent message from James. She needed his calm reassurance telling her everything would be ok.

Chapter 31

I was busy writing up my notes on the 4126999 case in my chamber, quite enjoying the fact that I actually had lots to write up and more importantly that the case was going well for a change. Well that is my opinion; others may not agree that it's going well and of course it could all change. Humans are very fickle, I find.

I closed my case file and patted the cover proudly, then popped it on the shelf with my previous cases (not many, I might add). I wondered if Hibissa would allocate me some more cases soon, or would he hold back and first judge me on my performance on this case? I felt that I had started to prove myself as a Guardian, and I so much want to be a fully qualified one, it has always been my passion.

I have to admit that I will miss Katie once this case is resolved, which hopefully will be soon for Katie and James. However I have a nagging feeling that there is still quite some work to get through.

My thoughts suddenly changed and I found myself wondering about the relationship between Hibissa and Bella; he obviously had a soft spot for Bella like I do for Katie and continues to 'pop' into her life when needed. Quite nice really, I thought. The entrance of Pascolli almost falling through our Chamber door suddenly and rudely broke my peaceful thinking time!

"Oi steady on" I said to Pascolli who was closely followed by Willow.

"Sorry" apologised Willow

"Don't apologise Willow, Nicoise is the worlds worst pupil for crash landings, isn't that right Nicoise?" laughed Pascolli

"I don't know what you mean!" I replied defensively knowing that I had had a few near misses in the past with my landing techniques.

"Anyway no time for idle chatter. James and Katie are meeting up again. Want to come along with me?" asked Pascolli

I checked my diary of 'likely future outcomes' and this meeting between James and Katie was not mentioned, "I have no record ..." I started to say

"The records are only a 'guide' Nicoise. Circumstances can change from minute to minute down on earth, you know that" Willow interrupted.

"Yes, but …. Oh very well, give me a moment to get ready," I said, slightly flustered for some reason unknown to me. Willow and Pascolli looked at each other slightly impatiently.

"Hurry up!" Pascolli barked.

"Alright, what's the big rush today?"

"James spoke to Carla!" Pascolli stated

"James spoke to Carla?" I repeated in true parrot fashion "When, how, why?"

"It seems as though Carla sensed something at the bar the other evening. She thought she saw Katie leaving and it got her thinking about unfinished business between them, so she called James to see 'how he was doing' and checking his counselling was going ok" Pascolli paused

"Go on tell him the rest" Willow interrupted not for the first time that day

"So, Carla, being Carla, managed to wrap James around her little finger, like only women can. He naturally felt she still liked him, and he got his emotions all confused. He told Carla that he had met up with Katie, who told him Carla had taken his cases away on purpose and that the 'nervous breakdown' was all a fabrication and what Carla wanted others, including James to believe"

"Shit!" I now blurted out

"Nicoise, language!" Willow scolded.

"Sorry, it's being around humans too long I think. I'm starting to sound and think like them," I said, "What did Carla say to that then?"

"She laughed and said that she had never heard of anything so ludicrous, and would have words with Katie 'to put her in her place!" Pascolli continued.

"That might explain her side kick's visit to Katie's place today" I added worriedly

"Carla went on to say she still had feelings for James, and that she had only urged that he stay off for his own good because she cared so much. She told him that, of course, he would get his cases back on his return to work and that she was just looking after things for him for the business. She is such a damned liar, and we are all now back to square one, as James has fallen for her crap!" Pascolli said

"Not really square one" Willow said

"No more like minus square one!" I added, "This is terrible, how did it happen? Why does James now want to meet up with Katie?"

"He's confused, I think deep down he realises that Carla is a bad apple and is using him, but being the love struck man that he is something is not letting him believe that. Maybe he is blanking it out. Now he thinks that Katie is stirring things up which is exactly Carla's plan, so he wants to confront her" Pascolli said very gloomily now.

"This is terrible I was only just thinking how well the case was going, looks like I jinxed it, its my fault, just my luck" I said feeling sorry for myself.

"Its not your fault Nicoise. It's not about you it's about Katie. She's just starting to get her confidence up and you were working with her beautifully" said Willow, I looked at him surprised he had just told me off in a sort of nice way, but complimented me too?

"Think of James. He was already a mess now he's going to be a bigger mess. It's my entire fault not yours" Pascolli said sadly.

"Guys, guys stop blaming yourselves. Shit happens, deal with, learn from it and stop whinging!" said Willow sternly

"Shit happens?" I looked at Willow who had only moments ago pulled me up for using that very word

"Different context Nicoise, great expression though don't you think ... human lingo," he laughed.

"We're wasting time talking, we need to go now," Pascolli said impatiently.

"Yes, you guys go. I will make excuses for your absences at the Assembly tonight" Willow added.

"Of course the Assembly, Hibissa won't be happy. What will you say?" I asked Willow.

"Don't worry I will think of something appropriate. Now go, quick!" he almost shooed Pascolli and me out of the Chamber.

With that we flew silently out into the cold evening air, through the chilly clouds and down to earth, to James' apartment. We just made it as Katie pulled up outside in her little red car. She had no idea of what had occurred or what was indeed now going to happen. Oh I wish I had not spoken earlier about how well everything was going. It was all too good to be true. The human road is always bumpy; ups and downs all the time. I shouldn't have tempted fate, things never stay the same for long.

Chapter 32

After quite a long time of deliberating what she should wear Katie finally decided on a silky blouse and jeans, and thought she looked quite respectable, even a little sexy. However, she needn't have bothered because as soon James opened his door, she realised this was not a 'date' type of evening.

James looked dreadful, unshaven, messy hair, probably unwashed and still in his pj's. He looked small and scared, a little like how Katie imagined a pig would look just before it went off to market after being put in one of the horrible lorries that she often saw crammed full of pigs.

"Are you ok?" Katie asked James very quietly. James didn't reply, he just opened the door wider for her to enter and glared at her. Without saying a word he walked back into the lounge leaving Katie to shut the door and wondering (1) should she follow and (2) had she done something wrong? She closed the door and made her way down the hallway to the lounge where James was pacing up and down. He stopped when Katie entered and pointed to the armchair in the corner.

"Have a seat," he almost ordered.

"Thank you" Katie replied, not really knowing what to expect. She had never seen James in such a mood before, and was not too sure she liked this silent and moody side of him.

"Carla called…" James stated and looked straight back at Katie to gauge her response.

"Oh, that's erm… nice?"

"No it's not 'nice' Katie, not nice at all!"

Katie stared down at her feet not really knowing what to think let alone what to say. So she said nothing and let James continue.

"Carla said she thought you and I were plotting against her, especially you!"

"Me! What have I done?" exclaimed Katie.

"You stole the case file from her flat for starters and planted it on my desk to try and get me on your side. You ensured her letters went out late, which caused her to lose jobs. You were lazy and incompetent in you role as her secretary and she said you were often a bit vague to her clients on her whereabouts causing her to look unprofessional!" James said all in one big deep breath.

"Sorry. I don't understand" Katie said upset and not believing her ears. "Did she really say that?"

"And a lot more besides. But quite honestly I can't be bothered to go through it all. She did say you were really jealous of her relationship with me? Is that true?"

"Well, I did like you yes. But you were my boss, I didn't think she was right for you that's all" explained Katie.

"So, you agree that you tried to ruin my relationship with her. Well guess what? You succeeded so well done. And I lost my job in the process" he turned away from Katie as he spoke, his eyes welling up.

"You've lost your job?" asked Katie with concern.

"Yes. Carla said that they're cutting backing due to the recession and as I'm 'unfit' to work they're letting me go!!" He sounded like he was going to burst in to tears at any moment.

"Letting you go? When? I mean when did Carla do this?"

"She called today. She was so upset, and was really nice about it. But she did say I had you to thank for my downfall, and that while you may look quiet and shy, really you're knifing and scheming and would do anything to get me?"

"I do not want you!" Katie was angry now "Why would I want someone who is so easily led by a woman; someone with no back bone. No James you are so mis-taken. I certainly don't want you. I want to help you, but I can see now how totally smitten and bewitched you are by Carla, you cant even think straight! You have absolutely no idea, that it is Carla and her boyfriend who are the knifing and scheming ones not me!"

"Boyfriend, you mean ex"

"No James. I mean boyfriend. He is not her ex. He's a ruthless con man who is in it with Carla to get everything they can from that business to line their own pockets. You said yourself that she sent an actor round to pretend to be a Counsellor. No normal person would go to that much effort don't you think?"

"She did it to help"

"Goodness you really don't know how pathetic that sounds. Wake up James!" Katie shouted.

"Mr Heath said he was in a play at the Princes" James said randomly completely changing the subject.

"What? What are you talking about?

"The Counselllor is in a play. Shall we go and watch?" James asked

"Why? So we can go and have a chat about the little scenario thought up by your Carla?'"

"Well yes. He may have answers. It might make some sense?" James said so sadly.

"Ok" Katie said, agreeing to watch 'the Counsellor'

"I'm so sorry ....I am sorry. I don't know whats wrong and right any more. I'm screwed up, useless, worthless" sobbed James which then made Katie cry and together they cried until they finally laughed at themselves crying!

For over an hour Katie sat on the settee hugging James. He was just so lost. She didn't really know what else to do; all she could do was be there. She didn't feel she could leave him.

The curtains were still open and Katie watched the day sky turn to dusk. James had fallen asleep in her arms. She said nothing, she badly wanted to move her arm that was tingling with pins and needles, but she didn't want to disturb James whilst he was so at peace.

"I'm sorry" James finally said in a small voice "It is Carla, I know. It makes sense. I guess I just didn't want to believe it, or to admit what a fool I have been taken for. You must think I'm so weak. I am so sorry" Katie didn't reply but she did think he weak.

"Katie, will you really come to the Princes to see Mr Heath with me?"

"Of course" Katie smiled "What night is it anyway?"

"Wednesday or Thursday whatever suits you"

"Perhaps I could get a group together, make a night of it? Shall I get a couple of extra tickets as well?" Katie asked (she also felt the back up of her friends might be needed on this night).

"Erm that sounds cool, yes do that" and with that he hugged her tightly.

Katie left quietly into the night, not really knowing whether to be happy or sad. Mainly she felt she should be happy because although James was very sad, he was finally realising the truth and was starting to understand that he was part of a devious 'game plan' by two clever con artists.

Chapter 33

Pascolli stayed with James and I followed Katie to her car. I slipped onto the passenger seat beside her to watch over her on her journey home; I could feel her sadness, confusion and anger all mixed up together. She drove in silence, not wanting to turn the radio on to disturb her deep thoughts. I could tell she felt very alone, and knowing Katie as I now do, I knew she wouldn't call anyone to talk it over, so I felt I should stay with her.

Katie was thinking negative thoughts, doubting herself; I could not let all my good work now become undone, so for every negative thought in her mind I willed her to have a positive one to counteract it. Gradually, as she pulled outside her flat I could sense her starting to feel calmer and more positive than she had at the start of the journey.

I followed her into her tiny flat, into the kitchen. She flicked on the kettle, with the intention of making a cup of tea. I smiled to myself thinking how wonderful 'tea' must be, as humans certainly seem to consume a lot of it!

Katie sat sipping her tea, and dunking in quite a few chocolate biscuits. I could sense she was now wondering what or who had caused Carla to act like she had. Why had she lied?

Eventually, Katie retired to bed, she tossed and turned for a while but eventually seemed to settle and fall into a nice sleep. She looked very young as she was curled up into a little ball on one side of her double bed. I felt that my job today was done, I had guarded over her and protected her; I felt that she had indeed sensed my calming presence. I remember Willow telling me that some humans actually could sense the presence of an angel, like Bella and Hibissa I guess. I hoped that one day Katie and I would have that angel/human understanding that Bella and Hibissa shared. I glanced over at Katie one last time before I left, she was dreaming and it was not a nightmare. No nightmare's for Katie tonight I commanded.

I peeped out of the curtains in her room and shuddered at the thought of the long journey upwards. I wished Pascolli were still with me, I preferred to fly with company than solo. I wondered if he was still with James? I decided rashly to go and check. Then we could fly back together, hopefully.

I was, as suspected, right. Pascolli had stayed with his case until he had fallen asleep, only James was still unsettled and tossing and turning in his sleep, chucking off his covers, pulling them back on pushing them off. His mind was busy and although he appeared to be asleep his mind was still working away, he was shouting out in his sleep. Pascolli looked worried not knowing what else he could do.

"Why not try and change his dreams, Pascolli?" I offered helpfully

"Goodness Nicoise we could get into trouble big time with Hibissa if we interfere again" he replied.

"No, we will just be channelling his energy to positive dreams rather than ...." I looked across at James still mumbling ".... well whatever he is currently thinking about. It worked with Katie. I actually think it's part of our duty Pas" James suddenly sat bolt upright shaking with fear, and sweat dripping down his reddish face. "Come on lets fill this room, his head and his soul with positive colourful prisms, it will help Pascolli – it's the only thing to do now"

"Your right of course" agreed Pascolli

We closed our eyes and summoned our most inner and positive thoughts, scanned every beautiful colour and concentrated on bringing the colours, the positivity out into the open, and into James soul. We thought of peace and tranquillity and meditated for a while, letting the visions become real for James in his mind in his dreams. Briefly I stopped meditating (something I struggle with, which I know is a little bizarre for an angel), I looked over to Pascolli whose kind face was all distorted where he was concentrating so hard to help James. I wanted to giggle because he looked so funny. However, I composed myself, closed my eyes and once again concentrated on the visions of calmness.

Eventually, after what seemed an eternity, the colours came followed by stillness. The room was alight with colour, the most amazing transparent colours dancing around. We watched James in his sleepy state look around bewildered at first, but then he relaxed and lay back on his pillows and watched the colours dance around him. Each colour represented a nice memory to him, he thought of each of these memories in turn, and gradually his mind and body began to feel relaxed. He closed his eyes and we knew he now felt safe in the field of colours that engulfed him. Pascolli looked across and smiled at him, I knew he was proud of what we had achieved as was I - just maybe I am getting the hang of this 'guardian' job, it could be quite satisfying at times like this!

"It's so beautiful Nicoise – we created this, wow!" said pascolli.

"We did, and yes it is beautiful, totally amazing" I nodded mesmerised myself now by the prisms of colours.

"We can leave him now. He will be safe now. We'd best get back" Pascolli said

"Shame, could almost drift off myself," I laughed

"I know what you mean, but we most go" Pascolli replied. We both looked over at James who was now gently snoring in his bed. Pascolli concentrated and the colours dimmed down to a fader more gentle prism of colour, like a gentle night-light guarding over a child.

"Ready?"

"Yep lets hit the sky"

With that we left.

Chapter 34

Katie was having one of those mornings where nothing went to plan. She felt tired after the late and intense goings on of the evening before. Her mind kept skipping back and thinking of James. Then Carla, then James. She could not concentrate one bit on the order she was supposed to be placing.

Bella was worried that the shop was not doing too well. Blaze had in his very own cheery style tried to convince her that it was the whole recession thing and not personal to her business, but still this did not reassure her. She in turn had been harder on Katie's to market the place. She was pushing her for new ideas and wanted Katie to bring the open day forward. All this was now adding to Katie's troubled mind, and now as if that was not enough the stupid computer had frozen; it wouldn't let her go any further than entering the password. It was really getting to Katie.

Blaze came happily marching into the shop. He was like a bull in china shop, his gangly long body always knocking something over in the cluttered shop. This time it was the cloth angels that fell off the shelf as his satchel swung round and hit the shelf.

"Blaze!" scolded Katie; she was not in the mood for such happiness and bounciness right now.

"Sorry Katie" he grinned and shrugged his shoulders. Katie did not look up she continued to type in the text of the order, muttering under her breath.

"What's wrong?" Blaze asked sensing her frustration.

"Oh nothing ... well this blooming order just won't send," she moaned.

"Let me have a look" he said. Katie moved off the chair for Blaze to try, where he sat and stared seriously into the screen.

"Aw there we are, that seems to have done it" he smiled after tapping away for just a few seconds.

"How did you do that?" Katie asked, quite impressed

"I do have some talents you know" he winked at Katie "How about in return you make me one of your super cups of tea and then you can tell me all about last night"

Katie shuddered at the thought of last night. Honestly she really did not want to think about it let alone talk about it, but dutifully she made the tea and served a customer in between. The customer left and the shop was once again empty, which Katie knew would not please Bella.

Blaze patted the stool next to him, indicating to Katie to come and join him. Katie brought across two steaming teas before sitting on the tall stool with Blaze.

"James wants to go and see that show at the Princes next week, to talk to that actor"

"What show? What actor?"

"You remember, the actor who pretended to be a Counsellor, he visited James on Carla's instructions. James thinks he might be able to throw some light on stuff and help understand why he would do such a thing"

"Well that is obvious I would have thought, he got paid, money for old rope and all that," said Blaze.

"I know that, but James thinks it could put a few bits of this puzzle into place. He just thinks it might help"

"Aw the puzzle ... what is the name of the play anyway?" asked Blaze.

"Actually I have no idea. It's on at the Princes though. Hang on I'll look the name up on the Internet" Katie typed in the details and waited for the slightly slow computer to come up with the answer.

"Flowers and Horses"

"What?" Blaze pulled a face

"You heard, do you want to come along too, Jane and Lucy are coming too"

"Do I have a choice?"

"No" laughed Katie at her friend

"Ok. I would love to accompany you all to the theatre. It sounds, erm, riveting. Does it say if they are using real horses?"

"Don't be silly Blaze, it's only a local thing. Anyway the whole point is to talk to Mr Heath. James was in such a state last night. Carla has fired him under the pretence that the recession has affected the business and as he is unable to work due to stress he is a liability!"

"Oh my, she is such a cow," exclaimed Blaze

"That's not the half of it. She also tried to convince James that this was all my doing, because I was jealous of her relationship with him!!"

"And were you?" Blaze asked

"Was I what?'

"Jealous?"

"What? No - well maybe a little, but not now. He's such a wimp, but I know I need to help him and would like some support here from you"

"No problem. When is it and how much?" asked Blaze very matter of factly.

Katie looked at the screen and looked back to Blaze after hearing him gulp his tea extremely loudly. "Wednesday at 7pm, there is one on Thursday but Lucy can't do that, got some birth club thingy to go to, oh yes its £19"

"£19!" Blaze almost spat his tea out in shock "You're having a laugh! £19? For a local show - to watch some 'pretender' to be in a show about horses and flowers, on a creaky old stage with moth eaten curtains? That's outrageous!"

"Calm down! I'll pay if it's a problem?"

"No, I'll pay, just can't see how they can charge that. Bet it's not busy at those prices"

"Shall I book your ticket now then?' asked Katie.

"I guess so" agreed Blaze.

So Katie booked the seats for Lucy, Carrie and Blaze (and one extra as not sure if she was getting the complimentary ticket James had mentioned).

Whatever the play was about really was irrelevant – the real issue was helping James understand things better and he felt that this Mr Heath man might be able to help. "All done," she said as she printed off the receipt email.

"Can't wait!" said Blaze with a hint of sarcasm in his voice

Katie kept herself busy or the rest of the afternoon, mainly concentrating on the grand opening and marketing. Katie had decided that the open day would be quite near to Christmas, so that would be useful for people buying presents. After a pretty slow afternoon money wise, Katie locked up and made her way over to see her parents.

"Come in dear" beamed Katie's Dad as he opened the door for her

"Who is it?" yelled her Mother from the kitchen

"It's me" Katie replied as she walked into the kitchen.

"Oh" replied her Mother in a her normal un-interested tone, she turned around to Katie "I suppose you want some dinner?'

"Do you have some spare?" Katie asked quietly

"Shepherds pie" her Mother replied sternly

"Erm, yes please" Katie said quite pleased because one of her Mothers best qualities was cooking. She made the most delicious home made dinners ever, unlike her own efforts.

The three of them sat around the pine table in the kitchen, where Katie chatted about the shop, telling them about the open day that she was working on, even her Mother seemed mildly interested. Then Nick strolled in, chucking his rucksack in the corner of the kitchen, and then pulled out a chair which made an awful scrapping noise against the floor.

"Budge up Sis" he said squeezing in next to her, as Mother served up a huge plate of pie for Nick (probably twice the size of anyone else's dinner).

"Cheers Mum, looks great" Nick said with a mouthful.

"It is" nodded Dad looking at his plate. His eyes caught Katie's and they both grinned thinking the same thought of how spoilt Nick was by his Mum.

"Working?" Katie asked. Nick did not reply.

"Let him eat his dinner Katie," said Mother quickly before Nick could reply

Nick finished his large mouthful and looked up at Katie "Enjoying your shop work?"

"Actually yes thank you I am"

"Sounds fun" added her Dad

"Looks like your eating too much of the cake to me" joked Nick

"Shut up!" Katie laughed, but inwardly felt a bit worried by that comment. Perhaps she should cut back. Her Mother got up and started clearing up and her Dad shortly followed to help. He knew his place! Nick leant over close to Katie.

"Do you think you could give me a sub sis?" he asked sweetly

"How much?"

"£100?"

Katie sighed. She had had this conversation so many times with Nick. It's not that she didn't want to help him, but this time it made her cross. She thought how lazy and selfish he was and that it was never a 'sub', she rarely got the money back unless he had a win at the horses, he owed her hundreds. She was about to say 'ok' when she heard a little voice in her head say 'no'. She paused before she replied to her brother who was awaiting her usual reply.

"No" Katie said strongly, obeying the voice in her head (*be stong and say no, say what you really think the voice had said*)

"No?" Nick repeated, not quite believing what his sister had just said.

"Look Nick, I'm not going to be able to help you out this time, things are a bit tight for me too you know" she said almost trembling, wondering how he was now going to react. He looked puzzled, shocked even, he certainly had not expected that reply.

"Oh, ok, sorry you're skint too" he replied, uncharacteristically "I didn't think"

"I can't keep giving you money Nick, I just don't have it, sorry" she said (*don't apologise, the voice said, no need to apologise*).

"I would pay it back," he added quietly

"You don't usually" Katie looked across at her brother; he looked quite lost for words and quite sad. At that point she nearly gave in but stopped herself from speaking. *("Stick to you guns" said the voice).*

"Ok no worries, I understand" Nick said, "Where's Mum?"

"She popped out into the garden I think"

"Mum?" Nick called as he got up and walked towards the back door that led to the garden. Katie knew exactly what his question to his Mum would now be, but she told herself it was not her problem. She suddenly felt quite empowered, quite strong, saying 'No' had not been too difficult and Nick had just accepted it really.

Katie smiled at her Dad - who had witnessed the conversation (as he had been drying up the dinner plates), he smiled back.

Chapter 35

Here I am, sitting in the huge Learning Chamber, listening to one of the incredibly old and boring mentors delivering a speech on the importance of note taking. I can't believe this dinosaur is taking the lecture; he probably still takes note on stone tablets by the look of him!

If we are to move forwards, surely we should embrace the whole concept of words on screens (like humans have). Why can't we learn from humans for a change? I think some of their ideas are totally cool. It's so frustrating here sometimes; everything has to be done in the same way as it has always been done because that is the way things have always been done.

I can see Pascolli yawning, trying to look remotely interested in the boring speech. Willow, was, of course eagerly lapping up and absorbing the knowledge from the elder mentor like a good guardian angel swot should.

The hands on the large stone clock at the front of the hall seem to refuse to move, time is standing still, trapping me in this boring seminar. I want to be out, I have things to do, I don't need to be told how to write notes by this doddery old angel - I especially want to get back to Katie's case – I am so excited because through my channelling, she had actually said 'no' to her brother; this was a real break through, a revelation.

I desperately wanted to tell Willow and Pascolli about this and even Hibissa, (I wondered how impressed he would be, well hopefully), but no I still have to sit here through this talk from an old 'has been' angel, who has no real idea about what the new modern earth was now like; he hadn't left the heavens and ventured down for a good twenty five seasons. It was doubtful he could even fly now!

"That's it," I thought, almost out loud – I shall write a report for new guardians. Yes, embracing the new earth, take some of the better ideas from humans, to help speed up angel processes, so we can deal with more cases and hence help more humans. Surely that had to be the way forward. Then I can present cheerful, useful seminars, which hopefully new guardians could relate too not fall asleep too! I was excited and started to scribble madly on my notebook, causing Willow, Pascolli and a few of the others to look around as they heard my quill vigorously scratching the stone tablet note plate, the ideas were flowing, I just could not stop myself.

"What on earth is he doing?" one of my neighbouring students asked quietly in Willow's ear.

"Writing" replied Willow, throwing a questioning look to me.

"Writing what? There's nothing to write about is there?" the Student asked.

"He obviously thinks there is!" Willow said

"Oh … right" replied the Student, pulling out his stone notebook from his satchel and listening more intently so as not to miss anything that the speaker was saying, (who really wasn't saying very much in between all his pauses and 'erms')

I also heard Pascolli whisper to Willow "What's he doing? His shopping list?" I pulled a face at him and Willow giggled, unfortunately just at the point that Hibissa was passing the aisle we were sitting in. He stopped dead in his tracks and glared straight across at the three of us. Even though I was not looking at him, I could feel his beady eyes boring into my face.

"Nicoise, Pascolli, Willow a word please!" he hissed in a loud whisper across the aisle, causing everyone around to look and snigger.

"Now?" Pascolli asked

"Yes of course now! Is that not what I just said?" Hibissa hissed again. Only this time it was a slightly more irritated hiss.

Willow threw me a hurt look, as he got up with a heavy sigh. I knew he was thinking that he always got into trouble when I was around.

We left the stuffy Learning Chamber and although the circumstances of our departure where not ideal, I was secretly pleased to leave and be outside in the fresh air.

"Maybe you could explain why you were talking whilst an important training session was taking place; have you no respect for your elders and protocol?"

Hibissa's question was obviously directed at me, whilst the other two looked down at their feet.

"No" I thought to myself, but Hibissa obviously reading my thoughts, glared at me with his very scary face.

"I despair of you Nicoise. Just as I think you are making improvements in your work, I see that I am wrong and that you are still as stupid as ever, always the joker. Well I've just about had enough and, unluckily for you, I'm already in a very bad mood" Hibissa said sternly.

I looked over to Willow and Pascolli who continued to look down at their feet. I could tell that they were concentrating on keeping their minds blank and clear so that Hibissa couldn't read their thoughts.

"What do you think you were you doing? Talking when you should be listening! Especially you Nicoise, you should be listening and learning"

"I was taking notes Sir" I showed my writing to him quickly so he could not actually see what I had written. He raised one of his eyebrows.

"What on earth could you have possibly been writing? You have written more words there than Kannel actually spoke!" he replied, causing Willow and Pascolli to look up, now interested in what my reply was actually going to be, as they too were curious as to what I had been writing.

"Well, truthly, I was making notes on the system that Kannel was speaking about Sir, and then adding my own ideas on how to improve systems specifically for new guardians dealing with younger humans in the new modern world, how maybe we could improve things and, speed things up" I smiled meekly hoping Hibissa would be impressed

"Changes?" bellowed Hibissa "Why would we want to make changes? This is how we work here. We are not humans; we do things how it is written for us"

"Even if it's not the best way of working? Has anyone ever really studied how much time we waste for instance? We need to adapt to keep up with... " I tried to finish my sentence but Hibissa interrupted.

"Enough! You do not know what you are talking about" Hibissa turned to Willow and Pascolli. They said nothing and continued to look down, not supporting me, not wanting to get involved.

"It seems you are alone Nicoise; I have no choice but to confiscate this ridiculous scribble that you have wasted your time on. Furthermore, you will now spend two days in the cooler!"

"But Sir, my case, Katie is at a crucial point ..."

"The Flowers and Horses play is the break point of the situation Sir" interrupted Willow trying to now help me

"Willow be quiet," barked Hibissa. "This is not your problem. Katie will have to cope without a guardian angel for a few days" Hibissa paused looking at me "She'll probably do better without you!" he finished cruelly.

That hurt, his words cut like a knife, I felt bad for Katie in her hour of need. It wasn't my fault – if the Seminar had been remotely interesting, none of this would have happened.

"Willow, Pascolli - back to training" ordered Hibissa "Nicoise, go to the Q box registration point and get one of the Harpers to take you to the Cooler - it will give you time to reflect on your career!" With that Hibissa stormed off making a gush of cool air blow over my face, Willow and Pascolli looked over at me with sad faces.

Willow flew to my side and whispered quietly "I'll go with Pascolli to the show and keep an eye on things" with that he was gone; I slowly made my way to the Q box registration point.

I made my way slowly to the Cooler. I knew what to expect. In all honesty the previous times had been justified but not this time. Hibissa just liked to pick on me, he really didn't understand. I felt sorry for myself, as I slowly got closer to the Cooler; I have to admit I am not too fond of being locked up, or being completely alone.

Chapter 36

Katie saw her chance and put her life in her hands as she ran across the busy road to join Lucy, Carrie and Blaze who were waiting outside the theatre, as arranged, by the stage door.

"About bloomin' time, its freezing!" complained Lucy as she kissed Katie on the cheek. Katie turned to Carrie and gave her a kiss too.

"Sorry" Katie apologised "You know me, someone always phones just as I'm leaving and it was Dad; didn't have the heart to cut him short"

"Yeah, yeah, heard that one before! Anyway where's James? I thought he was coming with you" probed Lucy

"He was" said Katie "but he texted me earlier to say he would met us inside a little later"

"Oh, bit strange" said Lucy.

"Not really - he probably felt little intimidated by all you guys being here" laughed Katie.

"Don't talk daft, everyone loves me," said Lucy, adding "But I know maybe people don't like it that I tell them how it is sometimes!"

"Erm you're not wrong there," added Carrie with a mischevious grin.

"Shall we go inside ladies or stand out here all night freezing?' asked Blaze very politely. Everyone agreed and duly followed him inside, through the narrow wooden doors, past the ushers and down a few steps to a rather tatty looking bar, albeit a well stocked one.

"What would you lovely ladies like to drink?" asked Blaze on arrival at the bar.

"Mine's a large red wine," grinned Carrie. Lucy threw her a jealous look as she mumbled that she would have lemonade, even though a nice wine would be far more enjoyable.

"Lets have a look at the bump Lucy?" said Blaze as her drink choice reminded him of her pregnant state.

"Why does everyone refer to it as a bump? I don't have a 'bump' yet I just look fat," moaned Lucy.

Blaze pulled a funny face at Katie, who smiled kindly at her grumpy friend.

"Lucy, you can get t-shirts that say 'I'm not fat, I'm pregnant,' perhaps you could order one off the Internet" added Carrie, trying to be helpful.

"Like I would be seen in one of them, honestly Carrie!" Lucy replied, horrified that her friend could even contemplate her wearing such a top. No, she was looking forward to a shopping spree soon to buy lots of pretty floaty maternity clothes, which couldn't be mistaken for anything else but still stylish and chic.

"What about you honey, what are you drinking?" Blaze asked Katie fondly, which made Carrie poke Lucy with a look that said '*see something is going on between them*'.

"Just orange juice please, no ice"

"Cheap round girls" said Blaze as he took his place in the queue at the bar. It appeared (as usual at such places) that only one person was serving and it was taking ages, causing people to huff and puff and generally be grumpy.

Just as Blaze managed to get served, an announcement advising everyone to take their seats as the show was about to start was being piped out through the bar area, causing everyone in the bar to moan at the barman.

"Take your seats," boomed out the Americanised pre-recorded voice, Blaze, Lucy, Carrie and Katie duly did as the voice instructed and made their way to the auditorium.

"Tickets please. Sorry, no drinks inside the auditorium" said the pan faced usher as they tried to enter the theatre.

"What? You're joking I've just brought these having waited ages to be served" Blaze exclaimed

"No drinks inside the auditorium" repeated the Usher on auto pilot tone "You'll have to drink them up now"

Blaze downed his pint in several large guzzles then slammed the plastic glass down on a small round pedestal, next to the door.

"Please can you put your litter in the bin in the bar, Sir" the Usher said, clearly enjoying her authority.

"Jobsworth" hissed Blaze as he dutifully complied.

"I've never seen you cross before Blaze" Katie said gently, quite surprised at the outburst from her mild even-tempered friend.

"Well, honestly. They take your money at the bar at the last moment, knowing you can't take drinks inside. It's ridiculous, in fact I feel a letter of complaint looming!" Blaze said.

"Lets' go in, come on we're down at aisle 'E', I wonder where James is?" Katie said, scanning around the crowd to see if she could see him.

"Strange. I wonder why he's changed his plan. We're only here because he wanted to see that Heath chap for goodness sake" said Blaze, apologising to people as he squeezed past to get to his seat right in the centre of the aisle.

As they took their seats, uncomfortable seats with no leg room, the stage curtains slowly pulled back to expose a very low budget set, full of flowery wallpaper. Blaze groaned loudly and Katie nudged him.

At the half time interval they could not wait to get up, especially poor Lucy who had not stopped moaning throughout the first half to Carrie who was sitting next to her. As Lucy stood up at the end of the row and stretched out a large lady in a turquoise jacket tapped her on the shoulder. Lucy and Carrie both turned round to the lady behind who was looking slightly fearsome.

"Excuse me, you might not want to watch this, but my son is in this play, and I for one would like to hear what's being said!" she said crossly.

"Oh, sorry I'm pregnant" Lucy said, which was kind of an odd thing to say in the circumstances.

"So what. I don't care if you're having twins. Just keep quiet, and have some respect for others" with that the lady huffed off.

"Oops" said Carrie

"Really, some people! Who does she think she is telling me to have respect." Said Lucy, angrily.

"Let it go ... it could be you in a few years time watching your son in a show" said Blaze. Carrie nodded in agreement and Lucy just threw her head upwards towards the ceiling.

"James still isn't here," Katie said worriedly

"No, it is a bit strange. I mean, he was the one that wanted to come and meet Mr Heath and put us all through this ... well this play thingy" Blaze remarked.

"Who is Mr. Heath?" asked Lucy

"He is Edward in the play" said Carrie

"Yes but who is he in real life" Lucy tutted at Carrie

"You know, the actor that the wicked Carla sent round to play with James head," laughed Blaze

"Oh yes I remember. I need the toilet, Carrie will you come with me?"

"Sure" sighed Carrie thinking of the likely queue for the 'Ladies', which would mean there would be no time to get a drink.

"Good thing you brought the extra ticket Katie" said Blaze, Katie nodded still looking around the busy auditorium for sight of James.

Carrie was right, as the queue for the toilets was pretty long. As they waited patiently in the queue, they heard snippets of conversations, which you really couldn't avoid in such circumstances. They were both busy listening but not really listening when something made them both stop and stare at each other.

"Sara! Hi, how are you? Still at the Accountants with Jayne?" they heard a ladies voice; the names Sara, Jayne and Accountant had sparked their interest.

"Hiya, yes still there. I've been promoted recently actually. James has left so Carla is now in charge! Got a grand a year more, and even get paid for coming along to this dump tonight!" Sara laughed (an annoying nasally laugh).

"Wow, cool, how comes?" the lady asked.

"I'm actually here with James. It's a long story, but Carla is worried about him so I'm kind of looking after him to make sure he does not do or say anything silly that could affect the business. Exciting stuff huh?" she laughed the awful laugh again.

"What do you mean 'silly?' Like what? Suicide?" asked the nosey lady enjoying a good gossip.

"God no. He was meant to be meeting some old colleague. In fact it's her job I've got now. But anyway, Carla ... oh here's my toilet ... Catch up soon. You look fab, text me" with that Sara entered the cubicle and the conversation finished, much to the annoyance of Carrie and Lucy who really were flabbergasted.

They looked at each other, but didn't say a word whilst in the toilets. Lucy took forever, which was frustrating Carrie as she wanted to get back to report to Katie, but Lucy, being Lucy, took her time even though she too wanted to get back and tell Katie.

The second half of the play had just started as the pair of them struggled back to their seats, making people stand up, some smiling and understanding others huffing and puffing.

Eventually they made it back to their seats and Lucy immediately leant across and tried to attract Katie's attention, who seemed oddly mesmerized by the strange pantomime type horse prancing across the stage. The crowd were laughing and Katie couldn't hear Lucy.

"Psst ... Katie!" Lucy almost shouted, and jumped when she received a strong tap again on her shoulder.

"If you don't shut up I'll report you to the Usher and get you chucked out. You really are disrespectful, why are you here?" hissed the woman behind

"Wait till the end, nothing can happen now" whispered Carrie to Lucy.

Lucy seething nodded at Carrie acknowledging what she had said. She turned to the woman behind and pulled a face then sat back and watched the silly horse prance around thinking that the turquoise Mac woman's son was probably the back end of that creature!

"Sorry I'll be quiet, but if you touch me again and I'll have you for harassment, I am pregnant you know!" Lucy hissed at the woman.

"Yes, you told me that earlier, you're boring me," said the woman.

"Oh shut-up!" barked Lucy really wound up now. She turned back to the play and tried to concentrate.

Finally, after a long second half, the play was finished. Carrie and Lucy were itching to get up and speak with Katie, but unbeknown to them she had slipped off to the ladies via the other end of the aisle just a few seconds previously to avoid the rush.

Blaze seemed to be the only one who had actually watched and enjoyed the play. This was strange given his protests at the beginning. The lights came up, causing everyone to blink and scramble to the exits. Blaze continued to just sit calmly and wait.

"Come on, get up lazy," laughed Carrie prodding Blaze.

"Where's Katie?" asked Lucy, seeing her empty seat.

"Loo. She's going to meet us in the Foyer" said Blaze.

"Oh God. Get up. Quick! James is here with a 'Carla' spy" shouted out Carrie

"Spy? What spy?" Blaze said continuing to sit.

"Sara, she used to work with Katie"

"Just move Blaze, quick!" ordered Lucy

"Bloody Hell woman" he moaned, but did as she said and got up.

"Katie doesn't know Sara is a spy and probably neither does soppy James, the idiot. If Katie says anything to James, you can bet it will get straight back to Carla. Sara's getting paid for tonight you know!" added Carrie "God this is really quite exciting, like a mystery on the telly" she added

"Grow up," said Lucy giving Carrie one of her legendary 'looks'. "Too late" she added as they finally had made it to the Foyer to find Katie chatting happily away to James and Sara.

"Shit!" said Blaze

"This is not good," whined Carrie, as they made their way across to them.

"James thought it would be nice for me to come along too, didn't you James?' they hear Sara say.

"I wondered where you were," Katie said to James

"Front row of course – the complimentary tickets?" James said giving her a funny look.

Did you manage to see Mr Heath?" asked Katie, turning her back on Sara

"Why would you want to see him? If we had back stage passes he would be the last person I would be wanting to see. Ugly man" said Sara.

"Sara, would you mind if I have a private word with James for a moment please?" Katie said, not really asking.

"Why what secrets do you have?" laughed Sara

"Leave it Katie. I don't need to see Mr Heath. I understand why Carla did what she did – it was to spare me any embarrassment. Look Katie I've got to dash, we're going for a nightcap aren't we Sara?"

"Why, yes of course, but there's no rush honey" she said, "it's good to see Katie, how are you? Where are you working now?" Sara asked, remembering she was there on a fact finding mission, not a date with a wimpy bloke.

"I am working at ...." began Katie.

Blaze charged into the middle of Katie and Sara and shook Sara's hand very strongly, causing her to throw Katie a questioning look. "Hi, how are you? Nice to meet you?" said Blaze weirdly.

"You are who?" Sara asked

"I'm Blaze'

"Blaze? Your boyfriend?" asked Sara turning to Katie looking horrified at the prospect that this badly dressed hippy guy could be her boyfriend.

"No" Katie and Blaze said together

"Well, lovely meeting you Sara. Come on Katie we must get that taxi we booked" Blaze said as he caught hold of her arm and pulled her gently away.

"Blaze!" she said wondering what an earth had got in to him tonight.

Blaze looked across at Lucy and Carrie for some support, but luckily Sara saved the day. Now bored and not really understanding her purpose in all this, she caught hold of James hand and turned to him.

"I am tired babe, can we go? And the play was awful wasn't it? Night everyone, bye Katie" she said.

"Bye Sara, nice to see you" Katie replied "Keep in touch. Oh, take one of my business cards, we're having an open day on ..."

"Not one of those awful cheap cards Katie. Wait till you get one of those fancy pink ones you've ordered" interrupted Blaze

"What pink ones?' replied Katie somewhat confused now.

"Can we go?" Lucy moaned "I am pregnant you know, I need to rest"

Katie looked puzzled, "Call me, James," she shouted across as she was being marched one way by Blaze and James was following Sara another way.

"Sure" James called back meekly

"Hey Katie, I'm glad that Blaze isn't your boyfriend, he has even worse clothes sense than you!" laughed Sara, having to get the last word in as usual.

James and Sara left, and as the others made their way out, Carrie in double fast 'Carrie speed' told Katie what they had overheard in the toilets earlier.

"I don't understand" Katie said

"What don't you understand?" Carrie asked

"Why is Carla so on my case? I've gone, she's ruined James' career, got the accounts she wanted so badly, and is creaming the business. What more can she possibly want?"She asked.

"You dummy. You know what she did and how she did it. You could expose her – that's why she is one your case" Lucy said

"Expose her - like going to the papers?" Carrie asked excitedly

"Shut-up Carrie" Lucy said looking totally exhausted now.

"Lucy's right. You could bring her down and stop her scam" said Blaze.

"She's dangerous and mean," said Katie sadly

"Yes she is. You have to be careful" Blaze said

"God, this is just so exciting. Just wait till I tell Tony" Carrie blurted out. Blaze, Lucy and Katie all turned and looked at her making her feel self-conscious.

"What?" she asked, as the others all rolled their eyes in despair at her.

"Come on, lets go and actually have a drink now the crowds are gone" said Blaze, but as they turned 'Happy the Usher' (as Blaze had named her) was standing right there.

"Can you all leave the building please?" she grumbled with a tiny smile at the corner of her mouth when she noticed it was that annoying ginger chap.

"We're going to have a drink," Blaze said calmly

"I am afraid, Sir, you will have to have your drink some place else, the bar is now closed," she said.

"Well thanks for nothing, Mrs Happy" said Blaze sarcastically.

Mrs Happy smiled a twisted smile to expose her yellow crooked teeth "Goodnight, hope you enjoyed the play" she held the door open as they all left the building.

"What a night" said Blaze as they stepped out into the street outside. It was now dark and cold outside and starting to rain.

"Didn't really go to plan did it? And we never got to see Mr Heath" said Katie gloomily.

"No, but you learnt a lot" Lucy said "And now you can act on it"

"Just what did Sara mean about my clothes anyway" asked Blaze remembering Sara's parting words, and laughing in an attempt to cheer up Katie who now looked quite miserable. Katie randomly hugged Blaze.

"Thanks for looking after me" she said

Blaze looked surprised, but happy as he hugged Katie back. Lucy and Carrie exchanged knowing looks. The 'hug' was abruptly brought to an end.

"Can we go home now, I'm tired and ..." Lucy shouted out.

"I am pregnant," everybody said in unison, which was fast becoming Lucy's catch phrase.

Chapter 37

I am sitting alone in the cooler, feeling a little sorry for myself. I mean, why does Hibissa always get the wrong end of the stick? Why does he never see what I have accomplished or what I am trying to achieve?

The room is very bland and grey; not white like almost everything else here in the angel kingdom. It's all very boring, very quiet and very frustrating. I want to get out of the cooler – I really don't enjoy my own company for too long. I am wondering how Katie and the others all got on at that theatre show thingy; did James find anything out about Carla's intentions through Mr Heath? Who turned up? How did it end?

I am, wondering what an earth Katie saw in James; honestly I know that I should see the good in everyone but I just see nothing - nothing good and nothing bad. People are strange, very complex creatures and, nearly always have some sort of hidden agenda going on with them.

My thoughts turn once again to Hibissa. All in all, I know he is a good mentor and has seasons and seasons of knowledge. Deep down he has our best intentions at heart, but sometimes he is just so wrong about how things are and how they should be done. Admittedly he often comes out with some cool sayings and phrases that make sense; for example I love it when he tells me that everyone has the power within themselves to shape the outcomes of tomorrow. I digress, however because, like all the old mentors, Hibissa is just so dated and unwilling to change, to modernise. How is the kingdom ever going to move forward with mentors stuck in the 'this is the way it has always been' psyche?

"*I have the power within to shape the outcomes of tomorrow ...Do I? Really?*"

If this were true could why haven't I been able to make Katie be the gutsier, assertive being that she needs to be? To sort out Carla for once and all, get over weaklings and negative people such as James and be happy?

Do I really have that power to shape outcomes, or does it have to come from Katie herself?

Of course, I remember reading about the sending of positive vibes and positive healing, but I can't for the life of me remember how it works. Heck, I wish I'd been a more attentive student!

A loud knock on the cooler door startled me and I lose my chain of thought. A small young cadet angel enters the room holding a tray, which he duly hands to me. Puzzled I look carefully at the items on the tray - some paper and different coloured feather inks, all neatly laid out.

"Hibissa sent these down for you," the cadet said in a monotone voice.

"Oh" I replied surprised and puzzled "What are they for?"

"To keep you mind busy, to continue your notes" he replied

"Notes?"

"Yes Sir, notes. Writing"

"Ah notes" I nodded "I see. Well thank you and please thank Hibissa"

"I will do Sir," he said as he left the room walking towards the door

"Erm excuse me, there is something else. Could you ask Hibissa if I could have some study books please?"

"Study books? I'm not sure that is customary Sir" the cadet replied dutifully.

"Well no, I guess not, but do you think you could ask anyway. I'm particularly interested in Positive Healing Studies".

"Why I'm reading up on that very subject at the moment Sir. I have the book in the office" the cadet replied slightly excited.

"Wow! I don't suppose that I could have a little read of your book this afternoon?" I asked nicely

The cadet looked very serious and I could hear his thoughts "No, not allowed" but my thoughts were stronger as I sent them across to him "Yes, yes it won't harm for a few hours".

I concentrated hard, and the serious face soon broke and a smile crossed the cadet's young face. "Why not, but only for a short session while I'm on shift" he said. "No harm"

"No harm at all" I reassured him, as he left the small grey room but soon returned with the book tucked under his wing. It was an enormous book!

"That should keep you busy for a while. There are some really good exercises at the back that you may like to try, I enjoy them," the cadet said, helpfully.

"Thank you – I will." The cadet said nodded and turned to leave the room, I said, " Thank you, much appreciated. I will be sure to spread the word on what a good example you are"

"Why thank you Sir. I would like to move up to train as a guardian, and get out of his job. It's just there's not many places available, not many guardians lose their jobs do they Sir? Well, unless of course they annoy their Mentor" he grinned knowing exactly what he was implying.

Cheeky rascal I thought, but to be honest he had a point. I really couldn't afford to upset Hibissa again, or I would be out of my job and, as this young angel had just told me, there were plenty of others waiting in the wings for an opportunity. I couldn't afford to blow it, I smiled at him as he left and closed the door. I turned over the first page of the slightly imposing book and started to read the minute text.

Very interesting, yes very interesting indeed, I thought. The time I now have on my hands is the perfect opportunity to study and absorb this knowledge. Hopefully I can even practise some of this distance healing too...

Chapter 38

Katie was wide-awake before her alarm sounded. She was not really sure why, considering she had had a late night at the theatre, but then she had been tossing and turning alot in the night wondering why James had gone there with Sara and not even let her know his change of plan.

It was also annoying Katie that it was her day off so she had no need to get up early, she could have had a nice long lay-in. But no, she was wide-awake and ready to face the day, whatever it would bring.

Despite waking up far too early, Katie felt positively chirpy, even happy, although she did groan when she saw her reflection in the bathroom mirror. In her rush to get to bed the previous night she had forgotten to take off her makeup. And there, looking back at her was the proof - black smudgy eyes and foundation still on, probably blocking her pores and likely to give her spots. She groaned again. However even the thought of spots didn't dent her good mood.

Whilst she was up she decided it was best to get her housework done first and out of the way. Then she would tackle the unwelcoming pile of ironing that needed doing. She switched on her radio and merrily began her chores, even though ironing was one of her pet dislikes and was always on her 'avoid till totally necessary' list.

As Katie placed a pair of carefully folded trousers on the back of a chair facing the window, she saw an image looking very much like Mrs Hogan walking quickly past. Nothing too strange there until she looked at the time and realised it was only twenty past seven. Where on earth could Mrs Hogan be going at that time of the day? Katie flicked off the iron and quickly dashed out, not realising she had not taken her door key with her.

She ran up the road until she caught up with Mrs Hogan, who, to Katie's horror, was in her dressing gown and slippers!

"Mrs Hogan" she called puffing from her unexpected early morning sprint.

"Katie?" Mrs Hogan replied not quite sure who was calling her.

"Mrs Hogan, where are you going?"

"I'm going to find Mr Hogan. He went to the pub hours ago but he promised he would be back to help with the dinner; he always carves the meat you know, that's his job not mine" she smiled.

Katie looked at her and felt a sadness come over her. Mr Hogan had been dead for years. Mrs Hogan really was starting to suffer from senior dementia Katie never imagined Mrs Hogan would end up like this, it was so very sad.

"I'm sure he has gone back home, you probably just missed him. Shall we go back and see?" Katie asked kindly, slipping her arm through Mrs Hogan's frail arm and gently turning her round back towards her home.

"Oh yes, you're right, he probably has" Mrs Hogan smiled; she looked old and small and very vulnerable.

Katie realised for the first time how much weight Mrs Hogan had lost, she used to be quite chubby, well maybe not chubby but cuddly, but not anymore. Her arm felt very small and bony. Katie felt a pang of guilt; she had been so busy with all the Carla and James goings on, that she had not noticed her elderly friend, become well more elderly, almost as if it happened overnight. She now looked so frail and old and Katie had not realised, not seen the changes. She would take her home and call her sister-in-law or nephew and explain that Mrs Hogan really needed more support now.

Mrs Hogan seemed more like herself once back in the familiar surroundings of her own kitchen. Katie put on the kettle and found some cakes albeit stale ones, Katie tried to avoid having a cake, but Mrs Hogan would not hear of it so she had to give in and eat one, which was very hard and dry now. Still, it pleased Mrs Hogan, who didn't seem to notice that the cakes were stale.

"Has Doreen been around lately?" Katie enquired about her sister-in-law.

"No she's in Spain, or France. No Spain, yes Spain" she nodded.

"Oh"

"Paul's has been round instead," added Mrs Hogan with cake crumbs bursting out from the side of her small mouth as she spoke.

"That's nice. Have you got his phone number?"

"By the phone I think, in my address book"

"Ok, do you mind if I use the phone and call him quickly?"

"Yes please do. Ask him round, it would be nice to see him. He is very handsome you know," she giggled. "Haven't seen him for ages"

"You just said he's been coming round while Doreen is in Spain?"

"Is Doreen in Spain, oh how nice"

Katie sighed and dialled the number. Paul answered (she felt a little guilty that she had probably woken him up). Katie explained to Paul, (who she had meet a few times over the years just to say 'hello' to in passing), the state in which she had found his Aunt and asked if he could come over. He said he would be round shortly if she could hang on there for a while.

Katie waited with Mrs Hogan who wanted more tea and cakes so Katie obliged. Paul eventually arrived, he knocked on the door and Katie let him in, he popped his head round the door to see his Aunt who beamed when she saw his face.

"Hello, my favourite Aunty how have you been? Heard you've been looking for Uncle?" he said.

"Don't be silly, Paul, he's dead!" Mrs Hogan replied very sharply. Paul raised his eyebrows to Katie and turned to face her.

"Mum is back home tomorrow, she'll probably have Aunty over to stay. I can stay here tonight if it helps?"

"That would be great if you could" said Katie "I'm just worried that she'll get out again and anything could happen to her,"

"No problem. How are you anyway? Still at Kyle's Accountants?" Paul asked.

"Oh God no. I left there a few months ago. I've got a new job now at a 'New Age' shop come coffee shop. It's really cool actually. We're having an open day to launch the place in a few weeks, you're welcome to come down or spread the word"

"I have some friends that like that hocus pocus stuff," he laughed.

"It's not hocus pocus!"

"You know what I mean," he said "So you're not working for James now. How is he doing? We went to school together you know, right smart kid he was"

"Well he's not there now either."

"Oh ... some sort of shake up there then?"

"Something like that. New management you could say"

"Oh right. That happened at our place, we had new management and they slowly but surely got rid of all the old managers and replaced them with their own. Always the same Katie"

"Erm, yes not really fair is it?"

"So, is James working somewhere else or still job seeking?" Paul asked

"Still looking I think"

Paul reached into his pocket and gave Katie a business card. "Tell him to give me a call, I work for this agency, and I could fix him up with some temp work if he is interested. It pays good, especially for smart guys like James"

"Thanks, I will. He'll be chuffed I'm sure" Katie said as she took the card from Paul.

"No problem, happy to help - even if he was a total geek at school" he grinned.

"What are you two whispering about?" asked Mrs Hogan

"The weather" grinned Paul. He had a lovely smile thought Katie; in fact he really was a good-looking bloke. Shame he had a lovely girlfriend already she sighed to herself – the good ones always do.

"I'd better go now. Let me know what's happening and if you need anything give me a shout. Oh and don't eat the cakes, they're at least a year old!" Katie laughed

Paul laughed "Ok I'll bear that in mind"

Katie said goodbye to Mrs Hogan who was delighted at having had two visitors in one morning.

Katie walked back to her flat. At he door she suddenly realised that in the rush to help Mrs Hogan she had come out without her keys. Even worse she remembered that she had the spare key indoors that she usually leaves at Mrs Hogan's because she kept forgetting to give it back after the last time she locked herself out.

"Damn" she said out loud. The only other key was at her parents. She would have to walk round there and hope they were in. So this is what Katie did convincing her that this was a positive outcome, as it would force her to walk and hence get some exercise for the day. Plus she would see her parents, which would hopefully please them; well her Dad would be pleased anyway!

Katie arrived a little out of puff, making a mental note to herself that she must start going back to the gym; she really had got out of the habit of going. She knocked loudly on the door, after a while her Mother answered.

"Katie? I wondered who on earth was knocking so early. Are you ok? Are you ill? You look very red and no make-up!" said her Mother all in one breath as she opened the door.

"No, not ill, just locked out!" she said entering her parents house.

"Oh for goodness sake, how stupid" her Mother scolded.

"It was a mistake Mum, I didn't do it on purpose"

"I didn't say you did, but you don't see me forgetting my key or your Father for that ..."

"Well I'm sorry I'm such a disappointment to you all. If I could just have my spare key, I'll leave you to your busy and organised schedule!" barked Katie, deliberately sarcastic.

Katie's Mother for once was speechless - Katie never answered her back. She did not know what to say. She must be ill, she concluded, reaching for the key from the key box in the hall way and handing it over to Katie in silence.

"Thank you, I'll return it later"

"Ok" Katie's Mother replied meekly.

Katie trekked back to the flat feeling strangely empowered. She had answered her Mum back, not wanting to be disrespectful, but she had answered her Mum back! Katie's Mum still spoke to her as if she was a naughty eight-year-old, forever scolding her and moaning. She couldn't remember the last time she had praised her.

Katie thought she should feel guilty speaking to her Mum like that, but she didn't - she felt good.

She smiled as she power walked home, making her face even redder still. She finally made it home; she checked the time and couldn't believe where the morning had gone, and what a morning! She checked her phone and saw that she had had three missed calls, one from Blaze, one from Carrie and one from James.

She dialled James' number. It rung for quite a while and just when she was going to cancel the call, a girl answered the phone.

"Hi, this is James's phone"

"Hello is James there?" asked Katie.

"Sure who is this?"

"This is Katie, I'm returning his call"

"Katie. Oh hi, it's Sara here. H's just coming, just putting his pants on ...ha ha only joking"

"Katie?" James said, obviously cross with Sara's little joke.

"Hi, just returning your call, but I can tell that you are ... busy"

"No its ok. Sara just popped round. I'm not really sure why but she did."

"Listen, I will catch up with you later, bye"

Katie finished the conversation quickly, not wanting to say much now that she realised that 'super spy' Sara was round there. That girl really was really taking her 'guarding/spying' duties seriously she thought. Katie picked up the phone and called Blaze, he would know what to do next; the next part of the plan needed to be discussed and she really wanted to hear his calming voice after her mad morning and then she would ring Carrie too.

Chapter 39

After a night of scribbling, thinking, reading and experimenting with sending positive vibes to Katie, I was exhausted and realised I had had no sleep. Not good for the mind or indeed your looks! I wandered over to the hard uncomfortable couch and lay down. No sooner had my head hit the 'pillow' I could hear loud voices, keys cluttering and the crashing sound of the cooler locks being unbolted.

The young Cadet entered the room and loudly shouted to me "Come on lazy bones, rise and shine, you're being let out a day early ...Hey what did you think of my book, any good?"

I couldn't believe my luck, out a day earlier, what joy! I so needed to be outside and free. Confinement is hell for us angels, although it did give me time to study and practise what I read, which I probably wouldn't have done in normal circumstances. I picked up the large book and handed it to the cheeky Cadet.

"Thanks, it was very helpful," I said.

"Hibissa wants to see you straight away" the Cadet ordered

"Oh, even before I have a bath?" I asked feeling rather smelly.

"I am afraid so Sir. Straight away was his instruction"

I left the Cooler and made my way back upstairs to the main building and along the endless corridors until

I finally reached Hibissa's Chamber. I sighed, wondering if I was in trouble as usual –I raised my hand to knock on the door, but it opened immediately and there, right behind the door was Hibissa, seemingly waiting for me.

"Come in and take a seat," he ordered, "I trust your experience in the Cooler was, well, shall we say rewarding?"

"Erm, well yes Sir"

"What did you learn?"

"Not to talk in Lectures Sir," I replied hoping that was the right answer, but not sure.

"No, no. What did you learn whilst you were in the Cooler?"

"Well ... it was actually nice to have some 'quiet' time away from the busy routine. I made some notes on the paper you sent down of possible or desired outcomes for my current case, did some meditation and tried to practise sending healing to my case from a distance" I replied.

I hoped Hibissa wouldn't ask me more about the positive healing as I didn't want to mention the book I borrowed as that would likely get that young Cadet in trouble. I concentrated on keeping my mind as blank as I possibly could.

"Good, sounds like your time was put to good use Nicoise, and I am glad you can remember some of your teachings!" he said with a glint in his eye. I guess he knew about the book anyway; basically he knows everything!

"Willow and Pascolli came to see me. They explained what had happened, and I feel that maybe I was a trifle rash with you. I do realise that you are trying and that you are having, lets say, moderate progress. Willow and Pascolli have kept an eye on case 4126999 and advised me that she answered her Mother back after years of her Mother controlling her a little too tightly, she has helped a neighbour and in doing so made a contact that may lead to work for one of Pascolli's cases that I believe you also know"

"A job for James really? Cool!"

"Erm, yes 'cool' as you youngsters would say. But be careful, we do not want her being too confident, it would not be her. Do you understand? You need to get the balance right, don't tip the balance"

"Yes Sir, I understand, balance everything out"

"You cannot change someone Nicoise, remember that. However, to make them feel positive and good about themselves is good progress"

"Thank you Sir" I couldn't believe what my ears was hearing.

"Anyway I summoned you here to discuss your notes" Hibissa said as he waved my notes about. "For me, they are too radical. However, there is a school of thought that suggests we need to look at adapting some of our procedures, so I am going to seek further advice and investigate a little further and see if there is anything in this review, reform or whatever you call it Nicoise"

"Thank you" I said again starting to sound like a parrot with no other vocabulary.

"I am not saying things should change mind, but continue working on your reform ideas Nicoise... in your spare time of course, and we will maybe speak about them again at some time in the future. And I mean do not work on them when you are in lessons!"

"Yes of course Sir"

"Off you go, Nicoise. Try and wrap this case up quickly will you, it's dragging slightly and I have a backlog of human cases waiting to be allocated, some which I may well allocate to you soon"

"Right" I said very excitedly "I will get straight on it Sir" I sounded incredibly keen, maybe just a little too keen I thought to myself.

"One more thing Nicoise"

"Yes Sir?"

"I would take a bath if I were you, the Cooler room is a little pungent" Hibissa laughed to himself as if he had just cracked a very funny joke, then pulled a 'you can leave face' and continued marking papers on his desk.

I took this as my cue to leave; I bowed my head in respect and left the Chamber. I flew down the corridors at speed, I was so happy. That was just the best session I had ever had with Hibissa, and it felt good.

Shame, that I actually missed seeing Katie answer her Mother back, I would have quite enjoyed that – although I had already seen her say 'no' to her brother.

Gosh, I am getting so good at my job. You could say I was in the same league, as Willow could you not? I visualised myself as a respected Guardian Angel as opposed to the joker trainee that I had been, because Hibissa did say a few more cases could be coming my way!

Chapter 40

Katie was with James at the Cobbles Bar, they were both sitting on tall stools sipping their lattes. Katie couldn't believe she'd actually got hold of James without Sara being there - she was like some of 'control groupie' around James. Katie observed James over her mug, and thought that he did actually look a little better, more like the James she knew and quite fancied all that time ago when she worked with him.

"Have I got something stuck on my face or something?" James asked randomly
"No?"
"Its just you're kind of looking at me rather intensely?"
"I'm sorry, I was just thinking that you look better"
"Better?"
"You know, more yourself?"
"Oh you mean I've washed and shaved today!" he laughed, paused and continued
"You know I do feel better. Even though I'm down, I feel like someone is looking out for me. It sounds weird I know, but some pretty shitty things have happened lately, and I really feel like someone is with me...does that make sense?"
"Yes" Katie said very seriously "It does. I've had the same recently. Perhaps we are both starting to go mad?" she laughed.

"Too late to start going mad, reckon I am mad now," said James a little gloomily "How's your latte?" he asked.

"A bit too sweet for me really" replied Katie.

They were both silent for a while. Katie wanted to question James about the Theatre episode the other night, but couldn't bring herself to mention it. James wanted to ask Katie why she was still concerned about him, he was quite touched that she cared, but he didn't say anything.

"How come your seeing Sara then?" Katie blurted out

"Don't have much choice. She seems to have taken it upon herself to check I'm ok, a bit like you I guess. What can I say, woman seem to want to mother me!" he laughed unconvincingly.

"Not sure I see Sara as the motherly type – how did you come to meet up anyway?" Katie asked.

"She called to say Carla needed some cases closing, and needed a few signatures and stuff, so we met up and she brought the paperwork round".

"Have you read it?"

"Nah ...Sara keeps asking me to, as Carla needs it back, but my plan is to make Carla come to me. If she wants it then she can come and get it" he smiled.

Katie sighed. He obviously still held that ever-burning torch for Carla. What on earth did that woman do to him, what was her secret, she wondered.

"Are you looking for work now?" Katie asked changing the 'Carla' subject.

"I have actually revamped my CV, so I guess that's a start"

"Do you remember Paul Williams from your year at School" Katie asked.

"Yeah, always had the girls after him"

'Well, he works for an Agency that deals mainly with Accountancy placements. I saw him the other day and he said to tell you to call him and that he could probably get you some work"

"Why have you been talking about me?" demanded James

"Not talking about you ..."

"You just said you spoke to Paul. Great, tell the world what a failure I am, why don't you?" James said angrily.

"What?" Katie stood up; she was shocked and angry at his outburst, and frankly getting tired of his ungratefulness. "I'm just trying to help you"

"Well don't. I don't need your help or the help of any woman in fact, you're all just interfering, scheming cows!" he shouted as he pulled his jacket off the back of the chair. "I'm off"

"Good. I've had about as much as I can stand of your self-pitying woes. Just go and look at yourself; you're intent on self-destruction. I've really only been trying to help you. I'll remember not to bother in the future" Katie put a fiver on the table "that's for my share" with that she got up and walked away trying to hold back her tears.

James continued sitting there just staring at he fiver, he suddenly scrunched it up and signalled to the waiter that he wanted to pay.

Walking, Katie wiped back a few tears, refusing to allow herself to get upset again, she wanted someone to help her. Why did things always seem to end up in a mess when she was involved? She felt a tap on her shoulder and looked behind her. It was James, and he touched her hand.

"I'm sorry, that was really rude of me. I am sorry, I just don't know who to trust anymore," James said out of breath where he had been running to catch up.

"You can trust me," Katie said.

"I know, I really think I can" James said, still holding Katie's hand. She did not let go either, not wanting to offend him. They stood in the street awkwardly for a few seconds, then James let go of her hand and gave Katie a big hug, she hugged him back, they pulled away at looked directly at each other, James then leant forward and kissed Katie.

Katie had wanted to kiss James for so long, dreamt about it even. However, this kiss was awkward and cringey, their teeth clashed against each other, and the kiss was nothing like she imagined or dreamt it would be. In fact it was awful, positively awful. As they stopped, James smiled at Katie, who nervously smiled back. Some children on bikes cycled past giggling, breaking the silence.

"Best get going" Katie finally spoke clearing her throat as she did so.

"Why? I thought we could get lunch?" James said looking slightly hurt.

"No. No, sorry I have to work on the open day schedule from home; it's only a few weeks away now. You should come and bring a friend"

"A friend?"

"Yes, someone you know?"

"I'm truly sorry Katie. I realise how much you've done for me. I promise I will make things good," James said.

"That's good. I would have done it for anyone you know – oh and here is Paul's card, I think you should call him, he seems very nice"

"I will and thank you again" he took the card and popped it in his pocket. "When can I see you again?"

"Soon" with that Katie kissed him on the cheek and as quick as she could ran across the road before he had a chance to repeat that first awful kiss.

Once she was round the corner and out of sight, she started to really run, even though her feet felt uncomfortable in heels. She didn't stop running until she reached her flat. As she arrived she was surprised to see a deliveryman knocking at her door with a huge bouquet of pink and white flowers. From what she could see they looked like orchids.

"Katie Johnston?" he asked reading from his list.

"That's me"

"Could you sign here please?"

"These are for me? Are you sure, there must be some mistake. Can you check?"

"There's a card" he handed her a small card.

Katie signed for the flowers. She opened her door and nearly tripped over the doormat because she couldn't see where she was going with this huge bouquet in front of her. She took them and laid them on the kitchen table. Surely James could not have sent these already in that short space of time? She read the card and smiled.

'Thanks for helping Auntie. You are a star. Be good to catch up sometime soon. Paul x'

"Aw" Katie said out loud thinking how very nice this was. She filled her vase of water after dusting it off (she didn't get flowers very often so the vase rarely got used). She arranged the flowers "Beautiful," she said smiling as she placed them on the sideboard in the lounge.

She wanted to call Lucy or Carrie but decided to wait. She really did need to get on with some planning work for the open day, she so was behind schedule and she really wanted it to go well for Bella and Blaze.

She retrieved the file marked 'open day' from her untidy drawer and sat down at her kitchen table with the intention to start working. Her phone bleeped loudly at her she checked the message.

'Hi, sorry again. Hope to see you soon, tonight maybe?"
Jxxx'

Katie groaned thinking that you should really be careful what you wish for in life because when you actually get it you often don't want it or it does not live up to expectations. Also James' constant use of the word 'sorry' was starting to irrate her. She knew she was guilty of saying sorry a hundred times and she made a mental note to stop keep using the word unless it was totally necessary. The 'kiss' was now an added complication to her life. She didn't want to hurt James or reject him, but she now knew he was not 'the one'.

"Where the heck is my guardian angel – I need you now to sort this mess"

Chapter 41

Back in my Chambers I was pleased to see my friends Willow and Pascolli. It felt like I'd been away for ages, when in fact it had not been that long at all. It just seemed like that, odd really.

"You must have impressed old Hibissa, for him to let you out early," said Pascolli

"Yes, what did he say to you?" asked Willow eagerly.

"Well one thing he did tell me was that you guys had explained to him what had happened, so gee, thanks for that," I said kindly

"We haven't seen Hibissa since the lecture" said Willow scratching his puzzled head.

"Really? He said that ....why would he say you had explained if you had not, that's a ..."

"Lie?" finished Pascolli

"Hibissa would never lie. Maybe he heard it as we think it?" Willow said defending Hibissa.

"That's well creepy. If he can now read our thoughts when we're not even in his presence, that's very worrying indeed" said Pascolli looking quite disturbed by the thought.

"I agree, that is creepy," I said

"Anyway, moving on, what else did he say?" asked Willow trying to keep positive and always see the good in everyone, as always.

"Well, he thought that my notes were, well perhaps not entirely to his liking I think he said, but he felt some of the points I raised were valid and should maybe considered further before dismissing. Hey and he said Katie's case is going ok, can you believe that? Oh yes, he also told me that I might get some new cases soon!"

"That's really good Nicoise, really good. You deserve a break you've worked hard on this one" Willow said. That meant a lot to me, I really valued Willow's opinion.

"We've all worked hard on 'your' case," laughed Pascolli "Enough praise, boring now"

"Cheers" I laughed

"We went to the theatre to keep an eye on things" said Willow "It was all a bit strange really. Carla now has Sara keeping a tab on James, a task she is taking very seriously. She gets paid really well for it, and has to ask lots of questions, especially about Katie!"

"Has Katie been different?" I asked, hoping that my positive healing had had some effect.

"Different? How do you mean?"

"Well, I practised some distance healing stuff while I was locked in the Cooler. Wondered if it had reached her really?"

"Can't say I'd noticed, though I guess you would know, she's not my case so I'm not really sure what she was like before?" Willow replied.

"Actually, James made a bit a twat of himself with Katie the other day when I was watching, and she seems to have completely changed her feelings for him, if you want my opinion?' chipped in Pascolli

"Really, tell me more" I replied getting closer to Pascolli. Willow looked up too with an interested glint in his eye.

"Well, she met some human chap called Paul ..."

"She met a bloke and I wasn't there to oversee?" I butted in.

"Well, when I say 'met' I don't mean 'met.' He's her neighbours nephew – you know Paul?"

"Oh yes, I remember"

"Well, when Katie told James about Paul and passed him Paul's business card so he could call about some temporary work, James flipped. He went crazy, and felt she was out of order speaking about him behind his back. Katie stormed off, he ran after her and kissed her!"

"Kissed her? After 'flipping' out? Sorry, don't think I understand?" I replied puzzled.

"Well, there was some arguing beforehand, but he did kiss her proper. You know the lips thing they do" Pascolli paused and pulled a disgusted face at Willow, who also mimicked him in his disgust at the details on kissing.

"She realises that James is not 'the one:' – So what do you make of that Nicoise?

"Not the one?" questioned Willow

"But I left the feathers. I thought he was the one she wanted?" I said, questioning my own judgement now.

"Yes, but Carla took one, don't you remember. It probably shifted the balance of probability of him being 'the one' I reckon" said Willow nodding as he spoke as if agreeing with himself.

"How can she tell?' I asked.

"I think they just know … their teeth clashed for starters, and there was no spark, no earth moving like female humans expect" Willow added.

"But she helped him, right?"

"Yes. In fact James has now called Paul, and he has a job interview tomorrow. I'm going to make sure he gets through it and gets back to work sharpish" said Pascolli firmly.

"Excellent. That's just what he needs. Too much time to mope around" Willow said.

"Does Katie like Paul now?" I asked

"He sent her flowers," Willow said. "He seems to have more to offer than that loser James"

"Hey watch it. James isn't a loser he's just going though a bad patch" Pascolli jumped in quickly in defence of his case, James.

"Ok, point taken. Shall we go and get some Sparkles?" Willow suggested, not wanting to upset his friend Pascolli. "Though on second thoughts I have actually got three case reports to write up"

"Lighten up Willow, a quick one wont harm surely?"

"Ok just one though" Willow said

"Come on Nicoise lets celebrate your freedom and good fortune with old Hibissa, God bless him," Pascolli laughed.

I didn't need asking twice, I needed some sparkles – the last two days in the cooler had been hard but a good learning curve; yes a positive experience in all.

Chapter 42

The shop was closed to the public. Blaze, Bella and Katie were in the back office drinking tea and talking about the 'Open Day', which was fast approaching and still much needed to be put in place.

"I'm not sure about that," Bella said.

"Why Mum, it makes perfect sense" Blaze replied.

"I don't know. I guess maybe. Katie, how is the marketing going anyway?" Bella asked turning directly to face her.

"Well, I put an advert in this weeks paper and they also gave me some editorial space, for a little feature on the shop. Look here" Katie passed her the local paper open at the page featuring Bella's business.

"Good picture ...not!" laughed Blaze as he peeped over his Mums shoulder as she read the article.

"Oh shut up" laughed Katie, cringing at the smiley picture of her and Bella in the article "I've also had the flyers back from the printers, which include that £5 off voucher that we spoke about if people spend more than £25 at the Open Day. Oh yes, they also mention the free herbal tea on entry.

"We should be careful about giving too much away Katie," said Bella looking very studious with her reading glasses balancing on her nose.

"I disagree Mum. I think a money off voucher and a free entry drink is fair enough," Blaze piped in.

"Plus, each ticket is put into a draw to win a prize" added Katie

"What is the prize?" asked Bella curiously.

"An hour with you!" replied Blaze, beaming as if that was funny. His Mum pulled a 'behave yourself' face and he stopped smiling immediatley.

"What do you mean an hour with me?"

"A reading. You know, customers that come here would love that. You have a reputation and, anyway, isn't it you that we're promoting as well as the shop?" Katie added.

Bella sighed looking a little grumpy; Blaze quickly changed the subject before his Mum had a chance to speak.

"Where have you distributed the flyers Katie?" Blaze asked

"Local Businesses mainly, you know usual hairdressers, beauty shops, dentists, newsagents. Carrie has been helping me and she took heaps of them to pre-school, toddler groups and so on. Actually I might do a leaflet drop this afternoon around the posh estate, do you fancy helping?" Katie asked Blaze.

"Yep, no worries" he replied cheerfully.

"I did speak to Rosie about her and her ladies doing some Indian Head Massages and Reiki treatments" said Bella looking a bit more enthusiastic now.

"Cool Mum"

"Katie, I can see you have worked really hard on this, thank you," Bella said.

"What about me?" asked Blaze joking with his Mum?

"And what about you exactly?" Bella replied, pretending to be all cross

"Haven't I been a help too?"

"I suppose" Bella laughed

"Don't thank me yet Bella. It might be a total flop. What if no one turns up? It will have been such a waste of your money" Katie said with a worried expression flashing across her face.

"Don't you start Katie, it will be fine, trust me. Hey Mum, what do you say?"

"There will be lots of people here I believe, maybe too many and a few undesirable ones" Bella said in one of her weird trance looks that she sometimes flipped into.

"Is that what you see Mum?"

"Oh no. Who are the undesirables?" Katie asked, now even more worried. "Do you think Carla will come?" she almost whispered her name as if it were forbidden to it say out loud.

"Well there is a chance. You have put it in the paper, and invited James who is abit volatile about his loyalties at the moment lets say. He could I suppose bring Sara who would tell Carla. But hey, lets not worry about what might be!" Blaze said.

"Oh no, I really don't want anyone to spoil it. Carla is going to ruin it, I just know. I hadn't really thought about the possibility of her coming along, cant really stop her either" Katie groaned.

"She will not ruin it Katie, believe me. Have faith, my dear" Bella interrupted Katie's hissy fit. "You will not allow it"

At that moment, before Katie could consider what Bella had just said, her phone bleeped loudly. She checked the message and then returned the phone to its pink case and slipped back into her bag.

"One of your admirers?" asked Blaze teasingly.

"James" Katie sighed "He keeps texting me and leaving messages. I've been trying to ignore him, but it's not working. He's not going away, I don't know what to say to him. I really don't want to 'see' him in that way! Just want to see him happy and back to the way he was"

"You can't ignore the poor man dear," Bella said. "You'll have to confront this and make it clear that you are no more than a friend. He sounds very confused to me, and clinging to people who show him an ounce of sympathy. Its not real Katie, speak with him honestly"

"Its not real? You mean he doesn't fancy me?" asked Katie, slightly put out by that comment.

"Women!" said Blaze raising his eyebrows "Never bloody happy are you?"

"Blaze be quiet" his Mother told him and then turned back to Katie "He just needs someone to lean on, someone to look after him tell him everything is going to be alright and right now I believe he thinks that is you"

"Oh yes I see, so he does not fancy me a tiny bit?" Katie said

"Of course he bloody fancies you a bit, you're cute Katie," blurted out Blaze, causing her to blush. "What time are you planning on delivering these flyers then?" asked Blaze, changing the subject.

"Shall we go now?" asked Katie, still red faced.

"No time like the present" Blaze said cheerily.

"I won't join you, I'm going to wholesalers," Bella added.

"Can we have a snack first Katieeee" asked Blaze

"God you're always thinking about your stomach" scolded Katie "Soup and roll?"

"Lovely. And that is so unfair, I do think about 'other' things you know. I'm hurt now" he laughed, and Katie pretended to thump his stomach. Bella tutted.

Bella followed Katie down the narrow corridor that led to the tiny kitchen. It was hardly bigger than a broom cupboard, but everything necessary was squeezed in there somehow.

"If Carla comes here, it could be a good thing" Bella said to Katie

"Really? How do you figure that out? Carla doesn't even know the meaning of the word 'good'. I really don't want any trouble on your big day Bella, things always go wrong for me" Katie blurted out surprising herself that she just said that to Bella.

"Trust in your angels Katie. Ask for help and they will guard over you. Believe me I know. I've experienced their help" Bella said.

"Do you really believe that?' Katie asked, not really believing "Do you actually have a Guardian Angel?"

"Of course. Everyone does. Mine is called 'Hibissa,' he has helped me many times over the seasons, sorry I mean years"

"Oh I'm not sure Bella. It is a nice idea, but if they exist where have they been in my previous troubles then?" Katie questioned as she stirred the soup in the saucepan on the hob.

"They won't help if you don't ask for help Katie, that is the key"

"So, if I asked to win the lottery I would?' laughed Katie

"No, you're being silly," laughed Bella. "Some guardians are human you know and around you in your environment"

"I really can't imagine anyone I know as my guardian, well maybe my Dad"

"You have good friends from what I have seen. Let people in Katie - let people help. Just remember that to receive help you need to ask for help. Anyway, I must go now, lots to do, got to get back and see that Mrs Nains, no doubt another crying session, poor lady"

"Poor lady" agreed Katie, now pouring the soup into two large bowls. Katie thought about what Bella had just said; she had a lot of respect for Bella and what she did for people. She gave them hope and raised their spirits. She was a good person. But 'angels' - some in heaven and some here, this seemed a little unbelievable and too 'fairy tale' for her.

Katie visulised angels, cute white little beings floating around and playing harps, she laughed. No these cute things were strictly for Christmas cards as nice as the concept was. You make you own luck surely she thought but who really knows.

Katie thought back to her conversation with James. He had said he felt someone was with him, helping him – and she had agreed she sometimes, especially recently felt that, but no, that was probably just a confidence thing... who knows, she dismissed the thought of angels and carried the two large bowls slowly over to Blaze who was patiently waiting for his lunch.

Chapter 43

Honestly, I am so cross after hearing Katie expressing doubts on angels. I mean, how on earth does she think she copes without one? If she continues with that chain of thought I won't be able to help her. I thought I was getting somewhere; I obviously need to try harder. A few more signs I guess would not go amis, though not too obvious as it could freak her out .... but on the other hand can I really do any more than I am doing? I am really trying on this case!

I need to keep to the plan. Yes, the plan, I wrote with my thoughts on the outcome of this case, or the desired outcome. I really can't afford for this case to go wrong. Hibissa won't give me those other cases if I don't succeed. I'm so excited about getting some new cases! Wonder who they will be, what their issues will be! I can't wait to see the other trainees when they realise, I like Willow, am becoming an accomplished Guardian. It will be so cool.

At that moment whilst I was fantasising about my fame, the chamber door smashed open. My chain of thoughts rather rudely and abruptly stopped. A puffed out Pascolli came charging in.

"Quick. You need to come with me to Earth. James is meeting with Carla. I could really do with your help. We need to keep him in-line, don't want Carla ruining the work and putting him under her spell again. Can you come now?" Pascolli asked very urgently.

"Of course, you've helped me often enough. Let me just put my file away and I will be with you" I replied.

We left our chamber and flew swiftly down to Earth. The air was fresh, with a slight bite to it. How I wished it was still the sunny season, this cold air was bitter at times and made travelling harder, although in honesty it speeded up the journey, in that it made you fly quicker to get you out of the cold. (I know I am a bit of a fair-weather flyer).

We eventually arrived at James' flat to find him and Carla sitting all very civilised in the lounge drinking coffee (shame she couldn't knock the coffee over, as we know that really annoys James).

"Very cosy. Not!" whispered Pascolli to me as we settled down to observe the proceedings.

"Sara tells me that you two are friends and that you went to the theatre the other night together. That's really nice to hear, I'm really glad you are feeling well enough to go out again. I don't like to think of you all alone and poorly here" Carla purred at James. She then looked around the tiny lounge and you could tell she was pulling her nose up thinking what a cramped pokey little place that he had.

"Sara is ok, but mad and loud" James replied, clocking her looking around.

"She is lovely. Just what you need, someone young, fun, and single!" Carla said.

"She's not my type," replied James.

"Really? You surprise me. Anyway, how have you been? You look smart where are you off too? An interview?" Carla laughed, flicking her long hair behind her in a flirty manner.

"Nowhere special" lied James "Thought I would make an effort"

"Ah, an effort for me?" Carla teased.

James did not reply, he just continued sipping his coffee rather loudly. Carla looked at him thinking his noisy drinking was quite distasteful.

"Have you seen much of Katie lately?"

"Now and again" he replied.

"Oh, not too regularly then? I thought last time you said she kept calling and interfering, Sara said ..."

"Sara talks about me to you?" James interrupted crossly, Pascolli gave me a look and I grinned; we both knew that people talking about James behind his back is one of his pet hates.

"No, no. She just mentioned that Katie was also at the Theatre the other night. Apparently she has some kind of open day at her new work ... a shop or something. When is that then?' Carla probed.

"16th at 2.30ish I think," James replied falling into the trap "She's worked really hard. Hopefully it will be a big success for her."

"Erm, I dare say. I might even pop over to offer my support for old times sake. Are you going James?" she fluttered her false eyelashes several times at James and moved a little nearer to him.

"Of course"

"Lovely, I will have someone to chat to, and have a coffee with ... remind me of the address again?" Carla was soaking up the information.

"Curiosity & Kittens, it's a kind of ..." James went on to explain all about the shop and what it sold. Pascolli and I groaned, this was not good, but yet we knew it had to be.

"This is her plan, to make an entrance at the event. You need him to stop blabbing on and get her out, before he tells her everything about Katie" I said firmly.

Pascolli looked at the large oversized wooden clock on the wall, which was an hour out of time. "Let's put the clock right, he has an interview in half an hour with that Paul chap"

"The Paul that Katie set up the interview with?" I asked smugly, knowing all too well that it was him.

"Well I guess she helped by passing on his card, made the contact" Pascolli replied quietly.

"Well - what's your plan with the clock then?" I asked impatiently.

"Don't know. I'm working on it. Be quiet, I can't concentrate with you going on"

"Charming! I exclaimed. I dutifully then kept quiet for Pascolli to concentrate on his plan.

"Do you have any notes on Mr Brownlow's case James? It would be a big help if you did. I just can't seem to find anything in the office these days" Carla asked now twiddling her hair round her fingers like a young girl. Pascolli and I pulled our noses up; She really was too much, so manipulative over this weak man.

"Will him to say no," I whispered to Pascolli

"I'm trying but can't seem to get through to him" Pascolli hissed back. "Will him too will you? Might help if there is double the vibes?"

"Ok" we both concentrate on sending James the vibes to say no, no, no, no.

"No" James said finally causing Pascolli and I to high five with glee "I don't think I have" he lied.

"Good on you James" cheered Pascolli to his case "Finally the worm turns"

"About time, he keeps re-lapsing though. Look at her now flashing her legs at him, she always uses that card on him and he just crumbles every time" I said staring at Carla in dismay "Does she actually have a guardian by the way?"

"Devil Guardian more like" Pascolli replied.

The clock suddenly started to make peculiar loud bird noises, something between a cuckoo and a pigeon. Although this clearly was not a 'Cuckoo Clock,' it made James and Carla nearly fall off the settee in fright, the sound was pretty horrendous almost like pre-historic birds.

I looked over at Pascolli wondering how he had managed to make the clock do that when I realised he was actually making the noises himself, he looked such a sight, and I rolled up with laughter. He glared at me, giving me one of his 'looks', but still I couldn't stop laughing, it was just so funny.

James' face was a picture - he was in total shock. He couldn't believe that after all these years he had just realised that the ugly clock left to him by his Grandad, was a Cuckoo Clock. Or was it? Was he going mad, he really didn't know. He suddenly realised the time and stood up.

"Goodness, I need to get going" he said.

"Sure" Carla replied staring at the odd clock "That clock is different, does it always make such a noise?" she asked.

"Actually, no. It's the first time I've actually heard it doing that, it must be going wrong. Guess I'll have to get it seen to, more money" James moaned still in shock, but at least realising that he needed to leave for his interview.

"It's truly awful James" Carla got up too, again flashing her shapely legs hoping to sway James from leaving as she needed to ask a few more questions. James looked quickly then looked away.

"It worked, the cuckoo worked," I laughed to Pascolli, who was holding his throat.

"Yes, but I can't speak now, it really hurt my throat" he whispered

"Oh dear, but it was worth it Pas, and very funny. Think you should be re-named Pascuckoo!" I laughed

"Very funny!" he growled at me in a husky voice.

He nudged me to show me Carla leaving. James shut the door behind her, and then came back and looked up at the clock, he touched it briefly, and then shrugged his shoulders. He then left the flat and made his way to his interview, he actually looked quite dapper and smart for once, probably the best I had seen him. He had improved; things were looking up for him. I was pleased for him.

More importantly to me I was pleased for my friend Pascolli, because this had been a hard case for him to work on (James was a very up and down sort of chap, more down in truth – quite depressive, not really what Pascolli was used to).

"Do you need me to stay for the interview? Wouldn't mind popping over to see how Katie is doing whilst I am down here" I asked.

"Nah, that's fine. I have good vibes about the interview. It's going to work for James, a new start for him getting that job. No, you go. And thanks"

"See you later then" with that we went our separate ways.

Chapter 44

Katie had been cleaning all morning on her day off as a favour to Bella. She had tidied up the treatment rooms and even the cluttered stock room and now, with Blaze's help, she was going to start on the actual shop ready for Friday's 'Big Day', which seemed to have come around super quick.

"Don't put that there" moaned Katie to Blaze

"Well where do you suggest I put it? It can't go over there because that crystal display is there!" Blaze replied

"Yes, but it could go there" Katie pointed "on the shelf"

Bella walked in chuckling away to herself at the bickering pair "You two are like an old married couple bickering away. By the way the treatment rooms look great. In fact I've never seen them look so sparkling"

"Well, you should try and keep them like that," grumbled Blaze to his Mother.

"Did you get out of bed the wrong side of the bed this morning dear?" Bella asked her tall gangly son. He grinned a false smile exposing his strangely very straight and white teeth, before he could reply two very official looking men walked in, one holding a clip board, the other gloomily following behind. They both flashed their identity badges stating they were from the Council.

"We've received some complaints about the business. We just need to ask you a few questions and do a quick check if we may?" asked the larger of the two men, while the smaller skinny man looked around the shop with his beady eyes.

"A complaint from who?' asked Bella defensively.

"It was anonymous, but we take all our complaints seriously. Are you the owner?" asked the man.

"Yes," replied Bella, still a little shocked that someone had complained.

"Firstly, we note from our records that you don't have planning permission for the signs outside. Are you aware that you need permission and that you are in breach of the regulations?"

"What, for one A-board?" interrupted Blaze incredulously.

"It's on the highway advertising a business," replied the officicial. "It needs planning permission. I have the forms here for you to apply, but in the meantime you need to remove it."

"Oh, I wasn't aware," said Bella meekly (not her usual confident self), she took the forms "I will get that sorted"

"So you will remove it, now?" the official insisted.

"But, we have an event tomorrow, being upstairs we need customers to know that we are here" Bella almost pleaded.

"What sort of event?" the offical enquired.
"An open day, an awareness day to show that we are here and promote what we do" Bella replied.

"Very nice indeed" he grinned, "Sounds nice. Are you thinking of having a raffle? If you are you need a licence. Our records do not show you applying for such a licence," the man said clearly enjoying his 'power'.

"We not holding any raffle" lied Blaze

The smaller, skinny man stepped forward and in a whiney voice asked, "Do you have hygiene certificates here that we could view? I can see you serve tea and cakes, and er hot food maybe?"

"Mainly tea and cakes" Blaze said

"Certificates?" he repeated

"I have mine in the office, I will go and find them if you give me a few moments" Bella said.

"I'll go and get it for you Bella I know where it is" said Katie.

"You work here? " the skinny man asked Katie.

"Yes" Katie replied.

"We would like to see your certificates too then please"

Katie didn't know what to say. She hadn't got any such certificate or been on any such a course. Bella certainly had never mentioned it; she looked over to Blaze not knowing how to reply.

"She's booked onto the next course at the Council" Blaze lied again winking at Katie.

"So, you don't currently hold a certificate. Is that what your saying?"

"That is correct, but I'm new and as my colleague explained I am due to attend one," replied Katie.

"Ok, I will just make a quick note of that. And you say you are booked on a course?" the man did not look up but just kept scribbling notes on his clipboard.

"Erm yes" replied Katie nervously, feeling uncomfortable about lying.

"Now we would like to look at the food preparation area, and the serving area please if you would be so kind?" he whinied.

"Be our guests" Blaze said winking again at Katie again to cheer her up, he then pointed in the direction of the serving area.

The smaller man pottered around, touched a few things, and looked miserable (probably because he couldn't find anything to moan about) and kept scribbling notes on this note pad. "Well" he said swinging around suddenly to face Bella "All seems pretty spotless. Excellent, I do like a tidy working area"

"So do I" Bella said, appearing again. She handed him her certificate.

"Good. All seems to be in order," the man said as he read the certificate, "I will need a copy of this at the offices please" he said handing it back to her.

"You just need to remove that advertising sign down please" the larger man chipped in, nobody said anything. "We'll be off and leave you to your day. Get the forms in to us for planning permission – it takes about 8 weeks for permission to be decided"

"8 weeks!" Blaze said loudly "But we have an event tomorrow!"

"Rules are rules," the large man said shaking his head and the smaller man behind copied, like two nodding dogs. "Goodbye" he said and the two men then left the premises.

"Well let's have three guesses as to who the anonymous complaint was from" Blaze said dryly.

"Erm, yep I've got it," said Katie

"Now come on you two," Bella said. "You don't know for sure. You should never just assume. There was no real harm done ..." She paused as she read the form in her hand "How much? Bloody hell! Bloody bureaucrats at the Town Hall!!" Bella grumbled after reading the fee for the planning application.

She handed the forms to Blaze, who raised his eyebrows when he saw the figure'

"Just for an A-Board?"

"Sort it out Blaze" Bella moaned

"Lucky you cleaned today Katie" Blaze said

"It wasn't that dirty," snapped Bella, obviously quite annoyed now.

"Come on let's keep going" Katie said. She'd never seen Bella cross before, but before she could start the door opened again and in strolled James.

"James? What brings you here?" Katie asked puzzled and slightly pleased.

"Thought I would quickly pop and see if you were here. Tried your phone a few times! Just came to say that Paul has offered me a fantastic job in London. It's a really good job, with good benefits. It's only a year's contract but that suits me. I have a really good feeling about it. The interview was piece of cake actually. Hey, talking of cake have you got any of that legendary cake you are always raving about?" James asked, positively beaming for the first time in ages.

"That is such good news James. Congratulations. I'm so pleased for you" Katie said. She wanted to hug him, but refrained in case he got the wrong idea again!

"Yeah, well done mate, I'll sort you some cake. Tea?" Blaze asked, to which James nodded. Blaze got up off the floor where he was seating and picked a box of angels up, and threw one to James "Here have an angel" he laughed and he went across to the serving hatch.

"Cheers?" James caught the angel and looked at it strangely thinking "weird chap."

"You don't have to keep it James," said Katie, watching his puzzled face looking at Blaze.

"Er, well its kind of cute I guess, like you. So I will keep it, could be my lucky omen. Yes everyone needs angels don't they Katie?" Hey I wondered if you could maybe go for a celebration drink with me when you've done here?" James asked.

Katie squirmed, not knowing what to say. She didn't want to bring him down while he was so happy.

Luckily Blaze once again came to her rescue as he brought cake over to James.

"No, no this little lady has lots of work today here. We can't possibly let her skip off today or I'll end up doing all the work and we can't have that," Blaze laughed. "Big opening tomorrow you know"

"Oh, yes of course, what time tomorrow? I will pop over." James said gloomily (back to his usual self).

"Well its an open house, so any time between 10 and 4, so whenever you fancy really" Katie said, thankful to Blaze for saving her again.

"This cake is scrummy" James said with his mouthful "Ok I will see you tomorrow" he finished his tea and cake and then gave Katie a kiss on the cheek and left.

"Oh deary me. He really does like you Kats doesn't he? Maybe you were just a little too helpful to him," joked Blaze. Katie threw him a dirty look and he laughed pretending to offended by her look.

"Shut-up will you and get on or we'll never be ready with all these blooming interruption's. Did you move the corner chest?"

"No you haven't asked me to?"

"Yes I did, you never listen!"

"Depends what your talking about" he grinned

"I get the message … I will move it now, don't stress, everything will be alright"

Chapter 45

Pascolli and I were enjoying our spare time at the Sparkles Bar. Pascolli was telling me some jokes and making me crack up with laughter. He has such a wicked sense of humour for an angel, it really shouldn't be allowed!

Sadly, Willow was not with us on this occasion, and although Willow is very studious, he still has a little grin at Pascolli once he gets going with the jokes.

"Big day tomorrow for our cases then?" Pascolli commented

"Oh yes. We need to be on top form. Better not have too many of these sparkle rays" I replied. "Do you think Carla will show?"

No sooner had I mentioned the name 'Carla,' we heard a groan, a sort of wailing. Pascolli and I exchanged puzzled expressions and looked across to where the wailing and groaning was coming from. There, slumped in the corner behind us, was Minjaa, a large, burly guardian who had been in my season at Angel School some time ago (although if I have to be totally truthful, I have admit that I never was too keen on this chap, very loud and a bit of a bully really).

"Minjaa?" I called gently "Are you alright?"

"Does it look like he's alright? What a stupid question" whispered Pascolli in my ear?

"Its just that name 'Carla." It makes me go cold whenever I hear it" Minjaa replied shuddering as he spoke and looking nervously around.

"Why?" Pascolli asked as we both pulled our stools over to where Minjaa was sitting.

"I have this case" he started and then sighed "Her name is Carla, and quite frankly she pushes me over the edge. She is awful, positively vile. I really don't like her and have no heart in helping her, which doesn't help the case or my stats for that matter. I really just don't feel I can work for her, it's not good for either of us really – what would you do?" He turned to us, his face all sad and questioning, not quite the bully that I remembered.

"Go and see your mentor. Who is your mentor, anyway? Ask for a case transfer and explain" I chipped in helpfully wondering if this was the same 'Carla,' which could be interesting to say the least.

"I don't think I could do that. Hibissa is my mentor and he is very strict on things like that. It would be failing and leaving her without a guardian..."

"Why is she is so bad?" Pascolli asked intrigued, as was I.

"Well, for starters she ruins peoples lives. Because of her this poor chap lost his job, dignity and all his cases that he had carefully built up over the years. 'Carla' thinks everything that doesn't go her way is this really nice lady's fault...Katie. That's right Katie, and now this Katie has organised some sort of event, not sure what, I haven't been down to earth for a while can't face it -

and this Carla is intent on ruining it. Frankly I don't want to be part of it" he wailed.

Pascolli and I looked at each other, both realising at once that this was indeed Carla's angel. (It is unbelievable really that such a human would have an angel but, we don't get to choose who we guard over, and even undeserving humans need looking after from time to time).

"If he gives up she'll have no guardian tomorrow, Hibissa won't have time to replace him" Pascolli sent me a mind message looking away from Minjaa in case he could read the message.

"Erm I know. Let's convince him to go to Hibissa, this is too good an opportunity for us to miss" I replied sending Pascolli a mind message back.

"Minjaa, I really think you should speak with Hibissa. He's not too bad you know. He is my mentor too, and I always find him fair" I said, telling a small white lie.

"Really? Hibissa would listen. Do you really think that? Are you a guardian now then Nicoise? I would never have thought that". Minjaa said, obviously shocked that I was succeeding. Honestly, the cheek!

"Yes, he would listen" I replied not commenting to his reference to my inadequacies. This wasn't the time or place and, besides, I wanted something from him, I wanted him to give up this case!

"He wouldn't listen, I don't think I can face him! I don't know what's worse really," he wailed again like a large baby.

"Come with us" Pascolli got up "We'll come with you now to see Hibissa"

Minjaa looked up and dried his eyes, smiled and then slowly followed us. I watched him bumble along; he really was quite chubby for an angel. He did say he hadn't been down to earth lately and you could tell he obviously didn't do much flying!

We eventually arrived at Hibissa's Chamber, praying he was not out at one of the many functions he always seemed to be attending.

"Come in" Hibissa bellowed after Pascolli knocked three times pretty loudly on his large wooden door. All three of us entered, Hibissa looked up quite surprised to see a 'group' of us.

"Oh, a group of you? Hello Minjaa, Nicoise and Pascolli. To what do I owe this pleasure?" he asked his eyes peering over his small glasses.

"Tell him" I pushed Minjaa forward who proceeded in telling him of his concerns about continuing working on the 'Carla' case.

Hibissa's face showed no expression as Minjaa whinied on and on, he just listened then, making me jump, he sent just me a mind message.

"You have nothing to do with this outbreak do you Nicoise? I mean Carla being without an angel would not be in your interest would it?"

"No Sir ... no. No interest. Just helping a fellow trainee Sir" I sent him a mind message back (first time I had ever done this to Hibissa, he looked up clearly impressed that I had finally mastered this skill).

Hibissa looked away from me and back to Minjaa who was still going on and on. Pascolli looked across and raised his eyebrows.

"This has obviously really distressed you Minjaa, and you were right to come to me with this problem. I will take the case off you as from now. Have a few days off, you seem stressed, then report back to me next week and I will reschedule a new 'easier' case for you" Hibissa said in a non-interested tone.

"Thank you Sir, but will this go against me?" Minjaa asked, worried.

"Not against you exactly, but of course a note will be made on your file"

"A note" Minjaa sighed. It was not good to have a 'note' on your records. You probably would never get a really juicy case again. Knowing this Minjaa looked down and sighed, but even this was better to him than continuing to help Carla.

(Carla even ruins angels, what a person – I sent this thought to Pascolli who nodded)

"I understand Sir. And thank you again"

"Good I am glad you understand. You can leave now Minjaa" Hibissa pointed to the door as he spoke. We all went to leave.

"Not you two – a few more moments of your time if you please" Hibissa said almost sarcastically to Pascolli and I.

"Oh dear – here it comes" we both thought.

"Don't think for one minute that I don't know what you two are up to. Encouraging Minjaa to give up his case. Granted he's clearly distressed by it, but a true guardian always sees it though to the end. I expect you are now pleased that Carla will be unguarded tomorrow, maybe a little vulnerable?"

"Vulnerable? I doubt she would ever be vulnerable Sir, she doesn't deserve a guardian Sir, with respect" I said bravely.

"Nicoise, every human needs one. They may not believe that or think that they do, but believe me they do. There are always two sides to people, remember that even if I have to admit someone like Carla is challenging. Anyway you do realise I will have to assign her to an experienced guardian, not a trainee? Hibissa smiled like a cat with the cream. (He could be very childish).

"Oh? Is that necessary Sir?" I asked.

"Nicoise, please don't ever doubt my judgement" barked back Hibissa with a face like thunder.

"Sorry Sir" I replied.

"Now go. I understand why you would hope that Carla is unguarded. It's sort of commendable that you both have initiative and commitment to your own cases, but rules are rules as I keep reminding you.... Good Day" Hibissa again pointed to the large wooden door. Its very intimidating when he does that pointing thing.

We left the chamber, a little confused by Hibissa's last comments. He always talks in riddles, never makes sense. You're never sure if he is scolding you or praising you. Minjaa was waiting for us outside.

"Thanks guys. Perhaps we could hang out tomorrow and get some sparkles," he asked eagerly.

"Not tomorrow, Minjaa we have a big day very big infact. It's make or break time," said Pascolli winking at me.

"Maybe sometime soon" I said to Minjaa, seeing the disappointed look in his eyes.

"Come on Pascolli we'd better sort out things for tomorrow and find Willow and get him on board"

"Can I do anything to help?" Minjaa asked hopefully.

"No" we both replied, and paused realising that the 'no' seemed very sharp. "Thanks though, enjoy your sparkles – you deserve them," I said kindly.

"Ah thanks again, feel so relieved" smiled Minjaa "See you soon"

"Yes lets find Willow, he will know what to do, he always does" Pascolli replied and smiled weirdly at Minjaa.

We flew off leaving Minjaa standing alone feeling half happy that he didn't have to deal with 'Carla' anymore and half sad in the knowledge that his 'book may be blighted.' He hadn't coped so he would be unlikely to ever get a really good case again, maybe easier cases with nicer humans would suit him anyway. Oh well, he would go and drown his sorrows at the Sparkles Bar no doubt!

Chapter 46

Everything looked clean, tidy and in its right place. Everything was marked up with a sale price, the raffle prizes were in place, and the cups and plates were gleaming clean.

Katie stood in the middle of the shop, smiling to herself. It looked perfect, but then she had a worried flutter come over her, that no one would turn up. What would happen if no one turned up, or worse if people came and didn't stay?

Katie could hear Blaze outside, cursing about something or other. She peeped outside and saw him battling with the long 'open day' poster she had got designed; the wind was quite strong and as soon as he fixed one corner the other side then curled up again. It was sort of funny but not. She knew she ought to go and help.

By the time she arrived Blaze was really moaning, his long hair being blown all over the show. He stopped when he saw Katie standing in the doorway.

"Well, a hand would be nice, don't just stand there!" he moaned, but nicely.

"Sorry" giggled Katie as she came over to one side of the large poster and held it whilst Blaze quickly fixed the other side. Once the sign was fixed they both went back inside.

The hands of the clock quickly whizzed to ten, the official opening time. Katie had kind of expected a long queue down the road, but when she nervously unlocked the door, she was disappointed to see just three ladies all dressed in purple looking quite windswept yet glowing as they stood outside in the wind waiting to come in.

Katie let them in, and they scuttled in grateful to be out of the windy weather. Bella was waiting to greet them with their free drink and raffle ticket once they had brought their tickets.

Soon it was half past ten and still no one else had turned up. Katie heard the disgruntled whispers from the practitioner's, who were eagerly waiting for their promised clients for their mini treatments of Indian head massages, reiki, reflexology and a whole host of other goodies. Katie was getting worried, they needed some customers and soon. Blaze saw Katie's worried look, he walked over to her putting his hand on her shoulder.

"Relax will you, it'll be fine. Stop your worrying and have faith," he said reassuringly. "It's still early"

"Is it? Do you think my marketing was wrong? Do you think no one knows about it? You really think it will pick up soon?" she blurted out in one big breath.

"Yes, it will pick up and soon, trust me, trust your angel" he replied smiling, Katie gave him an odd look.

"Angel?"

"Yes you know, your guardian. He will be here"

"Yeah right. Of course he's always here when I need him right?" Katie mocked.

"You must feel his presence sometimes Katie, surely?" asked Blaze.

Katie thought about it for a moment or two, then immediately dismissed the strange events and coincidences that had recently been occurring. Sometimes she did feel like someone was looking after her, and other times she felt very alone.

She looked at Blaze, thinking how weird he was sometimes, but then she couldn't imagine life without him now, he had become her rock, her best friend. She was about to reply and say something nice but the door crashed open and a group of ladies entered followed by Lucy, Mick, Carrie, Tony and young Toby holding his mum's hand.

"We're in business girly, get to your workstation" Blaze laughed.

Katie smiled a little smile and waved to her friends, quickly making her way to the refreshment area. Then Bella appeared welcoming everyone in her special 'Bella' way, warm and welcoming as if these people had known her all their lives.

Lucy and Carrie hugged Katie, and Tony and Mick gave her a quick kiss on the cheek.

"Toby is here too" Carrie smiled "And we managed to bring the men, against their better judgement!"

"Yeah yeah" said Mick "Hey it looks like you've worked hard Katie. You like your new job then?"

"Its good thanks" Katie replied.

"I'm really pleased things are working out. Hey, massages! Cool, I'll have some of that – excuse me ladies" Mick said, and with that he was gone, with Lucy scowling after him with her usual mean look.

"Men don't have treatments do they?" asked Tony curiously looking around.

"Course they do" Mick called back to his friend as he approached one of the massage ladies in the corner.

"He is such a tart, that man," laughed Tony eyeing up the cake, much more his thing "Tea please, got to be back at work soon"

A few more people turned up and the shop was starting to look pretty full now. The ladies in purple then all left, smiling at Bella as they clutched their new purchases. That's pretty much how the pattern continued for a while, people came in, bought things and left, which was the ideal scenario.

Katie heard her name being called and looked around to see her parents standing in the entranceway. Her Dad was beaming and waving like a puppy wagging its tail, her Mother was looking around the shop with her usual slightly disinterested look upon her face. Katie made her way across to greet them.

"Aw, thank you for coming" Katie said happily.

"Of course we would come, it's a pleasure" Katie's Dad beamed again.

"Yes, it is nice to see where you work" Katie's Mother added, withoutbeaming.

"Have a drink" Katie handed them both an herbal tea

"What is this?" Katie's Mother wrinkled up her nose whilst smelling the drink that her daughter had handed her.

"Green Tea"

"I'll pass if you don't mind. It looks very, well green really! ... No thanks" her Mother handed back the steaming brew. She looked across to her husband knowing he would not like it either but also knew he would not want to offend his daughter, and there he was gently sipping the hot tea clearly not enjoying it though. Katie noticed her Dad's face too.

"If you go over and see Blaze by the counter he will sort you both out a 'proper' cup of tea" laughed Katie.

"What, the man with the ginger knotty hair?" Katie's Mother grumbled, "He's your friend?"

"Yes, that's Blaze. And yes he is my friend. And they're not knots in his hair" Katie defended her friend. Honestly, her Mother never had anything nice to say about anyone, it really was quite tiresome.

Katie's Dad could see she was a little upset by the comment so started walking towards Blaze encouraging his wife to follow.

Blaze welcomed them in his usual excellent friendly manner, commenting on Katie's Mothers jacket, which made her blush slightly and she then warmed to this odd man, he made her feel quite special.

She sat down and listened to his soothing voice and he seemed to bewitch her, she actually really liked him. Blaze had an amazing way with people, it was almost as if he could really bewitch people with his charm and quirky personality.

The flow of people was encouraging, and Bella and the ladies doing the treatments were constantly in demand now, which was good. Bella looked around, she smiled and let out a sigh of relief. Things were going well, so far.

She noticed James come in with Sara, they looked a little out of place for some reason, a little odd, like they were not really comfortable to be there. James saw Katie and he tried to persuade Sara to go and have a treatment so he could be alone, but she was not having any of it. She had her strict instructions from Carla, to stick with James like glue!

Katie continued serving refreshments; she was so busy and hardly had time to stop and chat, the cake and tea were very popular.

Blaze on the other hand seemed to be the centre attraction; women flocked around him, wanting advice. Whatever they asked him about, buying once he had told them it was perfect for them, they always brought it – a born salesman really.

Katie caught Blaze's eye and he winked at her. It was all going so well. Maybe too well, Katie had a small nagging thought in the back of her mind that would not go away; a small doubt that kept bugging her, she felt sure something was going to happen and soon. She tried to think of her angel, the one that Blaze had assured her existed, and really hoped he was looking out for her.

Katie smiled as she spotted dear Mrs Hogan enter the shop accompanied by her very handsome nephew Paul. Katie blushed when Paul smiled across to her, he was way too good looking, yet so nice. She thought how nice it was of him to take time to bring her lovely little neighbour to the open day. She looked across to Mrs Hogan who was picking up everything and putting it into her small wicker basket. Katie smiled. Paul certainly had his hands full bringing Mrs Hogan; she was really becoming quite hard work. Katie felt a little sad as she realised Mrs Hogan probably needed a lot more care than she was getting, and may need to go into a care home, which she knew Mrs Hogan would totally hate.

"It's going really well" Carrie interrupted Katie's thoughts as she came over with Lucy.

"Bit crowded now and not enough seats really" moaned Lucy rubbing her pregnant stomach.

"You can sit down over there, ..." Katie pointed to a few wooden chairs tucked away in a corner.

"I'm pregnant, not desperate," Lucy snapped.

"Where are the boys?" Katie asked, quickly changing the subject

"Mick has had to go back to work. He did try and say goodbye, but you were busy"

"Tony is in his element – I think he's having a reading at the moment with Bella. He has spent a fortune!"

"Excellent" laughed Katie

"Tell us, who is that gorgeous man with your neighbour?" Lucy asked intrigued and looking Paul up and down.

"Oh that is Paul, her nephew. He helped me recently remember I told you when I got locked out?"

"Oh that's him? Very hot" Lucy said

"You're pregnant," added Carrie as she looked across to Paul to see what the fuss was about. "Wow you're right, he is hot!"

"He's ok, has a model girlfriend ... I think or did have" Katie looked across at Paul. Tony walked past them, pulling a strange face mocking the three women drooling over 'Paul'.

"He would be ideal for you Katie" Lucy said, "He's so good looking"

"Looks aren't everything," Carrie piped up

"Obviously not to you, you're married to Tony!" laughed Lucy

"Hey, you leave Tony out of this, he's lovely. Maybe a little more cuddly lately, but lovely" laughed Carried not offended by Lucy's usual rude comment. "Actually although he is nice there is someone else here who clearly likes Katie and is so right"

"Who? Not wet James?" asked Lucy

"Oh forgot about him. Yes he likes you Katie, but he is not the one. Blaze really likes you I can tell. I've been watching him look at you"

"Shut-up" Katie was embarrassed. "He's just my friend, just Blaze"

"Weird" Lucy said

"He's not weird" Katie said

"No I mean you couldn't seriously date someone who dresses like that. You'd have to re-educate him. And I mean, velvet jackets? Come on"

"He is the one, I'm telling you," insisted Carrie "Velvet jacket or not"

All three of them looked at Blaze and then over to Paul, worlds apart, but both really nice guys.

"No, Paul is just eye candy, Blaze is the one" said Carrie confidently.

"Eye candy, where?" Paul asked as he came over to them, with Mrs Hogan, catching part of their conversation, but having no idea he had been the main topic, along with Blaze.

"Hello Katie, it is so much fun here dear. Are these your friends Sara and Jayne that you use to moan about?" Mrs Hogan asked making all three laugh.

"No, this is Carrie and I'm Lucy. We are Katie's oldest friends from school, Sara and Jayne use to work with Katie" Lucy put Mrs Hogan right, speaking very loudly.

"She's not deaf," whispered Katie to Lucy.

"This is an amazing place" Paul said to Katie "You have really worked hard"

"He's even more gorgeous close up," whispered Carrie to Lucy who nodded approvingly at Paul. Katie knew what they were whispering about and threw them a disapproving look to shut them up.

"Have you tried the carrot cake yet Paul?' asked Katie

"No. I haven't" replied Paul "Heard its legendary!"

"Erm well you should get some 'legend' before it all goes, it's really the best," Carrie said

"Come on Auntie, lets go try some of this legendary cake then" Paul smiled at all three of the ladies, making them all melt.

Unknown to Katie, Blaze had been watching her and noticing how they were all in awe of Paul. He wasn't jealous as that was not his style, it was not an emotion that should be embraced in his opinion, but he wished Katie were talking to him.

Paul and Mrs Hogan came over to him, and he happily chatted with them as he served them up some cake and tea.

Katie suddenly spotted her brother, which totally took her by surprise, as she had not expected him to turn up today.

"I didn't notice you come in? Have you paid?" Katie asked.

"I came in the back actually. The door was wedged open. I've got no money, you don't mind do you Sis? Nice place actually quite hippy sort of place really, suits you. Any jobs going?" he asked cheekily. "Heard you're going to expand"

"Expand? What are you talking about?" Katie asked. She hadn't heard anything about expansion.

"I heard that Blaze chap speaking with some hippy old woman, probably his Mum, saying at this rate they would have to expand, and have a chain of 'New Age' shops – Cool idea, then maybe I could be a Manager of one huh?"

"Very cool, but I know nothing of it" Katie couldn't think of anything worse than having her brother work with her. Then she felt bad for thinking that, he was not so bad and he had made the effort to come and see her on the open day.

"Seriously Katie, much nicer place than the accountants" he said, stuffing almost a whole blueberry muffin in his mouth, crumbs spilling from the edges as he continued to talk.

Katie gave him a disapproving look and was just about to tell him off when their conversation was interupted by the main door being flung open. In entered the two men that had 'supposedly' been from the Council, followed by Carla and Anthony.

Carla as always made and impressive if not noisy entrance, she stood in the entrance surround by the three men all wearing black suits grinning.

"Wow what a babe!" exclaimed Nick, his jaw dropping down as he stared at Carla who was admittedly beautiful and always impeccably dressed with designer clothes and accessories.

"Shut up you numpty – that's Carla!" Katie hissed at her brother.

"Really, the bitch doesn't look like I imagined"

"Ssssh"

It was as if time stood still for a few seconds as everyone stopped and looked at this beautiful, but yet imposing and quite scary looking woman surrounded by her guards. It was like something from a film set.

The time passed and everyone continued what they were doing before she had entered the room. Blaze was suddenly right by Katie's side, as were Mrs Hogan with Paul, Carrie, Lucy, Tony, Toby and her parents. James and Sara hovered in a corner not really knowing what to do.

"Hello Katie, is someone going to take my ticket" Carla asked smiling her sickly sweet wicked smile flashing as always her dazzling white teeth.

Chapter 47

It was like a play, all the players were now on stage and the villain had just walked in, making an amazing entrance with everyone gasping, (well maybe that was a slight exaggeration, most customers there were totally oblivious to what was occurring). It was just that her dramatic entry was quite room stopping, and her beauty was striking. Yet she also had that evil edge that the villains' in plays always seem to command.

Curious Kittens was full of humans and unbeknown to them it was also full of guardian angels too. (Not every human has a guardian all the time, but at certain times during their life, when needed - some humans always need us though, dependant on us). Pascolli, Willow and I were obviously there, plus a few others we knew from lectures, just enough to say 'hello' to, but most interestingly, and a little worryingly, Hibissa was there. He came in when Carla had entered with her entourage of men.

"Who do you think he is here for?" I asked Willow and Pascolli

"He did say he would get an experienced guardian to replace Minjaa didn't he? Maybe he's the 'stand in'?" Pascolli said with a worried expression crossing his face.

"No, surely he wouldn't do that. I mean he is my mentor... He wouldn't would he?" I asked, not really sure what to think.

"He can do what he likes, he is Hibissa … one big joke for him no doubt" replied Pascolli getting even gloomier.

"He could be here for Bella or Blaze" piped up Willow optimistically.

"Of course, yes Bella …" I said with a sigh of relief. "Although he could still be here for Carla or one of her … men"

"Surely he can't be here one minute for Bella and then the next for Carla; that's just wrong" said Pascolli.

"Well maybe it's for one of these other humans. Who knows, watch for the signs, listen to his thoughts," I said looking around at the guardians, one of the older guardian spotted me and waved knowingly.

"That is Miccanna, he is pretty well known, perhaps he is Carla's guardian today?" said Willow hopefully.

We watched as Carla walked right up to Katie and into her area of personal space; she looked mean and disapproving of the shop.

"So, Katie Johnston, this is what you left my employment for is it?' Carla wrinkled up her sculpted nose (clearly not natural) "Bit pokey isn't it?" The two pretend Council officials with her laughed loudly as if provoked to big up their leader.

"What are you doing here?' Katie asked Carla directly facing her.

"What do you think? Thought I might have a treatment or buy some magic potion. I bought my ticket, I'm as entitled to be here as anyone else. I must say tickets are rather poor quality, I know a good printer ..." she smiled sweetly at Katie as she spoke. Katie had the urge to slap her, but resisted.

I could tell that Katie was fuming, she did not want Carla there, and she didn't want to see her, hear her or talk to her. Katie looked across the room to Blaze, but before she could attract his attention, Bella was by her side. She strangely took the tickets from Carla and pointed to the refreshments.

The situation was temporarily diffused and everyone that was slightly interested in the commotion carried on with what they were doing before Carla had arrived.

Carla seemed to relish in her own wonderfulness and looked almost as if she was floating around, looking at this looking at that, touching things and putting them back in the wrong places.

One of her men 'accidently' knocked a box of crystals with his arm, causing the crystals to crash down and go everywhere. Everyone looked across, and an atmosphere was starting to develop. It felt uneasy and cold. Some customers (maybe sensing tension) started to leave, which could have been coincidence but it felt to me like they were a bit freaked out by this strange woman and not really wanting to be involved with any further issues here.

Carla strolled glamourisly across to James and Sara who had been very quiet up to now.

"Thank you so much for inviting me today, it was a great idea – so quaint isn't it?" Carla said directly to James and Sara who both looked a little shocked.

Carla stared into a clear white crystal that she had picked up from the spillage; she seemed mesmerised for a few seconds and then threw it down and grinned at James.

"Katie has done really well here," James said nervously.

"Really??? I am surprised you think that James. Looks like a second hand junk shop to me. It won't survive; people don't want to buy junk and pebbles. Any way I'm glad to see you out and about. This is my boyfriend Antony, not sure if you have met before?"

Carla pushed Antony forward, who extended his hand out to shake James hand, who surprisingly, kept his hands in his pockets leaving Antony with his arm redundantly waiting.

"Oh dear me, James I can see you've been round Katie too long. You've even managed to pick up her bad manners. Honestly James, how rude. And we really felt that you might be ready to come back and work with us didn't we Ant?" she said

"I have a new job thanks" replied James looking directly at Carla.

"Really, how strange. Don't tell me it's doing the accounts for this place?' she laughed which set off her pack of hyena's. Carla glared at Sara. Who started to laugh thinking that was the right thing for her to do; she wanted to get paid for today.

"No. Although, that's not a bad idea - I would do the accounts if they wanted me to. You know, Katie was right about you" James said "I've been such a fool falling for your bull-shit!"

"Go James" Pascolli said as we watched James give Carla a piece of his mind. The icing on the cake here was when he turned round to Sara and told her to get lost!

"Look at Mrs Hogan" I nudged Pascolli and we watched as Mrs Hogan then came over and started telling Carla off as if she was a naughty child.

Carla found it amusing although she wasn't really listening to the old woman, she was eyeing up his sidekick Paul who she had just noticed. Paul however completely blanked her, which shocked her; Carla was not used to men turning away from her, she knew how to play men, rejection was not something she encountered from men.

The humans started to close in around Carla, all giving her dirty looks, or blanking her as Paul had, Carla didn't seem upset by it, she did however move away from the circle of humans all staring daggers at her, and continued to float around trying to look important; (she did feel a little threatened under that hard exterior I believe) her Anthony was constantly texting (irritating!).

"It is not going that well?" whispered Pascolli

"It's not going bad though" whispered Willow back "Could be worse!"

"I think it will get worse and very soon, it's brewing" I said gloomily.

"No, Bella and Blaze know we are here," said Willow "they trust us angels to help"

"They do? We're not really doing anything to help"

"We're here, our presence is here, and it makes them positive, which makes them act accordingly. So the more humans who feel our presence the better; more positive vibes working together to solve this problem" Willow said as if reading from a textbook.

"Oh is that how it works?" I asked.

"How do they know we're here?" Pascolli asked Willow

"They feel our presence, they sense Hibissa, and they feel a little chilly even"

"We make them cold?" I asked puzzled "not heard that before. Mind you, Bella has put her jacket on..." his sentence was interrupted mid flow as that clumsy man with Carla knocked a whole load of wind charms flying, making a terrific albeit tuneful crash. At the same time a beautiful terracotta sun dial with a happy face smashed into hundreds of pieces hitting some of the customers, including Katie's Mother who moaned loudly once with good reason as a bit fell on to her feet.

Carla seemed to think it was funny.

I watched Hibissa closely as he stared closely at Bella and then at Blaze. All of a sudden Hibissa was in between Bella and Blaze who both marched across the floor and stopped when they reached Mr Clumsy, as Willow and I had named him.

"Breakages have to be paid for I am afraid, that will be £50.00 please," Bella said very firmly but politely in the circumstances. Mr Clumsy looked surprised - and looked over at Antony for support.

"It was an accident. This place is way too cluttered, its no surprise accidents will happen. It's a health and safety risk this place" said Mr Clumsy "Will report it too"

"He's right. The organisation of the shelves, layout etc is all wrong, haphazard, no planning. The display was dangerous and could have hurt my good friend here," said Anthony.

"Rubbish" said Blaze at his Mother's side "I think you should all leave right now"

"Sorry, are you chucking us out of a junk shop?" laughed Anthony, very loudly so that everyone could hear. "Did you hear that honey? The ginger is chucking us all out!"

Carla turned around and glared at Blaze. I felt myself pushing Katie forward right in the firing line, I did'nt want to but she had to sort this out and now, this was her fight not Bella's and not Blaze's.

"Carla?" Katie trembled as she said the name out loud, she went to stop, I willed her on, willed her to be strong, willed her to believe, I then heard her small inner voice *"Come on guardian angel - are you here? I need your help? I need to be strong... Nicoise?"*

I couldn't believe it. Katie had sensed me – and she knew which angel I was (don't ask me how this happens but humans know the name once they know your there!) Katie had really called my name, yes my name 'Nicoise,' her guardian angel. Now I had to help, to do my job. I felt liberated; I was there for her. I caught Hibissa looking at me, he nodded, acknowledging what he had seen and heard. He knew too – even better!

"Sorry Katie were you calling me darling. Thought I heard a faint squeak," laughed Carla cruelly at Katie.

"Leave or I will call the Police" Katie said firmly and with her head up high staring straight at Carla's thunderous eyes.

"What ...leave now? But the party has only just begun" she looked over to Antony who deliberately pushed some candles over causing them to roll across the floor. A few more puzzled customers left, but all Katie's friends and family remained surrounding this awful woman.

"Why should I leave? You ruined my plans, you stole the folder, I know you did, you turned James against me ..."

"I did no such thing, all I did was try and let James know what your game was"

"Game? What game was that then Katie?" Carla asked.

"You know. I'm not going to spell it out. Please just, you are ..."

"A knifing corrupt bitch basically" interrupted James "And believe me, I'm going to get you struck off from every reputable professional register there is. You won't do this again," said James *(Pascolli was cheering him on from the sides).*

I looked over at James, and could see Pascolli right behind him. I smiled. James must have also asked for strength, for help, this was just so exciting and job satisfying – now I've had a taste of real guardianship I really want to climb the career ladder – wow!

I looked at Carla, there was no angel behind her, just greyness and anger, I looked over at Hibissa he had left Carla unguarded, he was here for Bella and possibly Blaze, and for us, his trainees, helping us with our cases. I felt quite humble and bad for thinking ill of him as I frequently did in the past.

Carla lunged forward to Katie her face fit to burst with anger, her skin was reddish and her eyes as dark as thunder "You Bitch, I ...."

As she lunged forward looking like she was actually going to hit Katie she tripped over a round pillow candle as it slipped under her feet undetected by her due to her deep obsession with hitting Katie. She fell hard on to the floor and yelped with pain or embarrassment (not really sure – hopefully both). Anthony was immediately by her side helping her up.

"Get off you bloody fool. It that was your fault you bloody knocked those over... Ouch, my foot really hurts" she yelped. Anthony eventually got her up. She looked around; everyone was scowling at her, not a pleasant sight. Young Toby was giggling; finding it hilarious; neither of his parents corrected his outbreak of laughter, indeed you could tell they also wished they could laugh out loud.

Katie's Mother pushed herself through everyone to face Carla *(Myself, Willow and Pascolli smiled, we knew this would be worth watching).*

"I'm not sure if you heard my daughter, but she asked you to leave" Katie's Mother said in a very schoolteacher tone of voice.

"Who do you think you're talking to? Can you not see I have just hurt myself? I will be sueing you know" Carla replied

"I'm speaking to you, and in case you didn't hear me LEAVE NOW!" shouted Katie's Mother.

"I can see where your daughter gets her manners from; she's a troublemaker and has ruined me" moaned Carla

"My daughter certainly is not a 'troublemaker' – she's the most genuine, hardworking and nice girl you could ever wish to meet. And if anyone has ruined your life it's 'you' and only 'you' with your greed. Now leave with your monkeys before we call the Police for disturbance of the peace for starters, damage, etc," Katies Mum said. "NOW!"

Carla looked around, she snorted and threw back her black hair with a 'I don't care' attitude and then limped to the door. She turned around at the door "If my foot is broken you will hear from my solicitor" she hissed, she signalled to her men to leave, and they all followed dutifully.

Once they had gone everyone started laughing and cheering, the shop was a mess, Bella walked across to the door and hung up the 'closed' sign.

"Free tea and cake for everyone I feel" she said smiling at Katie (she wasn't even remotely cross that her shop was a mess and things had been broken. On the other hand a lot of things had been sold, a lot of treatments given, bookings made, yes, in all not too bad).

She started clearing up the bits of the floor, everyone else started to help too, true team spirit. Blaze sorted out the tea and brought out a large tray of blueberry muffins and double chocolate muffins.

Katie went over to her Mum and kissed her on the cheek, something she rarely did. She was truly shocked, and proud, of her Mum and how she had stuck up for her. She really couldn't remember the last time she had heard her Mum praise her. Possibly when she did some good artwork at school? She looked around at all her friends and family and smiled, she was lucky.

"Thank you all so much, and I am sorry" Katie said looking around at everyone.

"You have nothing to be sorry for" Bella replied kindly.

"What a bitch" James snarled.

"Who is she deary?" Mrs Hogan asked all confused with the fuss.

"Good looking though ... wow she looked hot when she was angry?" Nick said smiling at the thought of Carla.

"Lets hope she learnt her lesson" said Katies Mum.

The human conversation went on and on, they all chatted away excitedly as they drunk their tea.

"Good work angels, you excelled" Hibissa said to us "We should go now, they will all be fine."

"We really helped didn't we?" I said in wonder

"Yes" Pascolli said, "We did"

"You guys were awesome," Willow said

"Katie asked for me" I grinned

"I know, it is a good feeling when you truly connect young Nicoise. Come we must go".

We left the humans chattering happily. They sat there late into the night ...we angels on the other hand left happy and satisfied; we flew fast and starting racing in the evening sky, (Hibissa even joined in – amazed the old guy can still fly!) - we too had fun.

Chapter 48

Everyone was sitting around drinking bottomless mugs of tea, served by Blaze and Bella. The mood was light and happy, despite all that had gone on.

Katie wandered over to Bella, who was over by the registration/ticket point, busily collecting up all the tickets.

"I am so sorry Bella"

"It wasn't your fault Katie"

"But the breakages. ...I'll pay"

"No, no. I wont hear of it. Do you know, we really took some money today? We had nearly 100 people though the door today, and some spent quite a lot of money. We have 23 new bookings too. So no, I don't want you to pay for the breakages.

Thank you for your good work on arranging everything, it wouldn't have happened without you, I would never have got round to doing it".

"Just doing my job," Katie replied, a little embarrassed. She was not used to getting praise, especially not from a boss and mother all in one day! "It was very cold in here though don't you think?" she said randomly changing the subject.

"Presence of angels" Bella replied matter of factly.

"Oh right! I thought it might be the boiler starting to play up!" Katie laughed.

"God no, I hope not. You'd better get Blaze to check it later! But no, it was the angels. They always bring a chill with them" she smiled at Katie's non-believing face "Katie you do know that Blaze is a lovely person don't you?" she said out of the blue surprising Katie with such a comment.

"Of course I know that Bella. Blaze is ... well he is Blaze. An amazing and lovely friend as are you," laughed Katie wondering why Bella needed to point such a thing out to her.

Katie's parents wandered over to her and Bella, almost not wanting to disturb them, standing there redundant on the sides for a few minutes until Katie's Mum coughed a false cough to get their attention.

"We need to get going Katie, need to cook dinner and feed Mr Syd"

"Mr Syd?" asked Bella

"Our cat" pointed out Katie's Dad who had been very quiet all throughout the afternoon, not speaking, commenting but definitely taking it all in as he usually did.

"It's a lovely shop Katie, and the cake is splendid. I wouldn't mind the recipe sometime Bella?" Katie's Mum said.

"No problem, I'll let Katie have it for you" Bella said.

"Bye Mum, bye Dad and thank you" Katie gave them both a peck on the cheek. Her Mum walked towards the door and her Dad stayed for a few seconds with Katie, he turned to her and whispered "We are both really proud of you"

"Thanks Dad" with that Katie's Dad caught up with his wife who was waiting at the door and he knew only to well not to keep his wife waiting.

Nick followed turning to Katie "Better cadge a lift if they are off – see you soon Sis. And well done" Nick said. "Remember my 'Manager job'" he added laughing as he caught up with his parents.

Katie couldn't really understand why everyone was saying 'well done'; she was only doing her job. Or did they mean the 'Carla' incident, finally sticking up for herself, perhaps that was it.

She smiled and acknowledged that actually she had done well, she had dealt with an issue, and she felt happy and ready to move on and chase her dreams without so many doubts. Yes, maybe she had done well. She looked up to the ceiling and inwardly thanked Nicoise whoever he maybe. Perhaps she dreamt up his name in one of her odd dreams, or perhaps she was going mad, but whatever had gone on today she knew she had felt that someone was there for her, guarding her, egging her on to say what she really meant, to be herself.

She wandered back to the main group of people that was left now, where she found Carrie and Mick telling everyone a really funny story about their son Toby. He was a funny kid, and always getting into trouble, but very lovable. Lucy was taking mental notes in everything Carrie was saying about Toby - probably noting that she would never let her child get into such trouble. Katie looked at Tony, he was in his element here, and he seemed to have really hit it off with Blaze, which would be handy Katie thought if they ever all went out. She stopped herself realising what she had just said to herself, which had shocked her and looked over at Blaze and thought "no ... maybe? Really? ..."

Mrs Hogan and Paul now got up to leave. Mrs Hogan hugged and kissed Katie and then the very gorgeous Paul gave Katie a peck on the cheek, which sent shivers down her back. Paul grinned, he seemed to be aware of the effect he had on women although he did not appear too big headed – part of the charm.

"Such a lovely party, Katie" said Mrs Hogan

"It was not a party Aunty" Paul corrected

"Well it seemed jolly and lots of lovely cake and tea ... can you bring some of those cakes round one day soon?"

"Of course I will"

"Good ...when?"

"Do you know I think we should do a yummy cake cook book, so many want the recipes?" joked Katie

"Why not, sounds like a great idea! Reckon that could be an earner you know" Paul added positively.

"Do you think?" Katie pondered for a moment; she had her serious head on.

"I think whatever you put your mind to you would make a success of it. You're pretty amazing you know, you just you don't know it" Paul said.

"Don't be daft," laughed, Katie, blushing as she brushed off the compliment as she always did.

"Perhaps we could go out for a meal one night soon?" Paul asked totally taking Katie by surprise.

"Erm …. Don't think your girlfriend would…."

"Oh he dumped her, too vain!" interrupted Mrs Hogan. Paul raised an eyebrow. Katie blushed, then James wandered over to join them wondering what Paul was talking to Katie about. Everyone stopped talking and there was an awkward silence for a few seconds although it seemed a lot longer. Then Blaze came over.

Carrie nudged Lucy, and Tony winked at Carrie.

"Like buses, men, either none on the horizon and you stand around waiting forever, or you get three turn up at the same time," laughed Carrie.

"She should go for Paul," said Lucy "He is fit"

"Lucy!" scolded Carrie

"I can look you know" Lucy moaned looking Paul up and down "I mean look at that bum"

"Calm down, don't get excited" Tony laughed, "James really likes her"

"Yes but he is so wet and drippy" Lucy said.

"No it's Blaze, Blaze is the one, you see" Carrie said

"I agree … Blaze is the one," Tony said nodding at his partner. "We'd better get going too honey". They all said their goodbyes and left. Mrs Hogan, Paul and James all followed, just leaving Blaze, Bella and Katie to clean up the mess, which they got stuck into straight away.

"What an afternoon" said Blaze to Bella as they washed and dried the dishes together. Bella saw them together, and made her excuses (to sort out some bits in the office).

"You were really amazing this afternoon," said Blaze.

"You're the second person to say I'm 'amazing' today," laughed Katie. "Plus I can't get over my Mum sticking up for me. I haven't done anything Blaze?"

"You stood your ground, and your Mum has always been proud of you Katie. Mums just don't always feel the need to go around bragging, I guess. Anyway, spill the beans who else said you were amazing then?" asked Blaze.

"Wouldn't you like to know? Anyway, what is this about a chain of shops ... Nick said something?"

"Oh that – it's just a dream, but I think you, me and Mum could make it work you know, its not such a bad idea"

"It would be hard work, but could be fun ... but erm money??"

"Yes, you and me, we could make it work" Blaze stopped realising how that sounded "and we..." he paused

"And we ..." Katie continued his sentence for him

"Could have loads of cake!" he said avoiding what he was going to say. He wanted to say that they could be together, but he knew that was not what Katie needed right now. She didn't need complications. However, she did have James and now that hunk Paul on her tail, he felt a little jealous – he wanted to say something but felt too shy, strange Blaze being shy.

He looked at Katie and smiled. He knew she knew what he was thinking; she was blushing, and looked a little flustered, she smiled at him and carried on scrubbing the dishes looking down so she did not have to catch his green questioning eyes.

"I will wait for you forever, you know Katie, I will always be here for you when you're ready" Blaze blurted out a little awkwardly.
"I know" Katie smiled then they hugged, the soapy suds going all over Blazes long red hair, causing him to stop and start chucking soap bubbles at her which lead to a soap suds fight in the tiny kitchen. Bella could hear the laughing and screaming, she smiled knowingly.

Chapter 49

I feel very tired after yesterday's events and the long fly home. I stayed up with Willow and Pascolli chatting endlessly about the outcome. We also spoke about alternative outcomes and what would have happened if this or that happened, and so forth.

Now, even though I could so sleep, I have to finish my report for Hibissa. Luckily and unusually for me I have kept my bookwork work up to date, so writing the report is not such a tiresome job as it has been in previous cases.

I pause and put down the ink feather pen for a moment. How I wished I had one of those computers that humans have, getting such work done would be so much quicker. I sighed, picked up my pen and started scribbling away, on my findings, my thoughts, and Katie's development. I paused again. I liked Katie; she has come a long way from when I was first assigned her. She has developed from a meek 'yes' people pleasing person into a stronger more assertive person finally happy being single and having a new purpose. She was well loved by her friends and family, very important for humans I find. Plus she finally believed in me, knows my name even, wow! What an achievement. I wish I could chat with her. It would be nice to chat to her, I feel I know her so well, but she knows nothing of me, or my existence, apart from a supporting presence and a chilly air.

My eyes grow heavy with tiredness, and my mind reverts to the large adverts I often see on earth about tiredness killing, I nodded, yes I can see that it could do that, maybe I should just have a little nap, before I continue …. 'NO' got to keep going, this has to be finished, I scribble on, my writing becoming more and more wiry and unreadable, my hand ached with cramp from too much writing.

I must have nodded off, because all of sudden I was rudely been shaken by Willow, who seemed very excitable.

"Wake up, Hibissa is on his way round here" he shouted

"Here – in our chamber?" I said looking around at the mess that lay about everywhere.

"Yes. You need to smarten up, wash your face, quick" with that Willow splattered a large wet sponge over my face causing the water to drip down my neck onto my white gown "oops sorry Nicoise" he said but continued washing my face to my horror. I sat up wondering why an earth Hibissa should feel the need to come here; we always get summoned to go and see him.

"What are you doing?" I asked Willow who was rushing about picking things off the floor.

"What does it look like, tidying up? Don't just watch, come on Nicoise, this is important!" Willow said in a rush.

Pascolli strolled in, giving me and Willow a temporary fright thinking it was Hibissa already "What's going on?' he asked puzzled at the activity in his chamber.

"Hibissa is on his way here to see me now!"

"Hibissa? Here? Now?" Pascolli repeated slowly in question form.

"That's right you heard, here, and now" Willow said panicking "Help us clear your mess will you?" Pascolli nodded and did as Willow said, not really understanding what was going on though.

"Why here? Are we or should I say you in trouble?" Pascolli asked as he hid things under his bunk bed.

"I don't know. You don't think I have to stand before the Grand Court do you? For collaborating on cases?" I asked

Pascolli gulped and went even whiter than normal, "Hope not"

"It could be good," added Willow not sounding totally convinced.

A cold air filled the room and we all turned to the door to see Hibissa, he had not knocked so we had no idea of how long he had been quietly standing there, I gulped nervously and hid the sheets I had just picked up off the floor behind my wings.

"Good day to you all. I have come to see Nicoise, but Willow and Pascolli now that you are both here, I would also like to extend my thanks to you ..." he smiled at Pascolli and Willow's shocked faces and added "... for your help yesterday. I understand why you felt it necessary on this occasion to work as a team rather than stand-alone. However, you should read up on your regulations and know the rules on such 'team' collaboration for future cases, but you worked well so thank you; now if you could leave me with Nicoise for a few minutes please"

"Yes of course Sir, and thank you" bowed Willow almost knocking into Pascolli as he bowed.

"I am sure your Mentor will speak with you Pascolli and I will speak with you soon Willow"

"We don't have to go to the High Court then Sir?" asked Pascolli

"Not on this occasion Pascolli, but like I said, the regulations are there for a reason, and rules do need to be obeyed or you suffer the consequences or worses still humans suffer through your failings. So please remember that, now I bid you good day" replied Hibissa.

Pascolli nodded, understanding now and followed Willow out of the Chamber, closing the door, leaving just Hibissa and me.

Hibissa turned to me, and then looked longingly at the wooden chair in the corner of my chamber. We stood in silence for a few seconds though it seemed it seemed longer. "May I sit, I took the stairs here to give you a little more time to tidy up, and my legs are not what they use to be, I should have flown"

"Of course, be my guest" I said surprised he even asked.

"I guess you are wondering why I am here?" he looked around my dingy Chamber, nothing like his luxury Chamber, "Goodness you know it is seasons since I have been to one of these chambers, it is a bit grim. When was the last time it was painted?"

"I really can't remember Sir, not for a very long time"

Hibissa took out his notebook and scribbled a few words " I will speak to Maintenance and see if we can get a paint scheduled in soon"

"Thank you Sir, I would appreciate that," I said not really truly bothered about the paintwork of the Chamber.

"Anyway I didn't come about that. No, I wanted to simply say 'Well Done.' I must say I am even surprised saying those words to you Nicoise, but Katie is a credit to your hard work"

I nearly fell off my chair. I am flabbergasted, never have I had such praise and from someone like Hibissa, I could feel my jaw dropping down, Hibissa laughed.

"Of course it could have been a fluke, she did meet up with Blaze and Bella, and they are very clued in humans, but on the whole it was your doing I believe. It will be interesting to see how you fare with your next case"

"Next case?" I said excitedly wondering what it would be. "Thank you so very much Sir"

"Don't gush Nicoise, it is not your style. Your next case will be even more challenging, I am really going to test you, and see if this was a lucky fluke or whether you really have the makings of a grade 'A' Guardian Angel." He paused and threw me over a dusty case folder making me sneeze (dust always does that, must be allergic) "Have you finished your notes on this case?"

"Almost" I lied

"Good bring them to me tomorrow then" he stood up, his willowy frame looking even longer and taller than usual "One more thing, I would like your to appear before the next spring meeting of the High Court"

My heart sunk, I knew this was all too good to be true, so Willow and Pascolli did not have to go but I did. How unfair, I thought. Hibissa just said I had done well, so why the High Court? Hibissa was obviously reading my thoughts, I could not retain them, and I felt sad.

"Nicoise you are not being charged with anything. Have faith. I have had time to read your notes on reviewing and streamlining procedures, protocols and I have to say, reluctantly, that we do need to - lets say - slightly modernise some of our procedures to cope with the forever changing human world. The human world is populating as a vast speed and we do not have the capacity or resources to meet all the requests, maybe and just maybe there is some merit in your ideas that could help us reach more people by streamlining and cutting out some of the bureaucratic red tape we currently go though. So I am asking you to prepare a presentation to take to the High Court, which I have to say is not going to be easy as you well know us Guardians are very set in our ways, perhaps bring one of those computer thingy's that you keep mentioning"

If I was shocked a moment ago by Hibissa's praise I was now lost for words, flabbergasted, amazed, excited all in one, in fact I could hardly breath I was that shocked. Hibissa looked happy too, a rare sight, I had an urge to kiss and hug him, of course Hibissa read this thought and quickly spoke out loud.

"I would rather you did not" he laughed, "You have one season to prepare this and I will allow help from your two friends. You still have your new case to work on as well, and you also still need to monitor Katie from time to time, so you are going to be extremely busy. Do you think you can cope with that?"

"Yes, yes I will Sir, I will"

"Good, then good luck, do not let me down, this is your 'big' chance, do not blow it young Nicoise" Hibissa got up off the wooden chair a bit awkwardly "Good Day" and left my untidy chamber,

I skipped and flew around knocking things over, I flew out into the corridor at super top speed, 'blow it'.... no I would not blow it, this was my break, my chance to really make a difference to humans and angels alike ... so excited, how a day can change your life.

<u>The End</u>

Lightning Source UK Ltd.
Milton Keynes UK
UKOW07f2051260115

245155UK00001B/69/P